Scott R Howard
Into the Mystic
Sorcerer's Magic
A Mystic Land Novel

Book design, cover, artwork, and text by Scott Howard.
Mystic Land map illustrated by Scott Howard.
Cover created with individually purchased stock photographs,
photo-editing and composition by Scott Howard.

Young Adult and Adult
Fantasy, Fiction, Adventure

ISBN (Soft Cover) 978-0-9893631-2-9
ISBN (eBook) 978-0-9893631-3-6

First Edition
Printed in the United States of America
Self-Published by Scott Howard
www.MyScottArt.com
Email: Scott@MyScottArt.com
Publication date: October 2022.

Thank You

I could never give enough thanks to my remarkable friends and family who have supported and encouraged me to chase each new endeavor generated by my creative imagination and willful ambition.

I doubt that any of my books would have been possible without the support of long-time friends, Beth Ray-Hofferth, Steve Moles, and Bruce Jones. Each of you have made a significant difference in my career and my life.

Special thanks to Wendy Williams, my collaborative friend and author of *Hooray for Breezy*, for your editing eyes and uncanny ability to see ways to improve this story.

And Mary Anne Ellis, for everything about you and your presence in my life. As a reading educator, college professor, and author, you were there to proof and edit, and every time I asked a question you always had the right answer. Most importantly, I am the luckiest man in the world to have you as my companion. I love you.

Dedication

To the memory of my father, Ralph "Gary" Howard.
His beliefs in positive thinking and the power of
our mind encouraged and inspired me to believe...
"You can be and do
anything you put your mind to."
- Scott Howard

Into the Mystic: Sorcerer's Magic

1 Becca...7
2 Lions and Tigers and Bears 16
3 The Wall 21
4 Shrouded Swamp 25
5 Visions 31
6 Gypsies 42
7 Revelations 55
8 Questions 65
9 Windy 80
10 Violet 89
11 Fellowship 97
12 Takoda Nemasket 108
13 The Storm 126
14 Alsaahir 140
15 Sorcerer's Fortress 154
16 Mystic Magic 165
17 Dire Decisions 176
18 Pixie 188
19 Elves! 197
20 Stratagem 218
21 The Quest 229
22 Sorcerer's War 242
23 Dark World 246
24 Necromancy 257
25 Reflections 267
26 Savage Swamp 281
27 Outside World 293

About the Author 299

The Mystic Land

1 Becca

Rebecca could feel the power of the stallion beneath her. The sounds of galloping hooves, panting horses, and beating hearts filled the night air. Swirling winds gusted across her face as she led the valiant warriors up the hillside toward the inevitable battle. She looked to her right, then to her left. The respect and appreciation she felt for these crusaders fighting by her side were beyond rapport.

A deafening roar from the hill's opposite side showed that their enemy was as prepared as they were. Fire suddenly swept across the ridgeline. Behind the flames lifted a single form. A vicious, angry face, burnt orange in color with blood-red eyes on an enormous scaled head, appeared above the wall of fire, followed by a long thick snake-like neck made of hardened leather. The light of the moon and stars seemed to disappear into the darkness behind the burnt-red body covered with deep slashes of blackened scars, lifted by massive wings that spread across the entire width of the hill.

In a flash, the immense dragon vaulted over the burning hillside, plunging downward upon them. The powerful forces exerted by its outspread wings toppled horses to the ground, tossing riders from their mounts like paper in the wind. Flames leaped from the dragon's jaws. Bravely holding her sword above her head, Rebecca glanced up long enough to see the sharp outstretched claws before falling forward to grasp the mane of her stallion for dear life. As the ferocious predator soared past, she felt the heat on her back and smelled the singe of her hair. She wondered if the cries of the warriors behind her would cloud her thoughts for whatever time remained of her life.

Nearing the peak of the hill, Rebecca turned to see the dragon circling back for another kill. This time, she knew it was coming for her. Indecisiveness raced through her mind. Stay atop her steed, or dismount to face the attacker one-on-one? Razor-sharp claws and teeth, rippling muscles, walls of fire, and the power of the enraged beast drew closer. Again, Rebecca bravely raised her sword, knowing it would have little effect on this angry monster. She could smell its' stank breath. She felt the heat of the dragons' flames engulfing her. Then, out of the fire, thick pointed talons wrapped themselves around her body, effortlessly lifting her from her stallion as it helplessly fell onto the burning hillside.

Suddenly, an old anti-war song jolted Rebecca from her nightmare.

Is this a dream
I can't tell the difference anymore
Reality should never involve war

Wake up, Wake up
This nightmare is all too real
Peace and love are all I want to feel

They call it an adventure
What do they want me to learn
If this is the truth, then why does it burn

No longer a child
I yearn to know me
I've earned my wings; please let me fly free

Rebecca reached across the pile of blankets and pillows to turn off her radio alarm clock and plopped back down on her bed. Wow, that dream felt too real, she thought. What caused me to have such an insane dream as that? She shook her head to shake the intense nightmare from her memory.

It didn't take long for reality to deliver more practical thoughts into her mind. Hey, it's Saturday, the first day of summer vacation. I have no school, and I'm not scheduled to work at the restaurant, so why did my alarm go off? Rebecca didn't have an immediate answer to that question, but after a few brief moments of consideration, she decided it was time to get up.

Rebecca Harmony Fields, nicknamed Becca by her family and closest friends, was considered a natural beauty even at seventeen, although she didn't see herself that way. Like most teenagers, she had not yet developed an abundance of self-confidence. As a young girl growing up in Rehoboth, a country town in Massachusetts, she had been a tomboy with no interest in dolls, dresses, or makeup. Instead, she loved playing baseball, basketball, soccer, swimming, and gymnastics, and she excelled in all of them. Rebecca could easily compete with any boys her age, although that did not necessarily attract boys!

Of course, beating boys in sports had its pitfalls. Until she started developing into a teenager, Rebecca had been taunted with nicknames like Becky Spaghetti and Stick. Nobody called her those names anymore, but the insults stuck in her mind and nagged at her self-confidence. She had just finished her junior year in high school with some of the highest grades in her class, received several athletic and academic awards, and was on the varsity cheerleading squad, yet she still felt like she was trying to find herself. It was time to begin considering colleges, although she still did not know what career she wanted when she grew up. That made selecting her college major and choosing a school more complicated, and her indecisiveness seemed to increase her insecurity.

Unlike many girls her age, Rebecca did not have a boyfriend. In fact, she had never even kissed a boy. The boys clearly showed their interests, but Rebecca was determined to wait until she met a guy who could accept her busy schedule and independence. The boys Rebecca felt most attracted to were the more intelligent and mature types at school, yet those boys seemed to lack the confidence to approach her. She had no interest in loud-mouthed boys who talked and acted like immature adolescents. Rebecca never understood how a boy might think pulling her hair would entice her to be attracted to him. Those were the boys she especially enjoyed embarrassingly beating in every sport and outsmarting in every school subject.

Nature gifted Rebecca with sparkling brown eyes that glittered like gold in the sunlight, extraordinarily long lashes, a contagious smile, dimples, and rosy cheeks on a radiant light-brown complexion. She never required makeup or even lipstick to look stunningly beautiful. Envious schoolmates accused her of spending hours a day in the sun or a tanning booth, yet she had never been in a tanning booth and rarely spent much time in the sun except for sports and traveling from one place to another.

An unusual trait in the women on her mother's side of the family is that they all looked almost identical when they were the same ages. Rebecca remembered seeing a photo of her grandmother as a child. She immediately thought it was a recent photo of herself, except she couldn't remember when the picture had been taken.

With long, straight black hair approaching the middle of her back, some people guessed Rebecca to be Egyptian or Native American. Her mother enjoyed boasting that when she was younger, people told her she looked like a young Cher, the musician and actress. Rebecca doubted that most kids in her generation knew who Cher was, but she knew. If people thought her mother looked like Cher, she must resemble Cher too, and Rebecca considered that a flattering compliment. Rebecca's grandparents were free-spirited hippie types who met at a big outdoor weekend concert in the 1960s. They both loved music, so they often traveled the country attending shows that featured their favorite bands. Her parents often brought her to concerts when Rebecca's mother was young. They influenced their daughter to play guitar, piano, and keyboards. But most importantly, she was gifted with an extraordinary singing voice that could only be comparable to the most talented singers.

Rebecca's mother, born Mary Anne Clover Fields, was known as Clover until her thirties when she decided that Mary Anne sounded more business-professional. Young Clover had intended to become a professional singer and musician. Around the age of twenty, she took a week-long vacation with two girlfriends, which turned into a two-month adventure. She supposedly met and had a heated romance with a handsome young musician from an unnamed New England town. Following the summer fling, neither of them stayed in touch. Less than a month after returning home, Clover discovered she was pregnant. Their beau-tiful love-child would become Rebecca Harmony Fields, nicknamed Becca. At least, that was the story Rebecca was told. Those flimsy details were never clearly confirmed in

Rebecca's mind, but that was all she knew about her birth father.

After becoming a single parent, Clover took a job as a server at a popular restaurant in her hometown of Rehoboth. The restaurant owners developed a close affection for Clover and Rebecca. They welcomed Clover and Becca into their restaurant and their lives with open arms. When the owners decided to retire, they offered to finance Clover's purchase of the restaurant – a deal she could not refuse. So, Clover reinvented herself with her more professional given name, Mary Anne. A few years later, Mary Anne changed the restaurant's name to Clover's Coffee & Tea Café, added a colorful hippie-style décor, and began playing the music of the 1960's and 70's, which often had customers joyfully singing along to the memorable songs.

Growing up in the restaurant taught Rebecca every position in the business, gave her a permanent part-time job through her teens, and positively influenced her love of that generation of music. Rebecca loved it all: rock, folk, pop, Motown, rhythm & blues, and soul. Rebecca could proudly sing the lyrics of almost any song from that era. Those influences inspired her to write songs, although she never dared to share them. Like her mother, Rebecca had an incredible singing voice. Still, she never felt enough confidence to sing in front of an audience, especially if it might result in being compared to her spectacularly gifted mother.

When Rebecca was seven years old, Mary Anne married a nice guy named Shawn. A year later, they brought home a son named Christopher. As a co-owner and creative director of a busy advertising agency in Providence, Shawn typically worked twelve-hour days, six days a week, leaving home before seven and not returning until after nightfall. Because her mother spent much of her time at the restaurant, Rebecca often felt like more of a permanent babysitter to Chris than a big sister. Sometimes the responsibility felt bothersome, sometimes he acted like an annoying little pest, but the truth be told, Chris was usually fun and humorously funny. She might not openly admit it, but Becca enjoyed the time and the closeness she developed with her little brother. With eight years of age separating them, there appeared to be few common interests, yet they always seemed to have a fun time together. Becca could see the love and adoration in his eyes and felt his appreciation for her attention. His pride in being seen anywhere with his big sister always made her happy to spend time with him.

Still wondering what might have influenced her to have such a strange, frightening, and yet so realistic dream about a battle with a dragon, Rebecca rolled out of bed, quickly splashed water on her face, brushed her teeth, ran the hairbrush through her hair, and headed downstairs. The television was on in the living room, but nobody watched it. Instead, she found Chris in the kitchen, slicing a banana into a bowl of cereal.

"Good morning, Chris," Becca greeted cheerfully.

"I sure would like some blueberries for my cereal," Chris responded.

"I sure would like to hear you reply with a good morning to me, Chris."

"Sorry. Good morning, Becca. Wanna go pick some berries with me today?"

Still trying to clear the morning cobwebs from her head, Becca's immediate response was a sarcastic laugh and a

resounding "No, I don't think so." Rather than face the
disappointed look on Chris's face, Becca grabbed a glass
from the cupboard and stepped to the refrigerator for some
orange juice. "Besides, it's only May," she commented. "Are
berries even ripe enough for picking?"

"Yes," Chris answered anxiously. Becca's question was
just enough reason for Chris to get hopefully excited. "I saw
some big juicy blueberries, raspberries, and blackberries
growing right down the road just a few days ago."

The room was quiet for a minute while Becca contemplated. With nothing else planned for her day, she couldn't
think of an excuse to say no. "Sure, Chris," she said. "I'll
go berry picking with you. Just give me a couple of hours
to wake up, shower, have breakfast, and get ready to go,
okay?" Christopher's huge grin was the only answer Rebecca
needed to know they were committed.

Following her shower, Rebecca considered what to wear
to go berry picking for a beautiful spring day in May, with
temperatures in the mid-'70s. She dressed comfortably in a
casual peach-colored button-up shirt with rolled-up sleeves
over a light blue-gray sportswear t-shirt, dark blue mid-weight
straight-leg jeans, black crew socks, and black leather ankle
boots just in case the ground might be damp or muddy. She
thought about wearing a baseball cap but instead decided to
put her hair in a ponytail with a suede headband, making her
look more Native American.

Mindful that it was the first day of her summer vacation,
Rebecca gleefully sang Alice Cooper's, *"School's Out for
Summer"* to herself as she emptied her school books from
her book bag onto her bed. She decided to keep a notebook
and drawing pad and checked the front accessory pocket for

essentials. Necessities included her wallet, a handful of pens and pencils, hairbrush, hand lotion, toothbrush and toothpaste, tissues, and a foldable pocket knife. Since the age of twelve, Rebecca's mother insisted that she carry a multi-use pocket knife for protection and preparation for any situation. At her mother's urging, she never left home without one. As a result, it became a habit to carry one of the several pocketknives she owned in her purse, backpack, book bag, or even her pocket, even though the only use she had ever found for them was to cut a strip of yarn or tape, or clip flower stems.

Rebecca scrambled eggs and toasted English muffins for Chris and herself for breakfast. Next, she made two sandwiches with peanut butter and red raspberry preserves for Chris and two with lettuce, tomato, and provolone cheese for herself. She packed the sandwiches, two quart-sized bottled waters, four granola bars, two apples, and a hand full of napkins into her backpack. Then removed the apples to make room for two medium-sized plastic bowls with snap-on lids for the berries they would pick.

Ready to go, Rebecca looked at Chris to ensure he dressed appropriately, checked her pockets for keys and cell phone, and glanced at the digital clock over the stove as they headed for the door. 12:12. I'm not sure if those numbers have any significant meaning, Rebecca thought, but she optimistically guessed they represented an extraordinary destiny.

2 Lions and Tigers and Bears

As the weather forecast projected, the sky was sunny and clear. Chris excitedly skipped along the country road, chattering about subjects that would usually only interest other nine-year-old boys, but Rebecca joyfully responded with laughter and entertaining comments. They traveled little more than a quarter of a mile when Chris stopped before a cluster of small trees and thick bushes.

"The berries are on a path on the other side of those bushes," Chris exclaimed. "Follow me," he called as he dropped to his hands and knees and began crawling under the thick hedges. Feeling doubtful but not wanting to ruin her brother's enthusiasm, Becca did as he requested. Despite branches grabbing at her hair, clothes, and backpack, she pushed through the bramble of prickly shrubs until it cleared at the other side.

She lifted herself into a narrow, leaf-covered path that appeared to twist through a mass of maple, oak, birch, and willow trees.

"You know Mom doesn't want us going into the woods, Chris," Rebecca warned.

"I know," he replied, "but Mom is afraid of everything. She thinks there are lions and tigers and bears in these woods!"

"Yeah, she's told me that too. I think she watched The Wizard of Oz too many times! We both know there are no lions, tigers, or bears here." Rebecca jokingly sang the familiar words, "Lions and tigers and bears, oh my!"

"Lions and tigers and bears, oh my," Chris repeated.

"Lions and tigers and bears, oh my," they sang together as

they marched along the path into the woods.

They walked fewer than fifty yards when they discovered the first bushes covered with plush red raspberries. Rebecca removed the plastic bowls from her backpack, handed one to Chris, kept a bowl for herself, and replaced the bag over her shoulders. As they picked berries, eating some and placing others in the bowls, they continued to talk, laugh, and wander further along the twisted path. Then, only a short distance further, Chris and Becca came upon lush blackberry bushes. And a few minutes later, they found some of the biggest, bluest blueberries either of them had ever seen. They seemed to lose track of time and place, but they were having a good time, fresh berries satisfied their appetites, and neither was on any schedule to return.

Rebecca truly loved hearing nature's sounds. The whispers of fluttering wings and singing birds in the trees filled her with joy as they strolled further into the woods. She could imagine songs and lyrics to sing with the birds. Chris broke the moment of quiet wonder, asking, "Who do you think made this path, Becca?"

"Well," she replied, "there's a lot of history in this area. In fact, in the later 1600s, a tribe of Native American Indians lived right here, in what is now our town of Rehoboth.

"Really?" he asked, stopping his berry picking long enough to look questioningly at his sister.

"Yes, Chris. Do you know of that hill of rock off of Route 44 named Anawan Rock?"

"Yeah, but I don't think I've been there."

"You'll probably go there on a fifth or sixth-grade class trip." Rebecca continued with her historical story. "Anawan Rock gets its name from the chief of the tribe. He was called Chief Anawan. They had battles with some English colonists who wanted to take their land. Some historians think Chief Anawan and his people lived at or near that big rock. Others believe it was a meeting place, a spiritual place, or a burial ground for the tribe. There are rumors that their artifacts might be buried right here in these woods."

"Really?" Chris asked again.

"It is said that when the English came to battle with the tribe, the Natives would retreat into the woods. They knew their way around the swamps, while the English didn't have the same knowledge of the area or the skills to find them. Some people say these woods are haunted by generations of people who got lost or died in the swamps."

Chris kicked at a pile of leaves under his feet. "Maybe if we look, we might find some arrowheads or hidden treasure."

"Maybe, but I doubt it," Rebecca responded. "It's been a few hundred years since they lived here. I suspect somebody would have discovered it years ago if anything were to be found."

Daydreaming about the history of the woods, they both got quiet for a while. The bowls they carried were getting full. New shadows were forming below the thick cover of the trees. They both knew it was nearing time to head for home.

Rebecca suddenly noticed that the woods had gone uncomfortably quiet. The birds were no longer singing. Even the buzzing of insects had reduced to absolute silence.

That's when a horrible, deafening noise came from behind the trees directly in front of them. "GrrrrrROAR!" it wailed. Chris and Rebecca both screamed. Still holding his bowl filled with berries, Chris turned and raced back down the trail from where they had come, screeching a heart-piercing cry as he ran.

Rebecca felt her heart jump into her throat. Moving only

by instinct, she bounded into the thick bushes. Stumbling in the thorny branches, she dropped her bowl of berries before staggering into the woods. Fear clouded her eyes as she ran wildly around large oaks and willows, bounded over fallen tree trunks, ducked under low-hanging branches, splashed through ankle-deep puddles, and raced through brambles of shrubs and bushes.

Even for an athletically fit seventeen-year-old teenager, the obstacles had to slow her eventually. With no concept of how long or far she had run, Rebecca finally looked over her shoulder to see if anything had followed her. With nothing in sight, she turned her head back in the direction she was running, just in time to keep from slamming into a long stone wall. It was the type of wall made many years ago with rocks piled on each other to mark property boundaries. This crusted old wall stood close to four feet high and stretched from left to right through the forest as far as she could see. Thick vines grew over and through the wall, and twisted trees with knotted roots grew out of the cracked and dirty rocks.

Rebecca quickly decided to climb over the wall of rocks to hide on the opposite side. She reasoned that if anything had followed her, it would not see her sitting behind the wall. Slowly, she began to catch her breath and collect her bearings. Except for knowing she was in the woods somewhere in Rehoboth, she had never seen this wall and did not know exactly where she was. Without a glimmer of sunlight peeking through the treetops, she was unsure what direction she was facing.

She reached into her pocket for her cell phone. First, she wanted to call Chris to make sure he was safe, then call someone for help to find her way out of these woods. Her concern for Chris was foremost on her mind. If the animal had not chased her, it might have gone after her brother. She would never forgive herself if he was attacked and she was not there to help him. She clicked on the phone, clicked on it again, and then a third time. It had no signal. How could the battery already be dead, she thought. It worked fine when I pulled it from the charger this morning. Rebecca felt defeated and afraid as she hid behind that wall, wondering what she would do now.

3 The Wall

A light fog settled into the treetops. Daylight filtering between the trees was becoming blurred in the haze. It's probably after five o'clock, Rebecca guessed. Without her cell phone, there was no knowing the exact time. She had been sitting with her back to the old stone wall for at least an hour. She knew she still had a couple of hours to get home before sunset, but she had no idea which direction to go.

Taking a drink of water from one of the bottles she had packed in her backpack, Rebecca realized that she was not feeling hungry even though it was nearing dinner time. Her loss of appetite might have been because of all the berries she had eaten earlier, but more likely, her stomach had not settled after the fright and running she had experienced that afternoon. She decided it would be wise to eat one of the granola bars to provide the energy to get home.

Thoughtfully stuffing the wrapper back into her backpack, Rebecca slowly stood up to look back over the wall of rocks. She could attempt to return the way she had come from, although her fear of the wolf or bear, or whatever had scared her, still had her too afraid of that choice. Perhaps she could follow the rock wall in one direction or continue forward the way she was already heading. Either way, the Rehoboth woods were no more than a few miles in any direction. Eventually, she would have to come out at a road or someplace she recognized.

Glancing over the wall one more time to scan the woods for any dangers, Rebecca gasped and instinctively ducked when a sizeable bird suddenly flew out of the shadows of the trees, passed only a few feet over her head, and landed on a branch no more than five yards away.

Because of its broad wingspan, Rebecca first thought it was a hawk, but after the bird settled on its branch, she could see more clearly that it was a stunningly beautiful owl. Creamy white feathers covered its body and wings, with reddish-brown feathered ears and tips just above its feet. Slightly longer and darker brown feathers at the ends of the bird's wings gave the appearance of long slender fingers. Large brilliant golden-brown eyes stared down at Rebecca from behind a band of dark gray color that wrapped around the owl's head like a bandit's mask. Feeling like the owl was peering into her soul, she cautiously fell back against the stone wall.

Grasping for any courage she could muster, Rebecca swallowed the lump in her throat to call out, "You startled me." She paused, almost expecting a response, but the owl only continued to stare. "You're quite a beautiful owl," she exclaimed. "Is there any chance you might know where I am?"

When the owl responded with a melodic "Hoot, Hoot," Rebecca jumped. To her, the sound was more like the cooing sounds of a dove than a magnificent owl.

"Might you suggest which way I should go to get home?" Rebecca cautiously asked.

"Hoot, Hoot," the owl appeared to reply, then it flew to the branch of another tree no more than five yards away. Then, again, it turned and stared at the girl.

"You think I should go that way?" Rebecca asked. She suddenly felt a foolish realization wash over her, "Look at me, I'm talking to an owl," she exclaimed. Dropping to the ground, back against the wall, feeling discouraged and unsure of herself, she wrapped her arms around her knees, placed her head across her arms, and began to cry.

The owl flew away a few moments later, following the wall to Rebecca's right. "Bye," she muttered, "It was nice talking with you."

Barely five minutes passed when the owl flew back, landing on the same branch it had first flown to several minutes before. "Hoot," it cheered.

Rebecca did not speak this time but wonderingly watched the owl. The brilliant sparkle in the owl's eyes gave her the feeling that he was watching and admiring her in return.

A few more minutes passed. Still deciding which way to go, Rebecca glanced left along the distance of the wall. Seeing it disappear into the thick forest of trees and foliage, she thought it looked impenetrable. The woods looked less dense and slightly easier to navigate to the right. Then, unexpectedly, she saw another movement on the wall, a small animal maybe forty yards away, skittering around trees and moving steadily in her direction. At first, she thought it might be a large squirrel, opossum, or a small raccoon. It disappeared behind trees, reappeared again, bounded over the thick roots and vines, jumped onto the wall's rocks, took a few cautious steps, and bounced back to the ground while maintaining a steady pace toward Rebecca.

Nearing less than twenty yards away, Rebecca was astonished to recognize the distinct features of a cat. Neither slowing nor quickening its pace; the mysterious cat swaggered up to just five feet away from where she sat in her layer of leaves, briefly glanced at the girl, took a seat, and began licking its front paws as though it was the most natural and expected thing to do.

Remembering a childhood friend, who had a cat

resembling this one, Becca believed it might be a Siamese or Persian cat called a Himalayan. Appearing rather large for a cat, it had white hair and face, with shades of tan on its ears, feet, and tail. Rebecca felt fascinated and mesmerized by its deep turquoise blue eyes.

"Well, hello, beautiful cat," Rebecca ventured, "Any chance you're here to rescue me?"

The cat's turquoise eyes fixed on her. It stood and walked toward the girl, purred as it rubbed its head and neck on her lower leg, then, taking a few steps away, it passed under the owl. Looking back at the bewildered girl, the cat vocalized a musical sound that captivated and moved her to rise and follow this unusual animal into the misty woods.

Rebecca glanced at the watchful owl as she took her first steps away from the wall. It appeared to wink at her, cooed an appreciative hoot, lifted off its branch, and flew ahead into the waiting forest.

4 Shrouded Swamp

The sun faded into a murky grey haze as the mist lowered itself into the swamp. Knowing she must have less than two hours of daylight, Rebecca wondered if she would make it home before nightfall. She closely followed the cat over a narrow, twisted path, cautiously trudging between deep pools of stagnant water and blackened moss-covered tree trunks. Scraggly branches reached down for her like skeleton fingers while the stench repulsed and discouraged her from venturing further into the mire.

The thickening fog around Rebecca's legs felt like it was rising from the swamp to slow her steps. It clung to her clothes in an attempt to pull her down. At times she thought she heard voices. Then she questioned whether the sounds were real or imagined. She instinctively focused on the cat, knowing it would be a dire mistake to stray from its path. Rebecca feared that one look away and her guide would be gone, leaving her alone to die in this noxious maze.

Movements skittered in and out of the mist at the sides of Rebecca's vision. Some she merely sensed as faceless and soundless shadows. Others scurried past in a blur of motion. Glowing eyes appeared to be watching as she passed. Then they blinked and disappeared into the fog. Recognizable sounds, such as croaking bullfrogs and buzzing insects, shared the mists with high-pitched noises, screeches of animals in distress, sudden splashes in the water, the rustling of tree branches overhead, and other indistinct noises fighting for attention. Every sound stretched her senses to the edge of fear. Her only consolation was to focus her attention on the movements of the mysterious cat.

Rebecca followed so closely to the cat that she almost tripped over it. Her most astonishing realization was that the cat seemed unnerved by sounds, visions, or anything happening around them. In some ways, the calmness felt comforting. In other ways, she questioned her sensibility in following an animal that didn't appear to be aware of imminent dangers coming at them from every direction.

Several times, when she felt most distracted by the movements and noises in the fog, Rebecca thought she heard the cat vocalize a sharp but gentle meow, pulling her attention back to their endeavor. Occasionally, Rebecca thought she heard the cat purring as if humming songs before shaking her head in doubt of her sanity. A few times, Rebecca thought she heard the cooing of the owl overhead. Then she wondered if her imagination was playing tricks on her. How could these animals be guiding her through this horrible, misty swamp?

Soon, the grey fog began growing darker. It became evident that she would not make it home before dark. She wondered if they would come out of these woods tonight or spend the night walking through this wretched swamp. While the woods grew dark, the noises grew louder. Although afraid and concerned, Rebecca felt grateful that she could still see the white cat. She forced herself to focus her attention on its back as they walked.

Suddenly, a rustling noise to her left caused Rebecca to freeze in her tracks. For a brief instant, she convinced herself that it was a figment of her imagination. Before taking her next step, something resembling a small two-legged animal dashed out of the darkness, and grabbed ahold of her leg, causing her to lose her balance. She tripped off the narrow strip of land where she had been standing, falling into a knee-deep stretch of slime-covered water and mud. The attacker jumped to her upper arm as Rebecca frantically tried to pull herself up. Face to face, it was close enough to see that it was like no animal she had ever seen. Although little more than one foot tall, its features were more human-like than any animal. It appeared to have a human face with only a thin patch of dark-brown matted hair hanging from the top of its head. The most shocking differences were flaming red eyes, a pointed nose, and a wide mouth with two rows of sharp teeth that menacingly grinned at her. Abnormally large hands, with long, pointed fingers, on thin stick-like arms, scratched desperately to hold onto the girl's upper arm near her shoulder.

Rebecca screamed in fear. She protectively swung at the attacker with one arm while desperately using the other to push herself above the water. The strike did not affect this creature, as it only dug its sharp fingers deeper into Rebecca's clothing. Its wide mouth snapped at her face. She rolled her head and body to the side in a troubled effort to turn her face away from the sharp teeth.

Abruptly, both Rebecca and the creature found themselves staring directly into the face of a massive white tiger. The animal's head was two feet wide. It was so close she could smell its heavy breath and feel the steam from its nostrils. There was not a moment to think or move. The tiger bellowed a deafening roar as it swung an enormous paw only inches above the shocked girl's face. The creature on Rebecca's shoulder had but a second to screech a loud wailing cry as the tigers' claws tore through its body.

Rebecca fell under the black, oily surface. Still struggling to regain her footing and composure in the deep mud, she knew she would be next to face the dangerous beast when she raised her head above the water. She thought it might be easier to drown in the wretched swamp than to face the brutal pain the monstrous tiger would inflict on her.

It wasn't a choice. Instinct forced Rebecca to raise her head above the surface to gasp for breath. As the water dripped from her eyes, she expected to see the massive head and a huge clawed paw smashing across her vulnerable face. Instead, she was met only by darkness and unexpected silence. She slowly sat up, wiped the water from her eyes, and looked around. The tiger appeared to be gone. Cautiously, Rebecca crawled to the spot of land where the attack had begun, allowing herself to drop face down to the ground. After wearily laying there for a minute, she breathed a heavy sigh of relief. Then, turning her head to one side, she found herself staring into the turquoise eyes of the unusual cat.

"Well, I am certainly happy to see you," Rebecca cried out loud. The cat gave a responsive meow, took a step forward, licked the girl's face, then sat back down and began to purr.

Exhausted, Rebecca pushed herself up to a sitting position. Leaning back against a tree, she gave herself an inspection for any wounds, which surprisingly were not as bad as she expected. She had scratches along her upper arm, just below her shoulder, where the attacker grabbed her. But, other than a few minor bruises and patches of mud and moss stuck to parts of her body, nothing else appeared to be harmed. She was surprised to discover that she was still wearing her backpack. The straps covered the same spot on her shoulder where the attacker had grabbed ahold of her, probably saving her from receiving more than minor scratches.

Another abrupt sound crackled in the branches. Rebecca gasped and quickly crouched against the tree. This time it was not a ground attack, nor the massive white tiger, but something was charging through the trees from above. She released her breath when she heard the cooing hoot of an owl. Her white owl with the gray mask flew out of the darkness, landing on a branch barely a few feet over her head. Its glowing golden-yellow eyes seemed to wink at her. Then it proceeded to speak in hoots and cooing sounds toward the cat.

Rebecca wondered, could the owl and the cat communicate with each other? Again, the owl glanced at Rebecca, winked, and flew off into the trees. Finally, the cat stood up, stepped forward to provide the girl with a gentle nudge with its nose, turned, and began to walk away. With little thought or consideration for other options, she pushed her weary body to her feet and moved quickly to stay close behind the precious cat. Hmm, Precious, that would be a good name for the cat, she thought. The cat looked back over its shoulder at Rebecca, then turned its attention to the narrow winding path. She briefly wondered if the unusual animal could have heard her thoughts. She shook her head as if to answer her own question. No, the cat was just checking to make sure she was following.

Rebecca noticed the sounds of the forest beginning to rise again. She thought the buzz of insects and the croaking of frogs was a good sign. However, her thoughts were mainly on the white tiger. Was it still nearby? What was a tiger doing in these woods? Why did it kill her attacker yet leave her alone? And how did it suddenly appear and disappear as it did? "I hope I never come face to face with it again," she shuddered, "but if I do, I hope it won't be hungry, and it will always be on my side."

Another thought suddenly occurred to her. What if that
tiger is the animal that scared her and Chris? "Oh God,
please let Chris be home safely," she silently prayed into
the darkening mists.

5 Visions

With her mind fixated on the day's frightening events, Rebecca fought to keep pace behind the ethereal cat in the darkness and the thick fog. She didn't notice when the ground first rose above the swamp. The twisted narrow trails and treacherous waters gave way to a grassy slope providing open spaces between trees with leafy branches. She first realized the change in terrain when she noticed the scent of pine trees. A few dozen steps later, the slope crested into a grove of tall pines. After enduring the toxic stench of the swamp, Rebecca became enthusiastic about the intoxicating scent of fresh pines. It reminded her of the sweet smell of a fresh-cut Christmas tree in her living room, except this was a hundred times more refreshing.

Mere seconds was all Rebecca needed to kick off her wet ankle boots. She had been sloshing in them since being attacked and nearly drowned by the forest creature. The thick bed of damp pine needles felt more comforting than she could have imagined before this frightful day.

Within the grove, the fog thinned enough to see a dozen yards around her and several branches upward into the canopy of trees. Rebecca felt genuinely relieved to see her owl friend peering down on her from a low-hanging branch. "Well, hello again," she exclaimed. The wondrous bird appeared to smile and wink at her. She grinned in response to the unusual circumstances.

Turning to find the cat stretched comfortably across a pile of pine needles, Rebecca asked out loud, "Is this where we're stopping for the night?" Receiving no reply, she slid her backpack to the ground and settled on a bed of pine needles under a large tree. Expecting everything in her pack to be drenched from her dunking in the swamp, she was grateful to discover the bag had been closed tight enough to keep its insides relatively dry. She took one of the lettuce, tomato, and cheese sandwiches out of the bag with a granola bar and the previously opened water bottle. She tossed small pieces of the sandwich toward the cat and the owl, but neither showed any interest beyond passing glances at the food. To suggest that Rebecca devoured the sandwich and granola bar would be an understatement. She practically swallowed it whole and quickly washed it down with half of the bottle of water.

Looking up at the owl, Rebecca announced, "With that beautiful mask around your eyes, I will name you Bandit." Then, turning to the cat, she declared, "And I've decided to name you Precious." Both animals just stared at the girl. She smiled reassuringly. That's the last thing Rebecca remembered before falling asleep.

The dream seemed to come to Rebecca almost immediately after closing her eyes. An angelic presence inserted itself into her semi-conscious mind. The vivid image appeared as a comforting mother with open arms and a soothing voice, offering solace to her fearful child. She had glowing dark tanned skin, a compassionate, loving smile, rosy cheeks, and light brown eyes that shined adoringly like a new mother seeing her baby for the first time. She appeared to be wearing a silky white dress, with a simple suede belt, necklace, and thin headband holding back her long dark hair. Her features reminded Rebecca of her mother. She was surrounded by a brilliant glowing light, creating the perception of a translucent angel.

"Listen closely, my child," she spoke gently but directly, "I have but one minute to share this message. I am your maternal great-grandmother in spirit form to serve as your counsel. In my native language, you would call me Nani. You are beginning a journey where you will encounter people unlike any you have known before. Some will become close friends and dependable allies. Others will present difficult challenges. To survive these challenges will depend on your ability to determine who you can trust and who can not be trusted. You must discover your strengths, find your magic, master your skills, and believe in yourself. Spirit Guides are with you, helping to lead and protect you. They can hear and understand you at this time, although you have not yet developed your senses to hear them. Listen closely, and you will learn to communicate with them. For the time being, trust your intuition. I will come to speak with you in the space between awake and asleep. Tonight, my time is ending. One final message," the angelic woman declared, "The owl is named Wisdom, not Bandit. The cat, which is not really a cat, is named Tempest, not Precious. And the nightingale is named Songbird. Awaken now to remember my message, then sleep well, my child."

Rebecca called out, "Wait, Nani, I have many questions. What kind of tests? What do you mean, find my magic?" Before she finished asking the questions, the woman's image faded into the darkness. Rebecca's eyes snapped open. She felt a shiver rush through her spine. For a brief moment, she wondered if it was a dream. Yet somehow, she knew this was real. After this day, even a visit by her maternal great-grandmother could not be entirely in her imagination.

She thought about her grandmother's message. It felt like a lot to grasp in a short time. Then she remembered her animal friends. Could they be her spirit guides? Rebecca raised her head from the pine needle bed. The owl rested on the same branch he had been on since they entered the grove. "Thank you, Wisdom," Rebecca called out. The owl blinked and responded with a cooing sound. The cat, which she was informed is not really a cat, curled up just a couple of feet away, appearing to be asleep. If she is not really a cat, what is she? Rebecca wondered.

"Thank you, Tempest," she whispered. Tempest did not appear to respond, as cats typically choose, but Rebecca thought she glimpsed a tiny smile.

Rebecca closed her eyes again. "Nightingale, what nightingale?" she questioned aloud as she fell fast asleep.

Instinctively, Rebecca reached across her bed with her eyes closed to shut off the radio alarm clock. But, when she came up with her second handful of pine needles, the previous day's memories abruptly reminded her of where she was. Please tell me that was all a bad dream, she thought, wishing she could turn back the clock for a one-day do-over. Cautiously opening her eyes, Rebecca was startled to see a pair of gleaming turquoise eyes staring back at her.

"Good morning, Tempest," the girl affectionately spoke to the unusual cat.

Tempest was lying barely one foot directly in front of her face. Whether she was staring amusedly, affectionately, patiently, or impatiently, Rebecca guessed, would soon be determined. Then, as if responding to her thoughts, Tempest crawled forward, pleasantly surprised the girl with a lick on the tip of her nose, and then sat back and watched.

Rebecca grinned. "What a wonderful way to wake up," she spoke aloud.

Rolling onto her back, Rebecca peered up to the branch where she remembered last seeing the owl. Wisdom was still there, but he was no longer alone. A beautiful bird, comparable in size to a blue jay, sat only inches away. It appeared to have reddish-brown feathered wings and tail, with a buff-white-colored chest and face. A pale-yellow plumage ran from the base of the bird's beak above its eyes to somewhere towards the rear of the bird's head. It sang a beautifully melodic song, blending whistles, warbles, and vibrating trills into a series of notes that Rebecca immediately felt was one of the most transcendent sounds she had ever heard.

Rebecca listened contentedly for several minutes, waiting for the bird to pause in its singing before lifting herself to a sitting position. Then, finally, she clapped her hands enthusiastically toward their morning guest.

"Good morning, Wisdom," Rebecca politely greeted the owl, "I hope you slept well." Wisdom blinked his eyes and cooed at the girl.

She then turned her attention to the new, smaller bird. "I'm guessing that you must be the delightful nightingale named Songbird. Is that a correct assumption?"

The bird whistled toward the girl, astonishing her with what she regarded as a genuine response to her question.

Rebecca stretched and began to ponder her circumstances. She quietly laughed at the thought that she had three animal companions she spoke to and seemed to understand her. More seriously, she's placed her trust in an owl, a nightingale, and a cat that might not be a cat to protect her and guide her through a treacherous swamp filled with dangerous creatures. She slept in wet clothes after fighting for her life with an angry imp-like goblin. And what about that white tiger? Is it still out there, maybe looking for her? How will her animal friends protect her from a massive tiger? Hopefully, her new friends will lead her out of these woods to go home. Her parents must be freaking out with worry about her, and she's still concerned about her brother. She wished there was a way to call them. It reminded her to recheck her cell phone, but it was still hopelessly dead.

Dense fog still hung in the air. The sun was not visible, but Rebecca felt relief for daylight filtering into the pine grove rather than darkness. She ate one of the peanut butter and raspberry preserves sandwiches she had packed for Chris and finished the bottled water she had started the day before. Taking note of the one unopened water bottle, two sandwiches, and two granola bars left in her backpack, she carefully repacked the empty bottle and sandwich bags. Then, she removed her toothbrush and toothpaste and stepped behind a tree to brush her teeth. Odd, Rebecca thought; she didn't feel comfortable brushing her teeth in front of her animal friends!

She wished she could take a hot shower. The foul smell of the swamp lingered on her wet clothes. I guess there's no reason to dwell on things I have no control over, she thought. Rebecca returned from behind the tree. Placing her toothbrush and toothpaste back into the essentials pocket on her backpack, a glint of light glanced off her pocket knife. Something told her that if she ever needed her knife, this could most likely be one of those times. She took the knife from her pack and slid it into her pants pocket. Rebecca pressed into her wet ankle boots. Although not filled with water as they had been the night before, they were still uncomfortably damp.

Slinging her backpack over her shoulders, Rebecca turned

to her companions to cheerfully announce, "I'm ready to go if you are!" Wisdom winked and flew in the opposite direction from where they had entered the grove. Tempest stood, patiently stretched each leg one at a time, yawned, shook her head like she was shaking off cobwebs, then sauntered off behind the owl. Songbird flew just far enough to stay within sight of the girl, landed on another branch, and turned back to watch for the girl to follow after the cat. Rebecca took a final deep breath of the pine forest. Then, letting the air release slowly, she allowed the fresh scent to register in her memory and took the first steps into the new day.

Tempest waited at the edge of the pines for Rebecca to catch up before beginning the trek down the hillside. The wilting leafless trees and dead moss-covered willows she had been unable to see in the dark the night before were now visible. As they moved lower down the slope, the fog grew progressively thicker. At the base of the hill, the ground flattened, and the stench of the swamp rose to meet them.

A short distance away, they heard Wisdom hoot. Tempest immediately turned to follow the owl's call. They approached a large willow tree where Wisdom stood on a broken branch lying on the ground. Looking up at Rebecca, he tapped one foot on the limb. Rebecca instinctively understood. Growing up in a country town, every kid was familiar with walking sticks. Such branches could become the staff of kings, a lance, or sword, or bent and tied with a string at each end to create a bow, with smaller sticks becoming arrows.

She lifted the pole-shaped branch in her hands. It was about five feet long and almost perfectly straight, with only a few notches protruding from its sides where smaller branches were once attached. It tapered from approximately two inches thick at one end to less than one inch at the other. Rebecca smiled at Wisdom. "Is this my hiking staff?" she asked. Wisdom cooed and flew up to the branch next to Songbird. She planted the smaller end of the staff into the ground. As she held it out in front of her, she felt a notch sticking into her hand where she felt most comfortable holding it. She quickly pulled out her pocket knife and cut the annoying piece off.

"Perfect," she declared, "that might be the most practical use I've ever made of that pocket knife. Thank you, Wisdom. I will proudly carry this walking stick."

Wisdom winked at the girl, lifted from his branch, and flew back into the thick fog. Songbird waited a moment before following. Tempest looked up at Rebecca, voiced a noticeable meow, and turned to follow the birds. Rebecca smiled. With staff in hand, she briskly followed after her guides.

Within minutes, the woods thickened, and the mists began to swirl. Rebecca wrapped her arms around herself as she moved closer behind Tempest. The cat hurdled over large stumps and squeezed between trees that Rebecca was slow to navigate. Low branches the cat did not notice scratched at her face, but she lowered her head and kept pace without comment or complaint.

The path often depended on jumping from one rock to another or balancing on long moss-covered roots stretching over deep ponds of oily black water. Rebecca was grateful for the hiking staff. It helped to maintain her balance. One wrong step would easily slip her into the putrid muck or bubbling pits of burning tar where every belch released a sickening stench. Rebecca pulled her shirt over her mouth and nose to protect herself from the toxic gases.

Dense swirling fog limited Rebecca's visibility to only a few yards. The sounds of bugs, animals, and indistinct noises grew louder as they moved deeper into the swamp. The one difference she noticed today was the whistling and singing of the nightingale. Songbird's melodic songs came from in front of them, sometimes directly overhead, but never far away. Rebecca thought she caught glimpses of the strange goblin creatures, similar to the one who attacked her the day before. But today, instead of hiding and racing past, they appeared to be dancing in dizzying twirls and twists. Is it possible, she wondered if they might be dancing to the nightingale's enchanting songs?

Tempest and Rebecca were crossing over a small island of land covered with dead fallen trees and heavy underbrush when Songbird's music suddenly stopped. The entire forest went quiet. A moment later, Songbird landed with a thud on a small spot of ground next to the cat, a small arrow jutting through her wing. The bird gently whistled to Rebecca, letting the girl know she was alive. Reacting quickly, Rebecca broke the arrow and pulled the attached piece through. She reached into her pack for the unopened water bottle, generously poured water over the open wound, and used tissues from her bag to wipe off the blood.

She had just finished cleaning Songbird's wound when loud screeching wails pierced the silence. Several impish goblins charged into the small clearing, intending to attack the travelers. There appeared to be about a dozen of the creatures. Their faces shared characteristics, like red eyes, pointed noses, and wide mouths with visibly sharp teeth, although each was somewhat distinct in size, weight, and overall appearance. Some were slender, some muscular, and some were surprisingly round. They varied between one and two feet in height. Some had long, ragged hair, while others had little or no hair. A few had beards, and some looked like females. Each seemed to bear individual distorted characteristics, including extraordinarily large or small hands and feet, twisted arms, legs, and necks. Deep scars replaced missing body parts. And they all wore pieces of moss, bark, and vines in place of clothing.

The creatures held sticks sharpened into knives and spears or carried wooden clubs. A few had handmade bows and arrows like the arrow shot through Songbird's wing. Impulsively, Rebecca swung her hiking staff at the first goblin to get near, striking its face and sending it tumbling back into the fog. Immediately, Songbird sprung in front of her, fiercely attacking the nearest creature, beak first into the goblin's eye. It dropped to the ground crying out in pain. Wisdom swooped from the trees, wings spread wide like a dark shadow, talons tearing and shredding the nearest creatures to bloody pieces. And that was when Rebecca discovered what Nani meant when she said Tempest is a cat which is not really a cat.

Tempest bounded in front of Rebecca, turned to face the assailants, and began to grow. In mere seconds the cat swelled into a giant, terrifying white tiger. Her back stood at least four feet tall, and her head towered at least two feet over her body. Muscles rippled everywhere. She roared so loudly; the sound echoed through the woods. Claws slashed, and teeth tore into the goblins. Pieces of arms, legs, and bloody body parts splattered in every direction. When the last few attackers turned to run, Tempest and Wisdom bore down on them like tiny fleeing bugs.

It ended almost as quickly as it began. Tempest, the fierce tiger, glanced at Rebecca before shrinking back to the size and form of the Himalayan cat. Then calmly sat down and began licking her paws. Wisdom flew the few yards across the open space to land next to the teen, still shaken by the attack. The owl looked into Rebecca's eyes and voiced a long soothing coo, spreading a calm sensation over her. Songbird warbled a soft melodic song. She was letting the girl know she was okay. Rebecca sat by a broken tree stump for a few minutes, catching her breath and feeling utter awe of her companions.

The travelers had barely restarted their journey when Rebecca began hearing voices calling her name. Turning toward the voices, she saw translucent images of people walking through the woods in small groups, searching for her. She recognized most as neighbors, classmates, police, and firefighters from her town spread out through the woods. Rebecca called out to them, "Here I am." But they didn't hear her. Some passed by only feet away, but they couldn't see her.

Her mother, stepfather, and her brother appeared. Rebecca felt immense relief at seeing Chris with her mother and stepfather. They moved slowly, huddled together, tears and concern displayed in their eyes. Her stepfather, Shawn, called out her name. Rebecca reached for them, but her arms passed through the ghostly apparition. Doubts entered her mind. Could she be dead? Maybe she entered a bizarre netherworld. Or is she losing her mind? Her senses told her the visions were genuine. Her friends, neighbors, and family were searching the woods for her. Yet, she was passing them by in these haunted woods. Rebecca felt hurt for the pain she knew they must be feeling. Somehow, she must let them know she's okay. Somehow, she must find her way out of this ghostly mist.

6 Gypsies

After the visions subsided, they traveled through the swamp for another two hours before Rebecca noticed that the terrain was changing and the fog appeared to be lifting. They no longer tread narrow twisting paths between dead trees and deep murky waters. The ground was drier. Leaves were beginning to appear in the trees. Rebecca could not yet see the sun or the sky, but she could see further as light filtered through the thinning mist. She felt a sense of relief to see a small white birch sapling. It meant she had survived the horrors of the swamp, and maybe she was nearing home.

Rebecca no longer followed inches from Tempest's tail. Instead, she and the cat now walked side by side. She commented on her observations and even asked questions, but other than an occasional glance in her direction, Tempest did not appear to respond in any recognizable way.

Wisdom was now visible, flying ahead of the group and watching for unexpected obstacles or encounters. After singing for more than two hours, Songbird only whistled to draw attention to occasional flowers or small animals, including a wild turkey, a pair of squirrels, and a tiny snake. None of which paid any attention to the travelers. Songbird gleefully fluttered around, displaying that her wounded wing did not seem to bother her. Rebecca felt an indescribable connection to the colorful bird. Each time the nightingale landed nearby, Songbird would peer into the girl's eyes with a look of caring and concern. Or, at least that was the impression she felt.

With the dangers of the swamp behind her, Rebecca

thought about her great-grandmother's visit the night before. It had to be more than a dream. One of Nani's messages was to learn to communicate with her Spirit Guides, who she now knew unquestionably were these three animals accompanying, protecting, and guiding her through these dangerous woods. "Trust your intuition," Nani said. Rebecca questioned whether Nani's visit could have been a figment of her imagination. But her intuition was telling her this entire improbable dream was true.

Suddenly, the four companions stepped through the wall of mist onto a hillside covered with tall green and gold grass. Yellow, white, and violet wildflowers and plush green trees stretched across the landscape. Random clouds floated in the sky, but overall, it was a spectacularly sunny day filled with energy and promises. The sun rested halfway between the top of the hill and the center of the sky. She guessed it was probably between ten and eleven in the morning, and they were facing east. Wisdom, Songbird, Tempest, and Rebecca headed toward the nearest tree for a much-needed rest. Songbird emanated a few cheerful whistles as she fluttered in and out of the tree branches.

Rebecca looked back to where they had entered the field. She was astonished to see the fog stood like a giant wall along the edge of the woods. From the ground to the tops of the trees, it spread in each direction as far as she could see. Settling against the tree, she placed her hiking staff in the grass beside her and stretched her fingers. Except for the few moments when Songbird had been shot with the arrow, the staff had not been out of her hand.

Rebecca quickly became aware that she did not recognize where she was. Not that she knew every field and patch of trees in Rehoboth, but she had assumed they would come through the woods to a familiar road, landmark, or house. She again tried her cell phone, but it still had no power.

Reaching into her backpack to retrieve the remaining two sandwiches and bottled water, Rebecca remembered that she had not seen any of the animals eat or drink since she began traveling with them the previous day. The snap-on lids meant to cover the bowls she and Chris had carried would work ideally as plates. She laid the covers top-down on the grass, proceeded to fill bottled water into one, and broke up parts of the two sandwiches into pieces on the other. Between pieces of lettuce, tomato, cheese, bread, peanut butter, and raspberry preserves, she guessed there must be something her companions would be hungry enough to eat. She placed the plates in front of her and asked the animals to "please eat." All three generously shared the meal while Rebecca finished the remaining sandwiches and water. She giggled amusedly at the sight of the owl, nightingale, and cat all drinking from the same water dish. She kept the two granola bars while quietly hoping food and fresh water would be readily available now that they were free from the retched swamp.

After lunch, Rebecca packed the bowl covers and sandwich bags into her backpack, and the group headed for the crest of the hilltop. Wisdom led the way, with Songbird close behind. The birds remained within the girl's sight, stopping in another tree barely fifty yards away. As Tempest and Rebecca walked close together through the field, she noticed that much of the tall grass was above the cat's head.

"Tempest, would you like me to carry you?" Rebecca asked nonchalantly.

The cat quickly increased his pace and distance from the girl, forcing her to run to keep up.

"You don't have to be sarcastic about it," she called out to the cat.

As they neared the tree where Wisdom and Songbird waited, Rebecca discovered it was an apple tree, abundant with lush red ripe apples.

She called out, "Thank you" to the birds, quickly picked six of the nearest fruit, and placed them in her backpack.

The two birds flew from the apple tree to a tall billowing oak tree at the top of the hill. Upon her arrival at the oak, Rebecca discovered a worn path only yards from the tree, where wheels had formed grooves in the grass. Tempest laid in the tree's shade. The birds appeared content in its branches, so Rebecca settled against the tree. Only minutes passed before the sound of horses could be heard coming in their direction.

A short distance away, where the path wrapped around a group of trees, a pair of work horses pulled an old gypsy wagon. Rebecca recognized the wooden box-like house on wagon wheels from history books. However, this horse-drawn gypsy wagon was not colorful like those she had seen in pictures. It was made of wood with no paint or color on it at all. In a seat at the front of the wagon sat a middle-aged man, wearing a large-brimmed hat shading his face. He looked strong, with a chiseled jaw, broad chest, and muscular arms. His skin was darkened and hard, like a man who had spent a lifetime working outdoors. His clothes looked faded and worn. They may have once been brilliant and colorful, but that day had long since passed.

Next to him sat a young woman, or perhaps a teenage girl. A reddish-brown bandana held her hair back behind her head.

She wore a plain white blouse and loose-fitting jeans. She had a radiant glow to her skin from an abundance of sunshine, but her features appeared to be a perfect mix of natural beauty and coarsened toughness. Rebecca immediately guessed she would rather have this girl as a friend than an enemy.

As the wagon neared, Rebecca stood up to greet them. The pair on the wagon appeared startled to see a girl standing alone under the tree. They slowed the horses to a stop and looked around carefully to ensure nobody else might be hiding behind the nearby trees.

"What are you doing out here?" the man called out to her from a short but safe distance.

"I've been lost in the woods since yesterday," Rebecca responded, pointing back toward the fog-covered forest. "I just came out of it this morning, but I'm still unsure exactly where I am.

"You just came through that forest?" the man questioned, doubting the girl's claim. Then, looking around suspiciously, he called out, "Are you alone?"

"I have a cat," she called back as she pointed at Tempest, "and a couple of birds who helped guide me through the swamp are in the tree, but no other people are with me."

The man quietly spoke to the girl riding beside him before signaling the horses to move the wagon forward. He brought the wagon to a complete stop as he pulled up next to the girl, The man spoke calmly, "For your safety, I suggest you come with us. You can bring the cat. I suspect the birds can easily fly if they wish to follow." He then proceeded with introductions. "My name is Aaron. And this is my daughter, Jillian, although she prefers to be called Jill. My son is in the back. Jules, come out here, Son," he called out.

Rebecca caught her breath when a handsome young man

appeared from behind the wagon. He was tall, slender, and fit, with black hair, dark tanned skin, and the most brilliant sparkling green eyes that Rebecca thought she had ever seen. He wore a white long-sleeve shirt with a dark green vest. Faded brown jeans tucked into black leather boots just inches below his knees. He held a handmade crossbow in one hand, with an arrow stretched across its barrel, pointed at the ground.

"My apologies for the weapon, my lady," apologized the young man. "You never know who or what you might encounter this close to the Sorcerer's wall."

"Sorcerer's wall?" Rebecca gasped. But nobody seemed to hear her concern.

"What might your name be, young lady?" Aaron asked.

"My name is Rebecca, although most of my family and friends call me Becca," she replied. "And this wonderful cat who accompanies me is named Tempest."

"You look familiar," said the father, "although I am unsure how I might know you. But, please, come to our home. Meet my wife. She will cook a fine dinner for us. We will all have an opportunity to talk and become acquainted." Then, turning to his son, he called out, "Jules, come ride up front with me. Let's give Becca and Jill a chance to talk first."

It didn't pass her attention that Aaron called her Becca.

Beaming an enthusiastic smile, Jill jumped to the ground from her seat on the wagon. Before Rebecca could say hello, Jill embraced her in an exuberant hug. "I already know we are going to become wonderful friends!" Jill exclaimed.

Rebecca watched Jules climb to the seat next to his father. I hope Jules becomes my friend too, she thought, then reprimanded herself for even thinking about him that way.

Returning to the tree to pick up her backpack and the

hiking staff, Rebecca looked around for Tempest, finding her sitting by the back corner of the wagon, patiently licking a paw. "Are you ready to go for a ride, Tempest?" she called out. The cat continued to sit and lick, seemingly ignoring the girl.

Peering upward into the tree's branches for the birds, Rebecca immediately found Wisdom and Songbird sitting quietly on a limb, staring back at her. Wisdom winked and gave his customary "Hoot" of approval. The unusually quiet nightingale appeared to nod her head toward the girl and whistled a few soft, comforting notes, which Rebecca was sure only she could hear. She thought Songbird seemed to say, "It's okay."

As Rebecca started toward the back of the wagon, a thought turned her back to the two men. Reaching into her backpack, she presented two apples she had picked only minutes before to the father and son. A third apple she handed to Jill. Then she looked up at the father to ask, "Sir, may I give an apple to each of your magnificent horses?"

For a moment, both men appeared somewhat speechless. They looked at each other, then back at Rebecca. Aaron's shoulders seemed to rise a little higher. Then, with a proud smile, he answered, "Of course, Becca, our horses would love it."

As Rebecca approached the large animals, she held out the apples and gently told each horse how beautiful and strong they were. She was happy that the horses did not have bits in their mouths. Instead, the reins were attached to harnesses around their chests. Rebecca took a moment to pet each horse along their neck and heads while telling them that she could see how hard they worked and how proud she felt to meet them.

Turning from the horses, Jill anxiously took Rebecca's hand and led her to the back of the wagon. Opening the door, Tempest immediately jumped in. The cat appeared to inspect the small cabin quickly before looking at Rebecca with a blink of her eyes and a nod of acceptance.

"Thank you for protecting me, Tempest," Rebecca affectionately whispered to the cat as she climbed aboard.

The cabin appeared to be about seven feet wide, twelve feet deep, and close to eight feet in height. Two wooden benches stretched along each side wall. Each bench was covered with a thin cloth cushion and a pillow propped up at the furthest end. The rear wall had a closet on the right-side corner; a waist-high counter stretched from the closet to the left side wall. Doored cabinets lined the back wall above and below the counter. Centered on each side wall, a small one-foot square open-air window with opened shutters allowed air and light into the room. The room was cluttered with household items, tools, supplies, and unusual oddities hanging on hooks or stuffed into overflowing wooden crates.

Jill closed the bottom half of the door while the top half remained open. She quickly invited Rebecca to sit while anxiously placing herself directly across from her guest. Jill was still grinning from ear to ear, obviously excited about the companionship of her new friend. Tempest, facing the girls, relaxed in front of the cabinets by the rear wall.

As the wagon lurched forward, Rebecca suddenly realized that this ride was not taking her home!

It felt like a short distance in the gypsy wagon, as far as gypsy wagon rides go. At least that's what Rebecca thought. On the other hand, it was bumpy, and the horse-drawn wagon moved slowly. She guessed they had traveled less than a mile during the half-hour excursion.

Jill did most of the talking. She would ask questions and then continue talking before Rebecca could answer them. She quickly learned that Jill and Jules were twins who were only a few weeks older than her. The teens spent a lot of time working with their parents at their farm home and an outdoor market where they had learned to trade goods. The market was where they were coming from this day. Jill told her how most people held old preconceived notions about gypsies. Although many people did business with her family, she had few close friends, which explained why Jill was so excited to welcome a new friend into her life.

At one point during the primarily one-sided conversation, Songbird settled on the open windowsill over Jill's head, surveyed the cabin, and shared an observant look with Rebecca. Then she appeared to silently communicate with Tempest in a focused moment of eye contact before flying away. Rebecca quietly giggled to herself, amused that Jill remained blissfully unaware of the appearance of the nightingale.

Jill announced they were home when the wagon made a sharp left turn and began climbing a slightly inclined hill. A few minutes later, the wagon came to a stop. As Rebecca followed Jill out of the cabin door, she heard Aaron tell the twins to take care of the horses while he introduced Becca to their mother. The gypsy wagon parked between the relatively simple house and a similar-looking barn, each built with plain wood boards. Even the roofs were covered only with wood boards. A large garden covered most of what they might call a yard, and an old-fashioned wishing well sat near the front door.

As Aaron entered the house with Rebecca and Tempest following closely behind, he called out, "Honey, we're home, and we've brought a guest."

A nice-looking woman with a friendly smile appeared from another room. Likely in her young forties, she wore long brunette hair pulled back in a bun. A long plain brown apron hung from her neck to below her knees. She held a long wooden spoon in one hand, with something caked on it that she had been preparing.

Aaron began the introduction, "Jasmine, this is...."

The spoon dropped to the floor. A look of shock replaced the woman's smile. "Clover, is that you?" she gasped.

A somewhat startled Rebecca responded, "My mother's name is Clover, or at least that's the name she once went by. Now she goes by her birth name, Mary Anne. My name is Rebecca. Do you know my mother?"

"Oh heavens, you look exactly as I remember her," Jasmine exclaimed. "And yes, your mother and I grew up together. We were best friends through most of our younger years." Then, picking up the spoon from the floor, she haltingly explained, "Please excuse me, Rebecca. I am preparing dinner. Aaron, would you please show our guest where she could tidy up? Rebecca, we will likely have much to talk about during and after our dinner." Jasmine then abruptly turned and left the room.

Aaron looked at Rebecca. "Well," he said, "I think I now know from where I recognize you. You do look much like I remember your mother. Follow me, young lady. I will show you where the wash room is. Do you have a change of clothes in that bag you carry?"

"No," she replied, "I did not know I would be here. After coming through the swamp, I must be a horrible mess."

"Do not be concerned. You appear to be the same size as Jillian," he offered, "I will have her get you a fresh set of clothes."

As Aaron led Rebecca from the room, he stopped to pick up one of three thick wooden pails of steaming water hanging from a hook over a fireplace filled with hot embers. He led her to a small room with a large wooden bowl set on a corner counter, where he poured the hot water. A chair was sitting next to the basin. A shelf held several folded towels and four hooks with robes hung along one wall. "The robes are clean," he said. "After you've washed, you're welcome to use one until Jill brings you fresh clothes. Leave your dirty clothes on the floor outside the door. Jasmine or Jill will clean them for you later."

Aaron opened a latched door along the back wall and pointed to an outhouse about twenty yards from the door. "If you should need it, there's the outhouse," he commented, then closed and latched the door. Then, returning to where they had come in, he pulled the washroom door closed behind him as he left.

Tempest sprawled on the floor next to the chair and closed her eyes, appearing to sleep. Rebecca felt somewhat confused by the outhouse, washroom, and lack of conventional plumbing. Add to that the horse-drawn gypsy wagon, and everything about this place felt perplexing. However, she was relieved to wash the unpleasantness from her body and change her filthy clothes. She had barely finished washing when Jill knocked at the door with a clean blouse, pants, underwear, and socks. Shoes were not included, so Rebecca took a few minutes to clean her ankle boots and backpack. Unsure about proper etiquette, she decided to place her pack and still-damp shoes near the fireplace and walk around in stocking feet until she needed to leave the house.

Rebecca asked Jasmine if she might help prepare dinner but was quickly reminded that she was a guest in their home, at least for today. While Jill, Jules, and Aaron took turns washing, she rested in a comfortable chair in the family room. There was little conversation as the family members hustled in and out of the room, knowingly managing their chores. Jasmine thoughtfully set water and food bowls next to Rebecca's chair for Tempest. The cat was not shy about eating every morsel from the food bowl and nearly finished the water.

While waiting, Rebecca observed that there were no electric lights, telephone, television, or even a radio. She wondered if this was a typical gypsy lifestyle or a religious choice. Windows were opened throughout the house to welcome sunlight and air, except for one wall covered by full-length curtains. Unlit candles were scattered around the room, waiting for nightfall. Finally, Jasmine called the group to dinner. A small kitchen and dining area, which Rebecca noticed, held no stove, refrigerator, or any electric appliances. Instead, an open fireplace set into an end wall, an icebox stood next to a large basin filled with water in place of a traditional kitchen sink. The table was big enough to seat five people comfortably, but the space to move around was tightly limited.

Jasmine had prepared a bountiful dinner with a whole chicken and a variety of freshly cooked vegetables from their garden. The conversation involved general questions from the family, although each response led to another curiosity or comparison of their lives. Rebecca told them her story of getting separated from her brother, becoming lost in the woods, following the three animals through the swamp, and her frightful encounters with the hateful goblin creatures.

When Jasmine asked if Rebecca's mother ever mentioned their friendship or journey into this land, Rebecca uncomfortably admitted that she did not remember her mother speaking about Jasmine or this place. "Truth be told," Rebecca confessed, "I still don't know where this place is!" Rebecca guessed she was about to learn something she might be better off not knowing.

7 Revelations

Jasmine began her story, telling first about three young girls named Mary Anne, Jill, and Elizabeth, who became best friends in elementary school. Around the age of ten, Mary Anne decided she wanted to be called by her middle name, Clover. The other girls decided they wanted to be named after flowers too. Jill chose Jasmine because it started with the letter J, and Elizabeth chose Violet because the color purple was her favorite color. They continually insisted that everybody call them by their chosen flower names until that's how they were known.

Throughout their teens, the three friends were inseparable. They went everywhere and did almost everything together. Nearing the age of twenty, Violet was the first to fall in love. And a year into their relationship, she became engaged to her wonderful, brilliant and creative young man. They intended to get married the following summer after he graduated from college. The three friends decided to spend a day together hiking and enjoying a picnic in the nearby woods to celebrate Violet's engagement. They began their hike at nearby Anawan Rock, where they could follow recognizable paths into the woods. When a thick fog consumed the woods, they lost sight of the trail and soon found themselves aimlessly wandering through the swamp.

After several hours, nightfall closed in. The young women desperately yelled for help from anybody who might hear them when a large shaggy brown dog appeared. The girls decided the wisest thing they could do was follow the dog. So, they clung to each other in the darkness while following the dog around twisted moss-covered trees, across narrow spots of land surrounded by deep pools of wretched oily water, and through patches of mud where bugs bit and strange noises frightened them. Twice they found spots of dry land vast enough for the group to stop and rest for ten or twenty minutes. They were tired, but sleep in that miserable swamp was out of the question.

Following the second stop to rest, the fog was so thick they could hardly see each other. Clover held on to the dog's fur. Jasmine wrapped her hand into the back of Clovers' belt, and Violet desperately held on to Jasmine's shirt at the end of the line. An ear-piercing shriek suddenly rose from the swamp. An instant later, Violet let out a frightening scream when she was violently attacked and forced into the water. Clover started to go after her when a vicious gang of small creatures with sharp fang-like teeth, clawed hands, and twisted bodies attacked the girls with branches, sharp sticks, and rocks.

Suddenly, a huge hawk-like bird appeared from out of the trees, screeching, scratching, and pecking at the faces of the ferocious goblins. Then a massive brown bear bounded out of the mist. Growling a maddening roar, it ripped into the little creatures, biting and tearing them to bloody pieces. The few small creatures remaining after the bird and bear destroyed their accomplices were quickly chased back into the mists by the fearless animals.

Shaken and afraid, Clover and Jasmine swiftly pulled a barely conscious Violet from the pool of retched swamp water. She had bloody scratches on her face, arms, and legs, a gaping bite on one cheek, a welt along the hairline of her forehead, and a deep gash across her stomach. Violet had swallowed much of the muddied water, gasping for air;

she was obviously in shock. Clover and Jasmine had minor cuts, scratches, bumps, and bruises, but none compared to Violet's injuries. They had to get Violet to a doctor but first had to find their way out of the fog-shrouded swamp.

Clover and Jasmine took turns holding and encouraging Violet while clinging to the dog through the remainder of their desperate journey. Finally, a few hours before sunrise, they limped out of the thick mist-covered woods. The dog led them to a small village of dried mud huts, where they found some people who could help them get medical attention for Violet. It turned out they had come into an old American Indian village. There were no medical doctors like the girls were familiar with, but there was a Healing Center with people trained in healing and natural medicines.

Jasmine and Clover soon learned that Violet had a concussion from the strike to her forehead. The bite on her cheek would leave a lifelong scar. And she developed a life-threatening infection from the gash in her stomach. In addition, she had a fever, constantly vomited, and became somewhat delusional, often screaming in her sleep from the nightmares of her terrifying experience. The friends spent many long hours by Violet's bedside during the weeks she spent in the care of the healers.

While Violet healed, Jasmine and Clover began to develop friendships among the locals. Finally, they learned of their location in a mysterious place the inhabitants had named The Mystic Land. A wall of dense fog surrounded the land, created by a Sorcerer four hundred years before to hide and protect what he perceived as his property. Few people made it through the mist to enter the land, and fewer left. The bodies of those who dared try to escape were often found mutilated at the edge of the woods. Most were never seen or heard from again.

The three girls each struggled in their own ways to accept that they would never return to their homes and families. Violet was especially despondent over her facial disfigurement and angry that she was lost to her fiancé and the future of her dreams.

When a few local women invited Jasmine to join them on a short trip to the Traders Market, she met an attractive gypsy trader named Aaron. They laughed, danced, told stories, traveled the land in his gypsy wagon, worked at the market together, and became inseparable in an exciting whirlwind of romance and joy.

"Aaron comes from a family that has been in the Mystic Land for several generations," Jasmine explained. "Most gypsies arrived here as a group after their caravan had been attacked in the late 1800s. It is their descendants who still live here."

Jasmine continued with her story. "During visits with Violet, Clover developed a friendship with one of the Native healers. They shared an interest in music, a love of animals, and similar spiritual interests. And they shared a mutual attraction for each other. A romance quickly developed. And since you are the same age as Jules and Jill, I am sure that is when they created you, Becca.

Clover kept the dog that had led them through the woods. She named it Insight. She also attracted other animals, including an unusual bird named Nani. Clover often talked with the dog, the bird, and other animals, as though having deep intellectual conversations with them. We began to wonder if Clover might be losing her sanity. Then, one day, after they had been there for about two months,

Clover announced that she was ready to return home. She claimed her animal friends had taught her the secret to passing through the mist, and they could safely guide the three of us through the swamp.

However, Violet was deathly afraid to go near those woods ever again. It also happened that I had just discovered I was pregnant," Jasmine confessed. "I announced my decision to stay behind to start a family and a life with Aaron. Clover told us that she would return with help to rescue us if she could. She talked about flying into The Mystic Land with a helicopter or sending the military. We cried, laughed, and hugged each other. The day Clover left was the last we saw or heard of her. I had always wondered if Clover made it home through the mists," Jasmine added, "until today."

Rebecca sat transfixed by Jasmine's story. She confided that her mother had never told her that story. She was warned to stay out of the woods but never explained why. In fact, she believed her mother was unreasonably fearful. Rebecca related that her mother had told her she had taken a short trip with two girlfriends, which turned into a two-month adventure. She had met and had a romantic fling with a handsome young musician from an unknown town somewhere in New England. Following the summer fling, neither of them had stayed in touch. Less than a month after returning home, Clover discovered she was pregnant, and Rebecca was the result of that relationship.

Following the revealing stories, Jasmine, Aaron, Jill, Jules, and Rebecca sat quietly around the dinner table before deciding it was time to clean up. Jules asked Rebecca if she might like to join Jill and him for some music at the gypsy camp, to which Rebecca cordially agreed. Jasmine reminded

Jules that Rebecca had a difficult two days with little sleep, so please not be out late. She then asked Becca to help her wash dishes before they left. It was apparent that Jasmine had something else she wanted to speak about with her. As they stood side by side at the basin, Jasmine quietly told her, "Becca, I still know your father if you might be interested in meeting him."

Jasmine agreed to keep Tempest at the house while Jules, Jill, and Rebecca went to the gypsy camp. But as soon as the front door opened, Tempest ran out. The cat waited a short distance from the door for the teenagers to join her. Rebecca did not have to look far to find Tempest watching throughout the rest of the evening.

The sun was setting behind them as they walked toward the sound of music drifting through the trees. Rebecca was surprised to see several gypsy wagons parked under the trees as they entered the camp. Jill mentioned that many of the gypsies lived in their wagons year-round. The campfires highlighted silhouettes of people, dogs, horses, cows, mules, sheep, chickens, ducks, and a few unidentifiable animals. Laughter and conversation echoed through the darkness.

They entered a clearing with huge bonfires at each end of a large open-air pavilion. Under the high roof of the pavilion, Rebecca guessed there must be close to seventy people playing musical instruments, singing, dancing, eating, and drinking.

"What are they celebrating?" Rebecca asked the twins.

Jules laughed. "Life," he replied. "Gypsies celebrate like this every night."

As the teens made their way into the crowded pavilion, bright-eyed young men asked Jill to dance, and teenage girls offered flirtatious smiles toward Jules. Still, in each instance, the twins politely said they had a guest this evening and would dance with them another night. Rebecca insisted they enjoy themselves, but the twins argued they wanted to spend this evening with her. She sensed several times that the siblings were competing for her attention.

After an hour or so had passed, Jill suggested showing Rebecca the lake. They walked a short distance along a wide path through the trees before arriving at the edge of what they called Mystic Lake. The moon and stars reflected beautifully off the water in the clear night sky. Rebecca was shocked to immediately recognize the lake as what locals in her hometown called The Reservoir. Yet somehow, everything around it appeared different. Jules explained that the lake was approximately a mile across at most points, and separate villages each bordered the lake. In addition, several rivers and streams ran to and from the lake, feeding freshwater to all who lived there. Jill added that the lands were rich in minerals and well-fed by the waters, allowing fresh fruits and vegetables to grow in abundance throughout the land.

As the three companions returned home, Rebecca heard a familiar whistle in a nearby tree. Looking into the tree's lower branches, she spotted Songbird and Wisdom watching her as she passed. Following behind the twins, Rebecca grinned and waved at the birds. She spied Tempest sitting and licking her paws behind the trunk of the same tree. No matter what dangers or circumstances she might encounter in this unusual place, she felt an incredible comfort and appreciation for those protective animals who watched for her safety.

Aaron was asleep. Jasmine was waiting when the teens returned to the house. She said that she and Aaron had decided that Jules could sleep in the wagon this night, allowing Rebecca to get a good night's sleep in his bed. Then, Jules would leave before sunrise to help his father at the market, while Jill and Becca would stay behind for a girl's day. Jasmine disclosed that she had much to talk about with Becca and thought Jill should be a part of the conversation. Everybody agreed. With no further discussion, Jasmine said goodnight and left the room.

Rebecca was surprised when Jules pulled open the two curtains spread across the side wall, revealing two nooks separated by a dividing wall. Each cubicle contained identical twin-size beds, bureaus with drawers, and racks of clothes along each side of the dividing wall. Jules grabbed a change of clothes from his dresser drawers and clothing rack. He bid goodnight to Rebecca and his sister and started toward the door.

Before leaving the room, Jules quickly returned to whisper to Rebecca, "I look forward to seeing you again tomorrow, Becca." She blushed and smiled shyly and couldn't think of a word to say before he disappeared into the night.

The girls called out "good night" to each other. Rebecca closed the curtain, kicked off her shoes, and fell onto the bed, still wearing her clothes. Tempest appeared around the curtain and laid himself on the floor next to the bed.

"Good night, Tempest," Rebecca softly spoke as her eyes closed.

Almost immediately, the angelic presence of Nani appeared in Rebecca's semi-conscious mind. A glow of light surrounded her like a translucent angel. Her silky white dress and long dark hair blew in a nonexistent breeze.

"Listen closely, my child," she spoke gently but directly. "Tonight, I want to tell you more about your animal guides. The spirits of ancestors, friends, and loved ones who have passed before us, often return as guides and guardians. Spirit guides help to lead and protect you. Every human is born with the ability to communicate with their spirit guides, but misinformation and limiting beliefs often separate people from that connection. As a result, few people believe, and even fewer ever strive to develop their innate abilities to connect with their spirit guides.

People who become angry, hateful, selfish, greedy, and closed-minded will never recognize their spiritual connections. Only those who are kind, compassionate, understanding, and open-minded to learning and self-development will discover the spiritual connection with their guides.

Rebecca, you currently have three Spirit Guides by your side. Wisdom, the owl, is connected to your intellect, logic, common sense, and ability to reason. He has superior insight, foresight, and eyesight. He was the true leader who guided you through the swamp. Wisdom could see you when you could not see him. He led you past several dangers that you never knew were there. When you first met Wisdom, you could not accept that the owl was communicating with you, so he went to ask Tempest for help. He knew you would feel a closer connection to a cat.

Tempest, the cat which is not a cat, is connected to your emotions. She is your protector. When you feel calm, Tempest will appear as a cat. But if you feel fear or danger, she will transform to defend you against anything threatening you. She became the tiger to protect you from the goblins in the mist.

Songbird, the nightingale, is connected to your heart.

She connects with your wishes, hopes, and dreams in all aspects of your life. She came to you for two reasons. First, her singing voice works like a Pied Piper to the goblins who cannot resist dancing to her music. When a goblin shot an arrow into Songbird's wing, she stopped singing long enough for the goblins to stop dancing and form an attack. Second, you have an extraordinary musical ability and singing voice. Only your lack of confidence holds you back from achieving all of your dreams. Songbird will help you dance to the music in your heart. Once you develop your confidence, you will have the skills to pass back through the mist if that is your choice.

Trust your intuition. Learn to listen to your spirit guides. Tomorrow night I will come to you again in the space between awake and asleep. I will have a few minutes to answer some of your questions at that time. Good night, My Darling."

Nani's image faded into the darkness. Rebecca's eyes snapped open.

"Good night, Nani," Rebecca spoke in a quiet voice. She thought about her grandmother's messages and briefly considered what questions she might ask the next night.

She leaned her head over the edge of the bed. "Thank you again, Tempest," Rebecca whispered.

Tempest purred.

Rebecca closed her eyes and fell into a deep, restful sleep.

8 Questions

Morning light filtered through the curtain when Rebecca finally opened her eyes. She could hear the sound of quietly speaking voices, but it was the intoxicating scent of breakfast that quickly helped awaken the rest of her senses. Glancing over the edge of the bed, she was surprised Tempest was not waiting there. As she rose from the bed, she felt enthusiastic about the eye-opening day she expected to lay ahead.

Pulling aside the curtain, she almost tripped over Tempest as the cat eagerly ate from filled food and water bowls.

"Good morning, Tempest," Rebecca greeted with a smile. Tempest briefly looked up at the girl before returning her full attention to her breakfast.

Jasmine and Jill called out in unison from the kitchen, "Good morning, Becca." Jill sliced fresh vegetables at the table while Jasmine was cooking, cleaning, and shuffling about the room.

Rebecca returned the greeting while pointing anxiously at the doorway to the washroom and outhouse. Jill laughed aloud and nodded approvingly, indicating for her to go in that direction.

"Breakfast will be ready when you come back in," Jasmine announced as Rebecca eagerly sped from the room.

Rebecca felt astonished to find the clothes she had worn through the swamp freshly washed and hanging from a clothesline strung from the washroom to a tree near the outhouse. Recognizable bird whistles echoed from a branch above the clothesline, where Songbird and Wisdom eagerly greeted her. Then, unexpectedly, Tempest abruptly darted through the doorway, guardedly looked about, and seated herself directly under the drying clothes. After all that had happened in the last two days, Rebecca gratefully knew she could feel safe and secure with the guidance and protection of these magnificent animals.

After brushing her teeth, cleaning herself, and brushing her hair, Rebecca returned to the kitchen with Tempest close behind. A plate with fresh fruits, vegetables, poached eggs, homemade bread with jellies and jams, and a tall cup filled with apple juice awaited.

"Aren't you going to join me?" Rebecca inquired of Jasmine and Jill.

"We've already eaten," Jasmine responded. "We feed the animals in the barn and have breakfast as a family before sunrise. We would have awakened you but thought you needed to sleep after your ordeal in the mists."

"Thank you for your consideration, and thank you for all you've done for me," Rebecca graciously replied. "You've made me feel so welcome."

"I'm sure you have questions, Becca," Jasmine pointed out. "Because we have many things to discuss and plans to be made, Aaron thought it best if we considered our options as a family. So he and Jules did not go to the market this morning. Instead, they are working in the barn and garden and will be in shortly to join us in our conversation."

Feeling an uncomfortable twinge of doubt about whether "family" meant the conversation would include her or be about her, Rebecca recognized that she would have to accept the results no matter how the conversation evolved. So, she prudently consumed her breakfast as if it might be her last home-cooked meal.

Hearing footsteps coming through the front door,

Rebecca hurriedly stuffed the last few bites of her breakfast into her mouth and then attempted to wash it down with the remainder of the apple juice. Realizing it was much more than she could swallow, her cheeks puffed out with the abundance of food in her mouth just as Jules and Aaron appeared around the corner. Rebecca's eyes went big while Jules broke out in laughter. Rebecca embarrassingly slumped under the table. In a moment, the kitchen filled with laughter.

The men left to wash off the dirt and sweat, and the women cleared the table before settling in for their discussion.

Jasmine began the conversation. "Becca, you are the daughter of my best friend. No matter how many years have passed, nothing will change that friendship. Aaron likes you, and our children already adore you. So, we want to invite you and Tempest to join our family and make our home your home for as long as you want. Are you interested?"

Rebecca felt tears well up in her eyes. She stuttered and stumbled to answer before crying out a grateful, "Yes. Thank you so much."

Jasmine continued, "Jules has offered to give his bedroom to you. He has always liked sleeping in the wagon. Now he's old enough to sleep there more permanently and sleep in the living room during poor weather. We will make arrangements for clothes. From my experiences in coming here, I know that you must feel some confusion. What questions do you have of us, Becca?"

"I have so many questions," she replied. "Where am I? Why don't you have phones, a television or radio, a stove or refrigerator, electricity or running water? How come you don't have a car? Is this a religious choice? What about…"

"Okay, Becca," Jasmine interrupted. "Because I came

here much as you did, I think I'm the best person to answer those questions before moving on to others. We are in a place named The Mystic Land. Its history is vague because there is no written history. Instead, stories pass from one generation to the next. I believe we are in our hometown of Rehoboth, yet the mists keep us hidden from the rest of the world. We exist in the same time and place as the people we grew up with but are unaware of the other's presence. In essence, the magic of the mist makes us invisible to those people, as they are invisible to us.

Aaron added, "The Mystic Land is surrounded by the wall of mists you came through. The land measures about six miles from east to west and ten miles north to south, although we are forbidden in the southern section because it belongs to the sorcerer and his army of trolls and mutants."

Rebecca gasped, "Sorcerer, trolls, and mutants?"

"There is also an area where the elves live." Jill chimed in.

"Elves, like at the North Pole?" Rebecca wondered aloud.

"Elves, like in the time of fairy," Jasmine replied. "It is said that they've lived here for thousands of years. They lived in unity with the Indians, but the elves decided to seclude themselves from the other races after the English colonists arrived."

"Sometimes, we see a few elves at the Trader Market," Jill exclaimed.

Aaron continued. "The story of The Mystic Lands says the Sorcerer declared this as his property even before the Pilgrims arrived in the sixteen hundred's. As more colonists arrived, he created the mist with magic to prevent others from venturing onto his property. However, warring English colonists and Native American Indians often ran into the swamps, got lost in the mist, and found themselves here, unable to escape through the shrouded swamps. Most people living here now are descendants of those who came through the mist. As years passed and more people arrived, the sorcerer used his magic to create creatures called goblins to scare away people who entered the mists. Those goblins evolved into the violent creatures you encountered in the swamps. Then the sorcerer magically created stone walls inside the land to separate the warring colonists, Indians, gypsies, and other tribes who were often at war."

"He made similar walls to keep people from his fortress in the southern section of the land, and he made a legion of trolls and mutants to guard his fortress from outsiders," added Jules.

"Sorcerer, trolls, mutants, elves, goblins… it sounds too unreal," Rebecca interjected.

"Remember Becca," Aaron commented, "You saw the goblins. As unreal as they may seem, the sorcerer created them. Some people believe the sorcerer is still alive. If so, he would be over four hundred years old. I am not aware of anybody living here now who has ever seen him. One common belief is that if the sorcerer were dead, the mist, all of his creatures, the walls, and everything his magic created would disappear. Since the mist and his creatures are still here, we assume he must still be alive."

Jasmine added, "Another result of the land being closed to the rest of the world is that no industry developed here. We have no means to create steel, metals, glass, plastic, electricity, or any modern conveniences you're accustomed to, Becca. Some pots and pans, knives, housewares, and a few weapons came through the mists with travelers. Some carried rifles, but those weapons were useless as soon as their ammunition ran out."

"That's why I carried a handmade bow and arrows for protection when we met yesterday," Jules added. "Most knives, tools, and weapons here are made from wood, stone, and bone."

"One way we are fortunate," Jasmine declared, "is that the soil is rich with minerals and the waters in the lake and streams are fresh. The air stays moderately warm even in the winter, so we have trees, vegetables, fruits, and berries year-round. Foods, natural medicines, and anything made with nature's materials is plentiful. Also, we don't have money in the way you are familiar. Instead, we trade for everything. Most people create handmade foods, cloth, clothing, and crafts. Even a person with nothing can pick fruit from a tree in the countryside and trade it for other items.

Aaron quickly added, "Animals are also plentiful. When the first horses, cows, chickens, and sheep were brought into the land, somebody was smart enough to breed them rather than eat them. As a result, there are now farms throughout the countryside. Many animals, eggs, feathers, wool, furs, and animal hides are traded. Even animal bones can be carved to create knives, small tools, and utensils. However, one law strictly adhered to in this land is that no animals are purposely killed for their hides, furs, or bones. Only meat for eating is legal.

"Which brings us to the next discussion," Jasmine interjected. "Aaron and I thought we would all go to the Trader Village together tomorrow. While Aaron, Jules, and Jill work at the market, I would like to take you to meet Violet. She needs to meet Clover's daughter and finally know that Clover made it back through the mists. Following your morning work at the market, Jules and Jill, would you escort Becca to meet Takoda Nemasket?" she asked.

"Do you mean Doctor Nemasket at the Healing Center?" Jill asked.

"Yes, Jill, Takoda Nemasket is Becca's father. They have never met. He does not know about her, and she will have to explain that she is the seventeen-year-old daughter of Clover Fields. It will likely be a shock to him, but I believe he will be receptive and welcoming once he realizes the truth of the situation. I expect each of you to act responsibly, with maturity and understanding. Do you understand?"

"Yes," all three teens answered in unison.

"You may stay overnight with friends in the Native Villages. But be home before nightfall the following day. Are there any questions?" Jasmine asked.

"No," Jill and Jules each quickly replied.

"I have a few more questions," Rebecca interjected. "First, Jasmine, if I understand correctly, you were named Jill but chose to be called Jasmine, and you named your daughter Jillian, but she chooses to be called Jill. Is that correct?"

"Yes," Jasmine responded with a laugh. The whole family chuckled with her.

"Second, did you tell me my mother talked with a bird she named Nani?"

"Yes," Jasmine answered, "that's correct. Why do you ask?"

"Because that's an old Indian name for Grandmother," Rebecca commented, not yet wanting to reveal her nighttime visits with her great grandmother.

Jasmine asked again if anybody had any further questions or concerns that they might want to discuss.

"I don't have any other questions, but I have something I'd like to share with all of you." Rebecca smiled as she spoke. "Please wait here for a moment," she called out as she dashed into the other room. Returning with her backpack, Rebecca pulled out the two plastic bowl covers and set them on the table, her notebook and drawing pad, and finally found the two remaining granola bars at the bottom of the bag. "I'm sorry, I only have two of these, but I think you'll like them if you want to share them."

Jules and Jill eagerly tore off the wrappers and broke the granola bars into bite-size pieces. Rebecca refused to eat any, insisting she wanted the family to enjoy them. They each moaned with joyful pleasure as they savored the tasty gift.

Jasmine commented that she might be able to make something similar using oats, grains, seeds, honey, and maple syrup, all readily available ingredients. She then gave attention to the pads of paper lying on the table. "Real paper!" she exclaimed. "Might you happen to have any pencils or pens in your bag, Becca?"

Rebecca reached into the essentials pocket and withdrew a handful of pens and pencils.

Jasmine had a look of absolute glee on her smiling face. "Becca," she exclaimed, "growing up, I loved drawing. I dreamed of being a famous illustrator. But, unfortunately, we only have very coarse paper here, and the only writing utensils are hay straws, feathers, or horsehair brushes dipped in a poorly made ink made from berries. May I use one page of your drawing paper and a pen or pencil to draw a picture?"

Passing the drawing pad to Jasmine, Rebecca then pushed the pile of pencils and pens across the table. "Jasmine, it would be my honor if you would accept this drawing pad and all the pens and pencils you would like as a gift. Please draw to your heart's content." She thought Jasmine could not have looked happier than she was at that moment.

Jasmine kept two pencils and two pens and handed the

rest back to Rebecca. "Thank you, Becca," she exclaimed. "You could not have given me a more valued gift. I will cherish it and use it with tremendous appreciation." Jasmine's eyes shined. Her smile spread so wide that her cheeks beamed like pink roses.

"We all have much to do to prepare for the market and our journeys over the next few days," Aaron announced, "I suggest we all get to work."

To Rebecca, the conversation seemed to end quite abruptly. All of a sudden, Aaron and Jules were out of their chairs. As they headed toward the door, Jules turned back. He winked flirtingly at Rebecca. Then, speaking only slightly louder than a whisper, he smoothly commented, "You look beautiful today, Becca."

"Jules!" his mother called out, "You behave yourself."

As Jules spun around, he walked face-first into the corner of the doorway. His hand grabbed his forehead. He did not look back again as he quickly raced from the room. Everybody else laughed out loud at his expense.

Rebecca felt complimented by Jules' playful attention, but she was wise enough to know that involvement with the amorous boy at this time would be utterly foolish for both of them.

Still giggling, Jill asked Rebecca if she would like to see the animals in the barn.

"I would love it." Rebecca enthusiastically replied. As the girls headed toward the door, Tempest quickly joined them.

Once inside, the barn seemed much larger than it had appeared from the front of the house. Two wide stalls held each of the workhorses. Rebecca stopped to hug and pet each of them. Jill explained that the barn had an enclosed hen house with two roosters, ten hens, and two dozen chicks. Separate stalls held a cow, three sheep, four turkeys, and several ducks and geese that wandered independently through the barn. The back door led to a fenced corral, although no animals were outside at this time, and roof-covered open-air pens held two enormous pigs. A female shared her pen with eight healthy-looking piglets, while a slightly larger male was kept separately.

The girls found Jules feeding the pigs. He explained that the adult pigs could become aggressive, so they were kept separate except for breeding. Neither of the girls mentioned the welt on Jules' forehead.

Back in the house, Aaron brought a basket filled with fresh vegetables from the garden. While Jill helped Jasmine with preparations for their dinner, Rebecca took Tempest with her to collect her clothes from the clothesline. Remembering Nani's directives to practice communicating with the animals, she especially wanted to visit Wisdom and Songbird. Not finding the birds at the tree where she had seen them that morning, she sang their names. Both birds immediately flew to the tree's lowest branch, a few feet above Rebecca's head.

"Hello, my friends," she called up to them in a melodic voice. She sat on the ground with her back against the tree. Closing her eyes in an attempt to relax, she could feel Tempest purring as the cat settled next to her. Well, that's a good beginning, Rebecca thought. She began asking questions of the birds, "How are you? What have you been doing? What have you been eating?" She tried singing the questions in her mind, but she didn't sense any response. As she became more comfortable, Rebecca could feel her eyes getting heavy. She quickly accepted that she would allow herself to take a short nap.

Standing on the edge of a high hill, Rebecca looked over sheets of golden grass layered with colorful flowers. She turned her face to the sunshine, feeling its warmth invigorate her body. Majestic fruit trees lined the river banks in the valley below. Flowing green and blue hills spread across the horizon beyond the river.

A voice beside her gently spoke, "It's beautiful, isn't it?"

"Yes, it's magnificent," Rebecca replied.

"Don't allow its beauty to lull you into forgetting the dangers that wait on the other side of the hills." the voice warned.

Rebecca looked toward the source of the warning. A stunning woman with shoulder-length white hair and bright turquoise eyes looked back and smiled at her. She wore a forest-green vest, tights, and boots, with a bow and quiver filled with arrows across her shoulder. Her fair-skinned body appeared toned with lean muscles. Rebecca noticed that her hair wrapped behind pointed ears.

"You're an elf!" Rebecca exclaimed.

"You don't recognize me?" the woman asked.

"No, I'm sorry, I do not. Should I know you?"

"I am Tempest." the woman answered.

Rebecca gasped. "Tempest, how can that be?"

"We only have a minute, Rebecca. With practice, we will soon learn to communicate together more easily. My message today is to stay aware. You are fortunate to have the support of this family. They are wonderful people, but they have their own lives and responsibilities. Stay open to learning. The twins wish to become close friends. There is much that they can teach you about survival in this land. Unfortunately, not all of the people here will be as kind. Be aware that dangers could be hiding behind lying eyes. Wisdom is being called away, although he will return as soon as possible. He also warns you to be cautious. Songbird and I will remain close while you navigate this journey."

"Becca... Becca!" She jumped awake. Jill called her name from a few feet away.

Rebecca looked about. Tempest had moved to a side of the tree where she nonchalantly licked and preened herself as cats do. Wisdom and Songbird quietly looked down at her from a branch a dozen yards above her head.

"Sorry, Jill, I must have dozed off," Rebecca explained as she lifted herself from the ground.

"Well, I apologize for waking you, Becca. You had been gone for a while. We became concerned, so I came looking for you. Dinner is almost ready. I'd be happy to help you with these clothes," Jill declared as she began removing Rebecca's clean clothes from the clothesline.

"Thank you, Jill. I feel so fortunate to have you as my friend. I can't imagine where I would be if I had not met you."

Rebecca was still trying to get herself fully awakened. Once again, an evocative message tugged at her thoughts. She wondered if it was a visit or a dream. Could Tempest have been an elf? She shook her head as she signaled for the mysterious cat to follow her into the house. Rebecca turned back toward the tree, allowing Jill to enter ahead of her.

"Wisdom," she called out, "if you're leaving, I want you to know how much I appreciate all you've done for me. I love you. And I will be looking forward to seeing you again when you return."

By the time Rebecca reached the living room, Jill had already folded her clothes. Aaron and Jules had pieces of wood and crude tools spread across half of the floor. Jules proudly announced they were building a new chest of drawers for her. Jasmine was setting the table for dinner.

Only minutes later, they were all seated for a relatively quiet meal. Aaron reminded everybody that they would wake well before sunrise to feed the animals and prepare the horses before leaving for the market. After dinner, Jill and Rebecca cleared the table and washed the dishes. Rebecca felt especially happy to see Aaron kiss Jasmine and thank her for her wonderful dinner. It was the first sign of affection she had witnessed between the couple. It filled her heart to know they still shared that love and appreciation.

The conversation was at a minimum throughout the evening. Jasmine sat at the kitchen table with her drawing pad, pens, and pencils. When anybody asked what she was drawing, they received a terse, "Wait and see," response. Rebecca used her notebook to begin writing a journal about her experiences. She felt overwhelmed with the attempt to write about this unusual experience. Who could believe it, she wondered? Jill seemed to flutter from one thing to another, deciding which clothes to wear. She packed sandwiches and fruit, then cleaned and organized the gypsy wagon. Aaron and Jules spent a little more time working on the chest of drawers. Finally, soon after the sun set, everybody retired to their bedrooms for the night.

Like the night before, Tempest slept on the floor next to Rebecca's bed. She wondered if Nani would visit with her again this night as her grandmother had told her she would. It did not take long for Rebecca to receive her answer.

Nani appeared almost immediately after Rebecca closed her eyes. The woman spoke in her gentile, comforting voice, "Granddaughter, we have but a limited time. So tonight,

I am here to answer your questions. What might you like to know?"

"Hello, Nani. Thank you for coming to me," Rebecca greeted. "Jasmine told me that when my mother came here eighteen years ago, she spoke with a songbird named Nani. Was that you?"

"Yes, my child, I came to your mother in the spirit of a bird. She was much like you at that time. Her spirit guides helped her find her voice and confidence, and we helped her return through the mist."

"Can you help me to return home?" Rebecca asked.

"Yes, Granddaughter. That is one reason I am here. Understand that purposefully returning through the mist requires more of you than mistakenly coming through to get here. The first time, your spirit guides led you. In returning, you must be a leader. That is why I speak of finding your voice and having confidence in your abilities. You must learn to communicate with your spirit guides while awake before you are ready to manage the challenges you will face."

"What do you mean when you say I must find my voice?"

"First, you must be ready to lead. You are young. Your mother was a few years older than you when she came through the mists. And her return was incredibly harrowing. Second, you have magic in your voice. The animals hear that magic which is why they are attracted to you. You have withheld your songs from the world. Allow the world to behold your gift to them. You must sing, my darling, sing!"

Rebecca felt startled by the suggestions and unexpected praise about her voice. But knowing she had only a short time to ask Nani her questions, she continued, "I had a dream today in which Tempest appeared as an elf. Was Tempest an elf?"

"That was not a dream, Rebecca. Tempest was communicating with you as I am communicating with you now. Tempest feels a strong affinity for you. She is now your guardian. She can appear to you in the form of various animals. You have already seen her as a cat and a tiger. She appears primarily as a cat because that is the animal in which you are the most comfortable. Several hundred years ago, Tempest was an elf in her human life. She was a warrior, guardian, and protector of the elfin kings and queens as she is for you now. She is also a distant relative to you, which is one of the reasons you carry her magic within you. We have time for only one more question, Rebecca."

"Are Wisdom and Songbird also distant relatives, Nani?"

"Yes," Nani replied, "They are both distant relatives to you. Wisdom was a brilliant intellectual, scientist, inventor, adventurer, author, philosopher, and teacher in his human life. Because his life was so celebrated, he chooses not to use his human name in his spiritual form. He prefers to be known only as Wisdom. Songbird is the most closely related to you. However, your connection to Songbird must remain a secret, as there are people in this land who would seek to harm her and possibly you if they knew of your relationship. Your ancestry will be revealed at the right time. For now, trust your intuition. Listen to your spirit guides. Tomorrow night I will come to you again in the space between awake and asleep. Awaken now to remember my messages. Good night, My Darling."

As Nani's image faded, Rebecca's eyes snapped open. "Good night, Nani," Rebecca whispered. She thought about her grandmother's messages, then closed her eyes again and fell into a restful sleep.

9 Windy

Everybody was up and awake well before sunrise. Opening her eyes before daylight felt contradictory to everything Rebecca was familiar with in her life, but she was certainly not going to complain to this family. She offered to help feed the animals but was nicely informed that this was not the best time to begin teaching her all that she would need to learn. So, while Aaron, Jules, and Jill took care of the animals, Rebecca remained indoors with Jasmine to help prepare for their day. She fed Tempest, rechecked the belongings in her backpack, and patiently waited to depart.

Rebecca had few reservations about the Traders Market. She expected it to be much like attending a Flea Market. However, she did feel concerned about meeting Violet. Rebecca did not know how to address that her mother had made it home while Violet had not. However, she felt the most apprehension over meeting her father. Takoda Nemasket. She repeated his name over and over in her mind. It's a fascinating name, she thought. Still, Rebecca knew little about him. And worse, he knew absolutely nothing about her. She tried imagining what it would feel like to meet a seventeen-year-old daughter he never knew was even born. Neither Violet nor her father knew of her or that they would be meeting her today. She anticipated it was likely to be an eventful day.

While the two of them waited in the house, Jasmine handed Rebecca a sheet of drawing paper. "I illustrated something for you, Becca," she offered. "It's a detailed map of the Mystic Land. During my first few years here, I felt so lost. I depended on Aaron to take me everywhere. I wished someone would have given me a map like this. So, I drew this map for you, using all I know of this land," Jasmine explained. "I've only been to the Elfin Woods one time. And I've never been below Mystic Lake, but I drew this map to the best of my knowledge. I hope it will help you as you travel around this land."

Jasmine pointed to where they lived and would be traveling to the Trader Market, where Violet lived in the Colonists' Villages, and where she would meet Takoda Nemasket at the Healing Center in the Native Villages. She showed Rebecca where bridges crossed the rivers and explained the three stone walls made with the Sorcerer's magic. "When the English Colonists and American Indians came through the mists in the seventeen hundred's," Jasmine clarified, "they were at war. It is believed that the sorcerer created the northern wall to separate the warring enemies and the southern walls to protect the property he claimed as his own. The rocks in the walls are somehow magically attached. They cannot be taken apart or removed. The walls are about four feet high. They can be crossed over, but horses, mules, carts, and wagons can only pass through at the crossing points."

Rebecca thanked Jasmine, complimented her on her illustration skills, and then placed the folded map into her pants pocket with her pocket knife.

As if on cue, Jill popped her head in to announce that they were ready to go. Jasmine, Rebecca, and Tempest readily headed out the door and into the back of the gypsy wagon. Jules rode in front with his father while the girls traveled together in the cabin. It was still not yet daylight. The weather felt comfortable. Jasmine left the top half of the door open, and Jill immediately opened the shutters on the side windows.

Finding her walking stick leaning upright in the back corner completely surprised Rebecca. Taking it in her hands, she told how the staff helped her through the swamp, including how she used it to defend against the goblins.

"It's a solid piece of oak," Jill commented. "It would be a beautiful piece of wood to carve if you had carving tools," she complimented.

"Would this work?" Rebecca asked as her pocket knife swiftly appeared in her hand.

Jill gasped. "What is that?

Jasmine quickly responded, "Becca, people here do not see stainless steel instruments like that. As standard an object as that is to you, it would have tremendous value in this land. Can I touch it?" Jill curiously inquired.

Rebecca pulled open the longest blade and handed the knife to Jill. "Be careful. It's sharp," she warned.

"I strongly suggest you keep that knife in your pocket," Jasmine continued, "unless you are alone or with people you trust with absolute certainty."

Within moments, Jill had taken the staff from Rebecca's hands, flipped the bottom end up, and carved a sharp point on the tip. She smiled proudly as she handed the staff and the pocket knife back to Rebecca. "With that knife, I would carve all kinds of things into that stick," Jill commented.

"I might just ask your help in doing that, Jill," Rebecca replied.

They traveled only a short distance. Sunlight was barely peeking over the eastern horizon when the wagon abruptly stopped.

"What are you doing out here?" Aaron called out from the front of the wagon.

Jill bounded to the closet at the back of the wagon. Then, with lightning-fast movements, she removed the handmade crossbow Jules had held in front of Rebecca a few days before, loaded an arrow into its barrel, and jumped to the nearest side window.

A female voice responded from a short distance away, "I'm just walking home."

"Why are you walking alone in the dark at this time in the morning?" Aaron inquired. "Are you alone?"

"Yes, I'm alone," she called back. "I work as a messenger. I delivered a package from a Governess in the Colonists Village to the Sorcerer's Fortress yesterday. The Trolls along the wall allowed me to pass on my way there, but a gang of mutants attacked me last night on my way back. I think a rock hit me from a slingshot. When I woke up an hour ago, I was lying in a pile of leaves on this side of the wall. They stole my horse and all of my belongings."

Aaron signaled the horses cautiously ahead. "Where is your home?" he asked as the wagon pulled up next to the young woman.

"I live in the Colonists Village near the Trader Market," she answered.

"We are going to the Trader Market. My name is Aaron," he offered. "This is my son, Jules. My wife, daughter, and our friend are in the back." "Girls, step out here, please," he called out.

Jill, still carrying the crossbow, Jasmine, Rebecca, and Tempest, stepped from the wagon.

"I recognize her from the market," Jill announced.

"May we ask your name, young lady?" Jasmine asked.

"My name is Windy," she answered.

"For your safety, would you like to come with us?"

Aaron offered.

Windy gave a cautious glance at Jill and the loaded crossbow.

Jill promptly pointed it at the ground. "My apologies for the weapon," Jill apologized. "You never know who or what you might encounter this close to the Sorcerer's lands."

"Wow! Déjà Vu!" Rebecca thought.

The four women and the cat each climbed into the wagon. It lurched forward, and the journey continued toward the market. With morning light filtering into the wagon, Jasmine noticed dried blood in Windy's hair and along the side of one ear. She quickly found a cloth and an ointment to help clean the young woman's wounds. Windy pointed out other bruises along her arms and legs where rocks had hit her. She told the women she had tried to outrun the gang of mutants, but she was not fast enough to outdistance the dozens of rocks being thrown and hurled with slingshots.

"The worst part is that I was given that horse and a stall at the stables yesterday as payment for delivering the package to the Sorcerer's fortress," Windy recalled. "Sometimes it feels as if every time I think I'm getting ahead, something knocks me back down."

"Windy, it could have been much worse for you than losing a horse you received only yesterday," Jasmine reminded the young woman. "I shudder to think of what cruelties the Sorcerer's trolls and mutants could have done to you."

"What are the mutants and trolls?" Rebecca asked.

Windy looked at Rebecca with wide eyes. "What are mutants and trolls? Where have you been?" she asked incredulously.

"Becca just came through the mists two days ago," Jill announced.

Windy's wide eyes grew even wider. "I don't think I've ever met anyone who personally came through the mists," she exclaimed. "Everybody I know comes from families of people who arrived here decades or centuries ago."

"I came through the mist eighteen years ago," Jasmine informed Windy.

Windy was fascinated. "There is so much I want to ask you," she announced excitedly. "But first, I'll answer your question about the trolls and mutants. I've heard that the sorcerer made them with evil magic. The trolls are big with huge, out-of-proportion muscles. Their skin is orange-brown, like burnt rust. Except for some minor size differences, their faces and bodies look alike. I don't know how they tell each other apart, and I don't think they care. Their only purpose is to protect the sorcerer, his fortress, and his land. Supposedly, the mutants are also made from the Sorcerer's magic, but they are distinguishable. They are all different shapes and sizes, but every mutant I saw had twisted and deformed bodies and faces. Most are bent and twisted as if made from branches and pieces of trees blackened with dark green patches like dead tree limbs with moss or mold growing on them. Their hands and fingers are like sticks. Some have weird patches of hair growing out of their arms, neck, and places that don't usually grow hair. Some have eyes, while others have holes or sockets inset into their deformed faces. I can't get the images out of my mind."

Rebecca confessed, "I hope I never meet any of them, mutants or trolls."

"Did you see the sorcerer?" Jill asked.

Windy shook her head, "No, I've heard that nobody has seen the sorcerer for many years. Some people think the trolls and mutants have taken control of the fortress, but I don't think they have the minds to control much of anything. Others say an evil witch has taken control of the fortress, trolls, and mutants. I don't know. I've not seen a witch either. I delivered a package to his fortress. It's a spooky place. It looks like a giant dungeon to me. I won't ever go back there no matter what kind of payment they offer,"

Windy curiously turned the conversation toward the three women. She was especially interested in how different the world was outside the mists. She'd heard stories but never personal experiences from someone who had lived there.

Rebecca found it difficult to explain her life. Windy had never seen or heard of a car, computer, television, telephone, or electricity. Jill and Jules knew of such conveniences because their mother had told them about life on the other side of the mist. But, to Windy, those were fantasy stories told around a campfire.

Nineteen-year-old Windy appeared to be of African heritage. Dark-skinned with hair pulled back in two long braids, her big brown eyes and every feature of her face glowed expressively. She explained that relatives on both sides of her family had been in the Mystic Land for several generations. She knew her maternal grandmother was Wampanoag Indian but was unsure of any other family histories before her grandparents. Rebecca told Windy she had just learned that her father was Wampanoag Indian, and she would meet him for the first time later that day. Something in that admission seemed to create an immediate bond between the two girls.

The conversation became energized among the four women. The remaining distance to the market felt like it passed in only minutes. As the wagon pulled into their market space, Jasmine told Windy that she and Rebecca would go to the village to meet a friend. Then, if Windy waited while they set out their wares, the three women could walk together from the market to her home in the Colonists Village.

The Traders Market buzzed with activity. Crowds of people cheerfully greeted each other, ready to offer their unique items for trade. Bartering captivated Rebecca. Clothes were traded for food, and furniture was exchanged for tools. Handmade blankets, baskets, jewelry, and eating utensils changed hands. Traders offered chickens, rabbits, sheep, and pigs. Many offers were accepted, some not. Rebecca expected a flea market but found it more like a carnival, exciting, entertaining, and fun.

A short while after arriving, Jasmine, Windy, Rebecca, and Tempest left the family members with the wagon and the crowds. Rebecca thought Aaron, Jules, and Jill were having such a good time they would hardly notice the three women leaving.

The girls dodged people, animals, and carts filled with goods as they ventured through the market. Tempest cautiously scooted between legs, around and under horses, mules, carts, and wagons Nobody seemed to notice the cat except Rebecca. Whenever she feared Tempest was about to be stepped on, run over, or squashed, the cat would magically appear ahead of whatever obstacle had intruded in her path.

Once they passed through the market gates, the activities and sounds diminished. Windy pleaded with her new friends to see where she lived. She wanted to be sure they would know where to find her whenever they came to the market. She lived in a long row of small one-room compartments. Each unit consisted of a door with a small window cut into it. Only a wooden number to the right side of each door distinguished one room from the next. Rebecca quietly compared it to a row of enclosed office cubicles.

They did not go into Windy's apartment. Instead, Jasmine reminded the young woman they had limited time to visit her friend before returning to the market. Not yet willing to let them go, Windy walked with Jasmine and Rebecca to their destination. As they neared Violet's home, Windy hesitated.

"I think I should tell you," Windy cringed, "this is the home of the woman who gave me the package to deliver to the Sorcerer's Fortress. It might have been an assistant to the Governor, or another person doing business here, I did not know the person, but I think you should know.

"Thank you, Windy," Jasmine commented. "I've known Violet since we were children but have not seen her since she married the Governor. So, we will be cautious." Jasmine and Rebecca hugged Windy and said their goodbyes, promising to see her again.

10 Violet

Before they approached Violet's home, Jasmine paused to speak to Rebecca. "Since the three of us came through the mists, Violet has held onto bitterness and resentment. A part of me sympathizes with her for all that she endured. Violet was physically and emotionally hurt. Before coming here, she was in love and engaged to be married to a wonderful man. I believe that losing that life of her dreams broke her more than the attack in the swamp. After healing from her injuries, she learned that she could never have children because of the damage across her midsection. Many lonely years passed before she met and married the Governor. He is a selfish, greedy, uncaring man, many years older than Violet. I suspect their marriage is merely one of their status and convenience. I hope that her meeting you, to know that your mother made it back through the mists, is the right thing to do. Still, I strongly suggest you withhold enthusiasm for your mother's life. If she asks questions, answer truthfully, but withhold exuberance. Do you understand why I am asking this of you?"

"Yes," Rebecca answered.

"Thank you, Becca. I will be there by your side. I will do my best to direct the conversation. However, if she makes you uncomfortable, please tell me, and we will leave. I expect we will be here for less than an hour. One other thing, Violet dislikes animals. Would you mind leaving Tempest outside? I doubt that she would be welcome in Violet's home."

Rebecca knelt and spoke quietly with the cat. "Tempest, you heard what Jasmine said. I have to ask you to find a place outside to wait. I promise I will be safe, and we will not stay long.

As she hugged Tempest, Rebecca closed her eyes. At that moment, she thought she could sense Tempest telling her, "I will do it, but I don't like it."

Violet's home, while still modest compared to many of the homes in Rebecca's hometown, was the largest building she had seen since coming into the Mystic Land. A tall picket fence wrapped around the property, with a wide dirt-covered driveway leading to the front entryway. Two large willow trees shaded the front yard. Two rows of multi-colored flower beds lined the front of the building. Yet, Rebecca noticed open and closed shutters in place of glass in the windows, even in this upscale home.

Even before Rebecca and Jasmine reached the entryway, the front door opened. An elderly, grey-haired woman wearing a grey dress with white trim waited in the doorway as they approached. "Hello, how may I help you?" she greeted.

Jasmine introduced herself and then explained to the woman that she was a longtime friend of Violet's, and they were hoping to visit or say hello to her while they were in the area. The woman invited them to sit on a wooden bench inside the doorway while she announced to the First Lady that they were there. Rebecca observed that while the house might be considered plain by the standards in which she had grown up, it had off-white painted walls, which was more paint than she had seen anywhere else in the past three days.

The woman returned a few minutes later, inviting Jasmine and Rebecca to meet with the First Lady in the garden. Rebecca and Jasmine followed the woman through a short hallway and a pair of open doors leading to a spacious backyard filled with various trees and flowers. In the center of the yard, a small table with four chairs nestled in the shade of a tall oak tree. A woman wearing a wide-brimmed hat sat in one of the chairs with her back to the approaching guests.

The elderly woman announced, "Madam, your guests are here to see you."

The seated woman rose and turned to greet Jasmine and her still unknown associate with a forced smile. Her smile disappeared from her face the moment she looked at Rebecca.

"Clover!" she gasped.

Rebecca started to speak, but Jasmine quickly moved her hand to the girl's arm, signaling her to wait.

Jasmine paused to allow the shock to settle before making introductions. "Violet, it is wonderful to see you. This is Clover's daughter, Rebecca. She came through the mists two days ago. She was fortunate that my husband Aaron was the first to find her at the edge of The Fringes."

Violet appeared speechless. She returned to her chair and signaled by hand for Jasmine and Rebecca to join her at the table. She gestured at the various fruits, homemade pastries, loaves of bread, and jellies on the table as an offer to help themselves, but she did not speak.

Rebecca knew Violet was the same age as Jasmine and her mother, but she looked twenty years older. She wore a faded lavender-colored dress with a pale-yellow sash tied around her waist. She was of average build with carefully styled shoulder-length hair that contained more streaks of grey than natural brown color. Her pale skin was aged with wrinkles. Her mouth had a downward frown, and her eyes sagged at the corners. A deep scar ran down her left cheek from ear to chin. Rebecca already knew about the bite Violet had received from the Goblin attack during her journey through the swamp, but seeing the deep pockmark on Violet's face filled Rebecca with emotions of empathy and discomfort.

As if called by magic, the whistles of a familiar nightingale drifted through the branches of the tall tree shading the three women. Rebecca did not have to look up to recognize Songbird's signals.

"Forgive me for my shock Rebecca," Violet finally broke her silence. "You look so much like your mother, an entire lifetime of memories flooded over me. I have so many questions about you and your mother I don't know where to begin."

"Obviously, Clover made it through the swamp," Jasmine interjected. "She discovered she was pregnant only a few weeks after returning home. Becca is only a few weeks younger than my twins, which means that Takoda Nemasket is her father. Becca is going to meet him later today."

Violet's intense stare began to make Rebecca feel uncomfortable. "So that makes you how old?" Violet inquired.

"I'm seventeen," Rebecca responded. "I just completed my junior year in high school.

"You are a beautiful young woman," Violet complimented, "I can't get over how much you resemble your mother."

"Thank you," was all Rebecca had time to say before Violet began asking further questions.

"I notice that Jasmine calls you Becca. I assume that is your nickname. May I call you, Becca?"

"Yes, of course, Violet. Rebecca is my birth name, but my family and closest friends call me Becca."

Violet continued, "How did you happen to come through the mists? Didn't Clover warn you about it?"

"My mother had warned me not to go into the woods but never told me about the mists," Rebecca admitted. "I went out to pick berries on a sunny Saturday afternoon. The next thing I knew, I was lost in the fog. I followed a cat through the swamp and ended up here."

"The goblins attacked her much like we were," Jasmin commented. "She almost drowned, but animals helped to save her. As a result, she made it through with only scratches and bruises."

"You are fortunate, Rebecca." Violet pointed at the deep scar on her face as she spoke. "Those demons nearly killed me. I do not wish that nightmare on anybody. Please tell me about Clover. Did she achieve her dreams of becoming a famous singer?

Rebecca grinned. She began to feel somewhat comfortable with Violet for the first time. "No, after I was born, my mother worked as a server at a nearby restaurant in Rehoboth. She later became a manager, and when the owners retired, she bought the restaurant. So now restaurant management occupies much of her time and attention."

"It sounds a bit lonely for you," Violet commented.

"I grew up in the restaurant." Rebecca admitted, "I have a permanent part-time job there as a hostess, server, assistant manager, dishwasher, and occasionally assisting the cooks. In addition, I have school and participate in a lot of sports. My mother married when I was seven. She and my stepfather had a son who is now nine. I spend a lot of time with him while they work. I never seem to find time to feel lonely."

"Well then," Violet responded, "I'm happy for you and your mother."

Rebecca sensed a little more resentment than sincerity in Violet's voice. She did not respond to the woman's compliment.

"You mentioned participating in sports, so you're athletic.

That's marvelous. Do you have other interests, or do you know what you might want to do for a career?" Violet boldly inquired.

"I like music," Rebecca answered, "although I'm certainly not as good a singer as my mother. And I like animals, so I've thought about becoming a veterinarian. But, decisions about colleges and my career make me feel a little overwhelmed. And now that I'm here, my future appears even more unclear."

"Well, Rebecca, it's been so many years since I've heard any songs from home," Violet gushed. "Would you be so kind as to sing us a song?"

"Me?" Rebecca felt herself shrink in embarrassment. Then she remembered the words of Nani persuading her to find her voice and sing. So, looking back and forth from Violet to Jasmine and again to Violet, Rebecca asked, "Is there a song that either of you might like to hear?"

Violet shrugged her shoulders.

"Something nice," Jasmine suggested.

After considering songs that might give Violet comfort and peace, Rebecca rose from her chair and began singing.

I see the sun peek through the clouds on a rainy day
I see the colors of the rainbow glistening through the rain
I see the flowers bloom in pink, yellow and white
I see the stars shine in the sky in the dark of night
In such a beautiful world

I hear the buzzing of the bees and waves on the beach
I hear the violins play and the songbirds sing
I hear the children laugh, and I hear myself think
What a beautiful world has been given to me
I am fortunate to have all of the friends that I do

I am grateful for the words I love you
For the air that we breathe and all the earth gives away
We must never forget how blessed we are for this day
In such a beautiful world

Rebecca did not open her eyes through the entire song. When she finally did, Violet was openly crying. Tears poured down her face.

Jasmine sat with watery eyes and an open mouth. She struggled to squeeze out the words, "Becca, don't ever again let me hear you say you are not as good a singer as your mother."

"That was magnificent," Violet added, "Your voice is angelic, Becca."

The women quietly recollected themselves before Rebecca broke the silence. "Violet, what is it like being a Governess?" she asked.

Violet gave a faint smile. "Actually, using that title is a common mistake," she said. "A Governess is a woman employed to teach children in a private household. My title as the Governor's wife is 'First Lady.' Most people think being the governor's wife is a life of elegance and decorum, filled with stylish parties and meetings with refined dignitaries. But in all honesty, it's exactly the opposite. The Governor is seldom home. And when he is, the house constantly has unscrupulous characters venturing in and out. Oh, I have a lot to be grateful for. I live in a nice home. I arrange events and maintain the house to keep me occupied. But it is improper for me to leave the house or be seen in public without being at my husband's side. I have an assistant who runs errands for me. The woman you met at the door is my husband's mother. She lives here, but I think she is mostly here to watch me."

All of a sudden, Violet paused. "Where are my manners?" she blurted out. "I am fortunate to have such a secure life. In fact, I have responsibilities that I really should be attending to today."

Jasmine and Rebecca understood Violet's hint that it was time for them to depart. As they stood to leave, each expressed appreciation to Violet for her hospitality. Jasmine stated how delightful it was to see her friend again.

They were turning toward the door when Violet inquired, "Becca, did you ever happen to meet or know a man named Shawn McGuinn?

"Oh yes," Rebecca responded, "Shawn is my stepfather. How did you know him?"

Immediately after speaking, Rebecca sensed that she had made a mistake. Jasmine and Violet stood in uncomfortable silence.

Finally, Violet replied in a broken voice, "I was engaged to be married to Shawn when your mother, Jasmine, and I got lost in the mists."

Rebecca stuttered, "I'm sorry, Violet. I did not know."

"If they are happy together, that is all that matters." ceded Violet.

Jasmine glanced at Violet, then took Rebecca by the arm as they started toward the door.

Moments after Jasmine and Rebecca left her house Violet summoned her assistant. When the woman appeared in the doorway, Violet called out, "Get me a messenger to deliver a letter to Alsaahir the Sorcerer."

11 Fellowship

The sun was nearly straight overhead while Jasmine, Rebecca, and Tempest hurried to get back to the Traders Market. Jasmine commented that they needed to help the family pack and prepare to leave. Still, the significantly smaller crowd surprised Rebecca when they entered the market.

Nearing the wagon, Aaron appeared to be bartering with a tall, muscular man wearing a variety of sheathed knives on his belt. Jules stood a few yards to the side of his father's shoulder, intently focused on the discussion between the two men. The women were surprised to find Windy feeding and watering the horses with Jill. Windy had changed into clean clothes, she had washed off the dried blood from the side of her head, and her hair was now in a ponytail.

Windy flashed her wide smile. She excitedly explained that she felt so restless after arriving at her home that she decided to return to the market to assist her new friends.

Jill announced to her mother that they had started packing their belongings onto the wagon but had held off while her father bargained with the man. "He might be interested in something they still displayed in their space." she declared. Jill also proudly reported that she had traded for ample amounts of honey, maple syrup, nuts, dried fruits, and two large boxes of oats to make homemade granola bars.

Jules ran to the wagon with an empty hand cart. He seemed to know what he wanted and exactly where to find it. He quickly filled the cart with gardening tools, various packets of seeds, a wooden pail, a large wooden bowl, and two hand-woven blankets before rapidly returning to the two men. The big man walked away after completing their deal, pulling the filled cart behind him. Jules raced back to hand one of two long knives in its sheath to his sister. They admiringly withdrew the long blades with ornately carved bone handles.

As Aaron approached the group, he solemnly addressed the twins. "You are both growing up. I am giving you these knives as a reward for your maturity and hard work. I am extremely proud of you both. However," he cautioned, "these knives are not flashy toys. They are weapons to be used for protection and necessity only. And I remind you that I can also take away what I give, so carry and use them wisely."

Jules and Jill graciously thanked their father, placed the knives into their sheaths, and placed them on their belts.

The group quickly packed the remainder of their goods into the gypsy wagon. Then, Aaron informed them that they would head east through the marketplace. When he and Jasmine turned south toward home, that's where they would drop off the teenagers to begin their walk to the Native Village to meet Rebecca's father.

Aaron spoke loudly enough for everybody to hear, "It will be approximately a three-mile hike. If you travel at a steady pace, you can walk three miles in one hour. If you walk more leisurely or make stops, it will be accordingly longer."

Not wanting to be left behind, Windy quickly asked if she could join them on their journey. "I could visit with my relatives while Becca meets her father." she pleaded.

"The gypsies always say the more, the merrier," Jules exclaimed.

"We already assumed you were coming with us," Jill added smirkingly.

When everybody laughed, they all knew no further approvals were required. Aaron and Jasmine climbed aboard the front of the wagon, while Jules, Jill, Windy, Rebecca, and Tempest climbed into the back.

The gypsy wagon lurched forward, moving slowly through the nearly empty Trader Market. Afternoon sunshine spilled through the open windows. The group cheerfully ate the lunch they had packed that morning, and Rebecca gave food and water to Tempest.

Barely twenty minutes passed before the wagon came to a halt outside the market's eastern gate. While the teens left the wagon, Rebecca took a moment to place her backpack over her shoulders, grab her walking staff, and speak with Tempest.

"Are you ready for another adventure, Tempest?" Rebecca asked.

Tempest spoke a short meowing sound and rubbed against Rebecca's leg as she swaggered toward the door.

Pausing for a moment, Rebecca tried to imagine what Tempest had said to her before admitting that she had no clue. She followed the cat into the afternoon sunshine.

Jasmine and Aaron shared hugs, kisses, and goodbyes with everybody before climbing back to their perch at the head of the wagon. From her elevated position, Jasmine starkly reminded the ensemble of friends to be home the next day before nightfall, "Or else!" she warned.

As Aaron and Jasmine steered the wagon south toward the Gypsy Camps and home, the eager teens excitedly began their journey to the Native Villages. Energies were high. They told stories and shared laughs about their lives. They followed the well-traveled dirt road through the picturesque countryside, stopping to pick apples from a plush tree and again at a row of raspberry bushes lining the roadway. Cheerfully, they greeted people as they passed in the opposite direction. Some travelers rode horses or horse-drawn wagons. Others walked with a mule or pulled a cart. And a few, like themselves, simply walked by with little or no noticeable belongings. All smiled and waved, and some cheered exuberant returns to the lively group of friends. They passed a few humble cabins, farms, and barns and briefly stopped at a small county store named The Trading Post, although they left without trading for anything.

They passed ponds where people fished and children swam in the sunlit waters. Flowing streams allowed them to stop regularly for fresh water. Jules and Jill refilled the water pouches they carried on their belts. Bees sang, and butterflies danced across fields of green grass and colorful flowers. A wide variety of birds fluttered through sweet-scented white birch, maple, oaks, fruit-bearing trees, and groves of cedar pine. Rebecca caught glimpses of Songbird flittering between trees, whistling songs to reassure the girl that she was always nearby. The sound of an owl in the distance reminded her of Wisdom. But sensing that she was in no immediate danger, she suspected the Owl was likely guiding another unfortunate person through dire perils in the misted swamp.

"May I ask a silly question?" Windy asked.

"It depends on how silly the question is," Jules remarked, followed by a giddy chuckle.

"Our mother always says no question is too silly," Jill responded.

Windy shyly continued. "I just realized that I don't know your last names. May I ask that, or is it too personal a question to ask?"

"I think that's a great question," Rebecca commented, "especially since I don't know anybody's last names either."

"Well," Jill replied, "I suppose that if we tell each other our last names, it should strengthen our friendships instead of making the question silly."

Rebecca spoke up first. "My full name is Rebecca Harmony Fields." she proudly announced.

Jules snickered. "So, your mother's name is Clover Fields?"

"Well," Rebecca grinned at the implication, "my mother's maiden name was Mary Anne Clover Fields. When she was younger, she chose to be called Clover. She's now married and known by most people by her married name, Mary Anne McGuinn." So, only a few older friends still remember her as Clover.

"I'm so confused," Jules laughed.

"Confused should be your middle name, Jules." Jill ridiculed her brother.

"My full name is Windy May Amahle. Windy added, "I got my middle name because I was born in May, and my African last name means 'the beautiful one."

"You certainly are beautiful," Rebecca complimented.

"This is May right now," Jill declared. "What day is your birthday?"

"I am nineteen today." Windy blushed.

Rebecca, Jill, and Jules broke out in cheers of "Happy Birthday" and "Congratulations."

"Do you have a birthday wish?" Rebecca asked.

"I think I already got my birthday wish," Windy replied. "Today, I think I met the best friends I've ever had."

The group was speechless for a moment. Then Jill, Rebecca, and Jules each hugged and kissed Windy and wished her a happy birthday. Windy fought to choke back her tears, but nobody commented or seemed to mind.

"We still don't know Jill and Jules' last names." Rebecca reminded them.

"Our last name is Verne," Jules spoke up. "Nothing fancy about that."

"We don't have middle names," Jill added.

"Wait a minute," Rebecca called out. "Your name is Jules Verne?" she asked the boy with a mocking grin.

Jules was not sure how to react. "Yeah, what's so comical about that?"

"You're serious?" Rebecca commented. "You don't know who Jules Verne is?"

Jules, Jill, and Windy looked at Rebecca as if waiting to be let in on a vital secret.

"Jules Verne is one of the most important French novelists of the late nineteenth century," Rebecca informed them. "He wrote a series of Science Fiction and Fantasy Adventure novels, including Journey to the Center of the Earth, Twenty Thousand Leagues Under the Sea, and Around the World in Eighty Days. They are still some of the best-selling books of all time."

"So having the same name as a famous author is not bad, is it?" Jules asked cautiously.

"No," Rebecca grinned, "I'm only surprised your mother never told you about your famous namesake."

"Let's keep moving," Jill commented. "We've still got about a mile to go."

No sooner had Jill's words been spoken when a loud voice called from behind a row of thick bushes, "You all stop right there."

The members of the group all turned at once toward

the sound. A scruffy-looking man of about average height, probably about thirty years old, stepped from behind the bushes. He wore an old gray cap tilted crookedly on his head. Unkempt hair pointed out from under the hat in every direction. Scruffy whiskers closely matched the hair on his head. He wore dirty, ragged clothes that looked like they'd never been washed and animal hides tied around his feet in place of shoes. He pointed an old civil war era sword at the group of friends.

A large brown hound dog standing at the man's side focused on Tempest, who sat calmly behind the four teenagers. Suddenly, about ten yards to each side of the shoddy man, two others appeared from their hiding spots in the bushes.

The big man on the left was at least six and a half feet tall and likely weighed more than three hundred pounds. He was cross-eyed, and his mouth hung open, displaying half a set of yellow and brown teeth. His ragged bowl-cut brown hair looked like an animal had curled up and died on top of his head. His shoulders slouched under a dirty brown t-shirt with massive holes in it. His knee-length cut-off jeans stayed up with a piece of dirty frazzled rope tied over his shoulder like a single suspender. Walking barefoot and with a bit of a limp, it was noticeable that he was missing three of his smaller toes on one foot. He dragged a massive wooden club resembling an oversize baseball bat on the ground as he moved into the road.

To the right stood a small, skinny, uneasy man with a crooked face and short hair that looked like somebody had hacked it off with a knife. He nervously muttered incoherently while chewing on something that looked like black tar as it dribbled from his mouth to his chin. He wore dirty jeans with holes, no shirt, and no shoes covering his filthy feet. He carried a large rock in one hand, a long wooden knife in the other, and several strands of rope-like vines hung over one shoulder. One could only guess his intentions with those vines.

"Well, what a pretty young bunch we have here." the man in the center of the trio announced as he pointed the sword in circles toward the group of friends. "Drop all your packs, those water bags, fancy knives, and empty everything from your pockets onto the road. Just do as I say, and you won't get hurt."

"Hey Dub, can I kiss one of them pretty girls before we go?" the skinny jittery man on the right asked the man in the middle.

Jules spoke up before the man named Dub could answer, "Why are you bothering us? We didn't do anything to you."

The big man on the left bounded into Jules, forcibly knocking him to the ground.

"Keep quiet, boy." said the leader. "If you know what's good for you, you'll shut up and do what you're told. Now, take everything you have and put it on the ground, or somebody is gonna get hurt."

Jules scrambled to his feet. The big man stood too far out of reach for the athletic boy to reach him with his knife but close enough to pounce on Jules with his club if Jules were to make any sudden moves. Jules had no choice but to remove his water bag and the knife.

Jill followed her brother's lead. Removing her water bag and the knife from her belt, she tossed the items on the ground. Windy wasn't carrying anything, so she stood in place without moving. Rebecca dropped her staff to the ground and quietly stood behind it.

"Take that bag off your back," the leader pointed his sword inches away from Rebecca's face, "and take everything from your pockets. All of you," he yelled.

Suddenly, a loud yelp came from behind the cluster of friends. The hound dog had moved around the group to investigate the cat. In an instant, Tempest transformed into a white tiger, ripped a paw across the dog's face, and pounced between Rebecca and the man holding the sword. With a swift swat of her huge claws, Tempest slashed the stunned man's hand, knocking his sword to the ground. The tiger roared so loud that the ground shook.

In the same instant, a maddened bird, screeching and flapping its wings, flew directly into the face of the small jittery man. In fear, the man swung his arm at the wild bird with his hand holding the rock. However, the bird proved faster than the man, dodging quickly to the side as the rock smashed into the man's own face slightly below his eye.

The three stunned thieves, screaming in fear, all turned and raced into the woods.

The angry bird swept after the big man as he ran. Viciously, she flapped her wings and pecked at his head, biting and ripping his ear. The big man swatted at the bird as if being attacked by a swarm of bees. But the bird was too fast, and the big man too slow to hit the nightingale.

Tempest stood in front of the group of friends, cautiously watching the men disappear before she shrunk back to the passive-looking cat.

Rebecca reached down to pet her protector. "Thank you again, Tempest. You are truly my savior," she praised. As she turned toward her friends, she found both Jules and Jill sprawled on the dirt road with shocked looks. Windy had disappeared.

"Windy," Rebecca called out. There was no response. "Windy," she called again, "it's safe to come out."

"Is the lion gone?" she heard Windy's voice fearfully

call out from behind a patch of bushes and trees.

"It's a tiger Windy, not a lion," Rebecca called back.

"I don't care what it is," Windy yelled. "Is it gone?"

"Yes, it's safe now, Windy," Rebecca calmly replied.

Windy hesitantly came forward into the open road, cautiously approaching her friends. Her head looked as if it was on a swivel, looking everywhere for the ominous tiger.

"I guess it's time I tell you about the cat which is not really a cat," Rebecca explained a shortened version of the story about her protector, who twice helped save her life in the swamps as she came through the mists.

Windy curiously and cautiously watched Tempest. "Well, I'm sure glad she's on our side," she exclaimed when Rebecca finished her story.

Jill and Jules were quick to agree with Windy's assessment.

Although Songbird did not return to the group, Rebecca noticed her in a nearby tree. In the excitement, nobody asked about the bird. With a giant white tiger in their midst, Rebecca thought that nobody even saw or remembered the bird. Since nobody asked, she decided to keep the presence of the nightingale to herself for the time being. The story of a cat who can become a tiger is enough, for now, she determined.

While gathering their belongings, they discovered that the three thieves had dropped their weapons as they fled. As a group, they decided that Rebecca had earned the sword, Jules was the obvious choice to carry the enormous club, and Windy would get the wooden knife, as she was the only person with no weapons for protection.

Jules informed Windy that the hardwood knife had been carved from a beautiful piece of red oak. "Those thieves gave you a valuable birthday present, Windy," he commented.

"They were probably stolen weapons, not theirs to

give," Windy commented.

Rebecca asked Jill to carry and take care of the sword, explaining that she couldn't comfortably carry her hiking staff and the weapon.

Jill proudly accepted. "Of course, we'll have to find or make a worthy sheath for this sword and Windy's beautiful oak knife," Jill acknowledged.

As the friends began the final stretch of their journey to the Native Villages, the enthusiastic chatter steadily returned to what it had been before their encounter with the thieves. Again, they found a common bond. "Together we stand," they each pledged.

12 Takoda Nemasket

The first indication that the friends were nearing the Native Villages was the round grass huts called Wetus that appeared in clearings between the trees lining the dusty road. Rebecca recognized the Wetus from photos in her history books but was fascinated to discover that people here still lived in them. Windy pointed out that families grouped the huts to share the duties of farming, cooking, cleaning, building, and raising children.

Rebecca realized she was already growing accustomed to seeing wishing wells in the front yards and outhouses in the back. Barns were plentiful. People owned horses, cows, and sheep. Chickens, ducks, geese, and turkeys roamed freely about the properties. Plush gardens lined the edges of the family communities. Rebecca felt astonished to see so many tall corn stalks, red tomatoes, and rows of fresh ripe vegetables ready to be harvested in May.

As they passed the small clusters of homes, people would wave and call greetings. Children with beaming smiles ran to the road to say hello. Several wanted to pet Tempest, but the cat was always quick to move out of reach of the excited kids. Just past midafternoon, the friends reached the Native Villages. Various buildings, homes, and huts lined the widening road leading to the heart of the community. A large circular wooden building centered the town. Other roads led outward in several directions from the round building like rays of sunshine. Coming to a stop about fifty yards in front of the building, Jules gently took hold of Rebecca's hand. She felt surprised by his daring move but comforted by the kindness of his gesture. She decided to allow her hand to stay in his, at least for now.

Jules' voice quivered as he spoke, "This is the center of the Native Villages, where the leaders meet and most commerce occurs. If any of us get separated, this is where we will wait to find each other. The road on the right leads to the Healing Center. Takoda Nemasket is the Chief there. Most likely, that's where we will find him. Becca, do you feel ready to meet him now?"

"I believe I am as ready as I will ever be," Rebecca replied. Then, turning to Windy, she asked, "Would you like to join us to meet my father, or are you anxious to visit your family?"

"Oh, I already know Doctor Nemasket," Windy remarked. "I've not seen him for a few years, but he helped deliver me into this world."

"He delivered us too," Jill exclaimed with a wide smile. "I think he delivered almost every child in the Mystic Lands over the past twenty-five years,"

"My mother and grandparents live between here and the Healing Center," Windy commented. "They would be happy to see that I've come with my new friends. Before we meet your father, would you like to take a few minutes to meet my family?"

Jules and Jill looked at Rebecca, who nodded in agreement, "Yes, I would love to meet your family. Windy," Becca asked, "you mentioned that your mother and grandparents live here. What about your father?"

"My father died in a work accident when I was a little girl," Windy replied. "Supposedly, he was crushed when a pile of logs fell off a wagon. My mother never remarried, but she is surrounded by family here. She has her parents, uncles, aunts, cousins, brothers, and sisters with their spouses and children."

Rebecca let go of Jules' hand with a kind smile in his direction. They hurried past the large building at the center of the village and turned right at the road Jules had indicated. Windy directed them onto a path leading to a collection of about a dozen Wetu huts. In the center of the cluster of homes, a group of people excitedly gathered about a large campfire. Some sat at tables, participating in robust conversations, while others helped with the cooking. "That's my family," Windy anxiously announced to her friends.

The conversations quieted when the family noticed the teenagers coming toward them until an elderly woman excitedly shouted, "It's Windy!"

The family raced to greet Windy and her friends. Windy attempted to make introductions, but she was overwhelmed with hugs, kisses, cheers, and celebrations.

Windy's mother began to cry. She tearfully told the crowd she had been thinking about Windy that entire day. She had prayed for her safety and wished she could see her daughter on her nineteenth birthday. Finally, her prayers and wishes had come true.

Everybody cheered, "Happy Birthday, Windy!"

Rebecca, Jill, and Jules were offered food and drink and made to feel quite welcome. Tempest attempted to stay outside the circle of people, but even she received a generous share of attention and plenty to eat and drink, especially from the young children in the crowd.

Rebecca was fascinated to see that Windy's extended family consisted of a diverse mix of African, Native American, and Caucasian heritage. The children were a blend of mixed races, yet the diversity never seemed to be acknowledged by a single person in the group. If anything, this appeared to be one of the most joyous families Rebecca could remember ever being around. If only the rest of the world could be so open-minded, she thought.

Nearly an hour had passed before Windy finally announced that they were on their way to meet Takoda Nemasket at the Healing Center. She explained that they were not seeing him for medical reasons but did not explain why they were going. Then she asked if she could return to stay for the night and whether there might be a place for her friends, to which they generously offered beds, food, and space in their homes.

Once again, the friends gathered their belongings for the final stretch of their journey to meet Takoda Nemasket.

The Healing Center was a vast building behind a beautifully manicured green lawn. As far as the eye could see to each side of the property, deep green trees fronted the edge of the Wampanoag Woods. A wide gravel driveway led from the road to the front of the building. Open-air covered parking stalls lined the sides of the driveway where a few horses and wagons waited for their owners.

Colorful flower beds and trimmed hedges skirted the front of the plain-colored building. Tall open windows with shutters to each side and awnings above peeked outward toward the lawn. A pair of doors stood open at the center of the broad structure. A few people came and went, but the Center did not appear overly busy.

Rebecca asked Tempest to wait outside the Healing Center while she and her friends went in. She didn't sense any concern from the cat as Tempest promptly padded her way to the underside of a thick bush near the front door.

As they entered a large lobby, it felt as if the eyes of every person watched with some concern the group of teenagers carrying a sword, heavy club, sharply pointed staff, and several long knives.

With an uncertain look and a forced smile, one of three receptionists sitting inside the doorway cautiously greeted them, "Welcome to the Healing Center. How may we help you today?"

Jules confidently stepped forward. "Our apologies for carrying weapons in here," he spoke loud enough for every person in the lobby to hear. "We walked from the Trader Market today. Our parents thought it wise to carry some protection. We mean no threat. We are wondering if Takoda Nemasket might be available to meet with us," he asked. "If so, would you please tell him that Jules and Jill Verne are here to see him? It is important."

The receptionist stated that she would check on his availability. She then invited the group to sit in the waiting area while she left to find the doctor. The lobby was comfortably spacious, containing several cushioned benches, tables, and chairs arranged to serve as a waiting room and meeting area for patients, visitors, and health care workers. They sat on an extended bench and placed their possessions against the wall.

The receptionist returned a few minutes later, telling the group of friends that Doctor Nemasket would be joining them momentarily.

Rebecca began feeling overwhelming sensations of emotions swelling up inside of her. Anxious questions raced through her mind. What if he doesn't believe she's his daughter or simply denies the relationship with her mother? What if he doesn't like her? For two days, she had been feeling excited about the possibility of meeting her father, but now she was feeling anxiety and fear. Maybe this is all a mistake, she thought. Perhaps I should change my mind and leave.

She was about to give in to the urge to get up and run out the door when Jules' calmly rested his hand on hers. This time, Rebecca felt no compulsion to pull away. Instead, she smiled a nervous grin as she glanced upward to look into his eyes. He smiled a compassionate smile in return. His empathy and support allowed a sense of relief to wash over her. Without a thought, her fingers wrapped within his. No matter what happened in this meeting with her father, she was comforted to know she had caring friends. Especially this thoughtful young man who was by her side.

A tall, statuesque, middle-aged man, wearing a loose-fitting white shirt and pants, entered the room through a doorway at the furthest wall. Looking briefly about the room, he began walking toward them. Instantly, Rebecca knew that was him. He was the father she had always imagined him to be. He was modestly handsome, with all of the most noteworthy features of an American Indian chief. Dark hair, naturally tanned skin, deep brown eyes, chiseled jaw, obviously fit, and he carried himself with an alluring confidence.

The four friends all stood at once. When Jules, Jill, and Windy stepped forward to greet him, Rebecca cautiously stayed behind. She felt so lightheaded she almost sat back down.

The man's broad smile beamed as he raised his arms in a welcoming gesture of friendship. "I am told some heavily armed teenagers are here to see me. I doubt I should have any reasons to be fearful of my favorite twins," he boldly exclaimed. One by one, Takoda greeted and embraced each of his visitors. "Jules, what a strapping young man you've become. And Jillian, you are more beautiful every time I see you." He gave Jill a small polite kiss on one cheek and then stepped toward Windy. "Oh my, is this the wondrous Windy Amahle? She grinned at his recognition. "You have grown into a young woman since I saw you last. How long has it been, Windy?"

"About three or four years," Windy shyly replied.

"Today is Windy's nineteenth birthday," Jill announced.

"Nineteen years! You've grown more than a little since we first met," Takoda responded with a huge smile. "My, how time flies. Happy birthday Windy."

He was already looking at Rebecca as he hugged Windy. He took a step forward to greet her, then seemed to hesitate. He glanced back at the twins and looked again at the doe-eyed Rebecca.

"Something tells me we have never met unless you were a very young child," he said to Rebecca. "However, you look like a beautiful young woman I once knew. Is there any chance you're related to... No, that cannot be possible. Who might you be, young lady?" he inquired.

Rebecca took a moment to gain her composure before she began to speak. She took a deep breath and started, "My name is Rebecca. I believe you knew my mother, Clover Fields when she was in the Mystic Lands about eighteen years ago. She made it through the mists when she left here and learned she was pregnant a few weeks later. I am the result of that pregnancy. If it is true that she had a relationship with you during the two months that she was here, I think I might be your daughter."

Takoda paused for barely a second before responding, "Rebecca, I believe everything you just said is true. I am likely your father. And if that is so, you have just made me the happiest and most proud man on this planet. May I hug you?"

Rebecca choked up. As she and Takoda embraced, she began to cry. "I didn't think you would accept me," she sobbed.

"Rebecca, we have much to learn about each other," Takoda tearfully responded. Then, looking at the group, he asked, "Are you all available to come to my home for dinner and get acquainted? I live very close."

Excitedly, they all began talking at the same time. Once the details were thoroughly discussed and worked out, Windy decided to spend the night with her family while Rebecca, Jill, and Jules visited and stayed at Takoda's home. They agreed to meet Windy at her family's home later the following morning to make the return journey together.

The teens again hoisted their possessions and stepped outside to see Windy off. Takoda asked Windy if she might like an escort. "We have some handsome young men working in the Healing Center who would be happy to see you safely home," he offered teasingly.

Windy expressed her appreciation and mentioned that her family lived close by, she had grown up in this neighborhood, and it was still daylight. "All reasons not to be concerned for her safety," she confidently stated. Everyone took turns giving Windy hugs and wishing her a happy birthday before she turned and headed down the driveway.

Returning his attention to Rebecca, Jill, and Jules, Takoda indicated that they could take a shortcut through the Healing Center, as he lived only a short distance behind it.

"Oh, but I have a cat with me," Rebecca announced, pointing toward the bush where Tempest waited. There she sat, staring at a singing nightingale sitting on top of the bush. An outsider might have thought the cat was eyeing the bird as its next meal. Only Rebecca knew that the two animals were communicating.

"Looks like Tempest has made a friend," Jules commented.

"We cannot take the cat into the Healing Center," Takoda explained, "but we can take the scenic tour around the outside of the building."

Rebecca kneeled, closed her eyes, and spoke in a low voice to Songbird and Tempest. "This man with us is my father. We will visit with him and probably spend the night at his home. He lives close by, somewhere behind this Healing Center. Songbird, would you please follow Windy to make sure she gets home safely?"

Although she did not hear an answer to her question, Rebecca believed she felt a surge of energy tingling through her back and neck. So that's what intuition feels like, she thought. When she opened her eyes, Songbird gave a sweet-sounding whistle and winked at the girl before spreading her wings and flying after Windy.

"Wow," Takoda quietly commented to Jill and Jules, "I just flashed back eighteen years. Rebecca is exactly like I remember her mother!"

They departed then. Takoda led the way with Rebecca at his side. Takoda asked Rebecca about her mother and her life growing up. Jules and Jill had already heard Rebecca's story, so they followed quietly behind, allowing the newly found father and daughter the opportunity to become acquainted. Tempest kept pace with the group in her usual catlike manner, sometimes following behind the twins, bouncing forward to walk beside Rebecca, or occasionally darting under a bush to inspect a movement only she had observed.

As they rounded the corner to the back of the Healing Center, everybody stopped to gaze in amazement at the spectacular garden covering several acres of land. Rays of sunshine brightened the rows of flowers, fruits, vegetables, grains, and herbs. Colorful butterflies fluttered in and out of the light like sparkles across a magic garden. Several workers tended the land, attempting to accomplish all they could before sunset.

Their path followed the garden's edge toward a tall line of trees. Takoda explained that almost all medicines, herbs, salves, potions, and elixirs used in the Healing Center and the foods to feed more than two hundred healthcare workers, healers, patients, and daily visitors came from the garden.

They entered a shadowed dirt path into the Wampanoag Woods. It was wide and tall enough for a single horse-drawn wagon but not wide enough for two wagons to pass by each other.

Trees of all sizes and shapes towered over their heads. Rebecca found herself taking deep breaths of the fresh forest air. She thought Mother Nature herself must keep the gloriousness of these woods. Wetus and cabins settled in clearings between trees, and treehouses that looked like fairies created them spread across branches.

Takoda asked Rebecca how she happened to come through the mist.

She told him about getting lost in the woods, the swamps, and the attacks by the goblins. She talked about her animal protectors and how she had been so fortunate to meet Jules, Jill, Aaron, and Jasmine.

About a quarter-mile into the woods, Takoda directed them off the path toward the front door of a nice-looking country-style log cabin. "This is my home," Takoda declared as he opened the door and invited them in. It was quiet and dark on the inside. Takoda hurried to get the kindling lit and a log placed in the fireplace. He then offered to make a dinner of fruits and vegetables while they continued talking. "I've been very fortunate," he explained. "The Healing Center graciously gave me this house as a reward when I reached twenty years of service. Two years later, I became the Chief of Medical Services. Or, as some call me, the Chief Indian Medicine Man!"

"Did you ever marry or have children?" Rebecca asked.

"No, that's where I've been less fortunate," he responded. "I've had a couple of relationships, but primarily I dedicated my life to medicine and healing. A healthy relationship is challenging when you spend most of your time engaged in your profession. If I may be very truthful with you, Rebecca, I was more in love with your mother during the short time we were together than any other woman I've since met. Meeting you today feels like Heaven opened up for me. I now have a daughter. I may have played only a small part in bringing you into this world, but the world blessed me by bringing you into my life."

"I've only been here for a few days. I don't know if I dare to go back through the mists or if I might decide to stay." Rebecca glanced at Jules as she spoke, then felt guilty for doing so. Common sense told her that deciding to stay or go would not depend on a relationship with a flirtatious seventeen-year-old boy.

"Can you sing like your mother?" Takoda asked.

"I don't think I can sing half as well as my mother," Rebecca shyly responded, "but some people tell me I have a nice voice."

"Before your mother left here, she told me the keys to returning through the mist were her connection to the animals, her singing voice, and her self-confidence. She claimed that the animals had taught her that," Takoda reminisced. "Until you came here today, I always wondered if she made it back through the mists or not. Now I know. I've seen your connection with Tempest and a bird. I believe that if you have a voice and confidence like your mother, you could return to your home if you choose to do so."

Rebecca quickly changed the subject. "My mother told me that my father was a musician. Are you still?"

Takoda bellowed a loud laugh. "I love music but was never gifted as a musician. So, your mother's ability was a big part of my attraction to her. I encouraged your mother to pursue her talent. And I give your mother credit for giving me the confidence to believe in my abilities as a healer and pursue my dreams in medical services."

"You're one of the most heralded and respected people in Mystic Lands!" Jill added to the conversation, "Our mother told us that you were the primary person behind the building of the Healing Center, the Conference Center, and the new school here in the Native Villages. Is that true?"

"Well, that's a very generous compliment by your wonderful mother," Takoda exclaimed. "Please express my sincere gratitude to Jasmine for her thoughtful compliments, but those buildings required this entire village's imagination, support, and hard work."

"Tremendously accomplished and humbled too," Jules interjected. "If not for this man, the Native Villages would still be a collection of wigwams and wetus. Nobody has made a bigger difference in this community than you, Doctor Nemasket."

Again, Takoda laughed out loud. "I can see that praise runs in this family. I admit to having used my position to get some important progress acted upon, but I am but a small breeze in a big forest. Furthermore, I am not officially a doctor. I understand that achieving the title of doctor requires many years of education outside the Mystic Land. I can only claim excellent on-the-job training over the past twenty-five years. We are both adults. So please, call me Takoda, or if you must be formal, you may refer to me as Mister Nemasket."

Jules grinned. He obviously liked being referred to as an adult, especially by a man he so respected.

Takoda asked about the sword Jill had carried. They told him about their meeting with the three thieves, including the part about Tempest not really being a cat.

"I am aware of stories of animals with similar reputations," Takoda responded. "Some call them spirit animals, others believe they come from the time of fairies, and some think they are the good magic that compensates for the evil in the mists. In addition, I am aware of an Elfin princess who claims to speak with these magical animals. Perhaps I could introduce you."

"The sword is a Confederate officer sword from the civil war period," Takoda informed the teens. "Most likely, someone came through the mists at that time, and the sword has been here ever since. The swords usually came in a protective metal sheath attached to the soldiers' belts. After all these years, it's anyone's guess what happened to the sheath or how those thieves ended up with the sword. Many similar weapons inherited by relatives have traded at the market."

"While I finish preparing our meal," Takoda inquired, "Rebecca, would you please sing a song for us?"

Rebecca was startled by the request. This is the second time she has been asked to sing today. "Is there a song you would like to hear?" she asked.

"Have you written any songs of your own?" Takoda asked.

"Yes," she timidly replied, "but I don't usually sing them to other people."

"Please sing one of your favorite songs, Takoda responded.

After considering for a moment, Rebecca rose from her chair and began to sing.

There are times in every life
When the road gets hard
And the rain pours down
When your heart gets broken
And tears fill your eyes
That's when you will find me there
That's when I'll be by your side

There are times in every life
When times get rough
And you need a friend
When the night is long
And sleep is short
When it feels like the pain is all around
That's when you will find me there
That's when I'll be by your side

There are times in every life
When things just don't go right
And all you need is a break
A spark of friendship, a little light
To brighten the dark of night
That's when you will find me there
That's when I'll be by your side

When Rebecca opened her eyes, Jill and Jules stood in front of her with their mouths ajar.

"Becca, I had no idea," Jill muttered.

Jules just stared. Rebecca thought it might be the first time she had seen him speechless.

Even Tempest, who Rebecca thought was sleeping by the fireplace, starred at Rebecca as if magically enchanted.

She turned to ask Takoda if he liked the song. She didn't have to ask. His hands covered his mouth as tears rolled down his face.

After collecting himself, Takoda remarked, "Rebecca, I thought I would never hear another song that could compare to your mother's voice. I was wrong. Even your mother's voice never brought tears to my eyes like you just did. Today, the angels brought you to me."

The room was silent while Takoda set the table with plates, utensils, platters filled with cut fruits and vegetables, bowls with sauces, and containers with various juices, teas, and flavored waters. He thoughtfully placed two dishes with food and water next to Tempest. Although the cat had eaten well at Windy's family gathering, she ate heartily of Takoda's offerings.

The conversation picked up during dinner. Takoda asked Jules and Jill about their lives and updates about their parents. He told fascinating stories about his experiences in healthcare and the enjoyments of working in the Healing Center.

When the subject of their plans for the next day arose, Takoda said he would have to be back at the Healing Center shortly after sunrise, but they could stay and sleep as late as they wanted. He offered them a ride with a pair of young workers who would be traveling to the Trader Market with herbs, teas, salves, ointments, bandages, and medical supplies in the late morning. He then showed them where the washroom was located and made sleeping arrangements. The cabin had only two bedrooms, so they decided that Jules would get the guest bedroom while Jill, Rebecca, and Tempest slept in the living room area. They thought it a fair arrangement for one night since Jules had generously given up his bedroom at home to Rebecca.

Following hugs and a fatherly kiss on Rebecca's cheek, Takoda brought out a pile of blankets, said his goodnights, and retreated to his bedroom. The teens each took turns washing and finally turned in for the night.

Jill whispered as the girls were getting comfortable, "I don't think I've ever had a single day filled with so many experiences, Becca."

"It was quite a day," Rebecca agreed.

"I wish it never had to end," Jill added. "I wish we could stay like this forever."

"I could have done without the three thieves," Rebecca responded. "At least none of us were hurt."

"Ha, I'll never forget the look on those fools' faces when Tempest turned into a tiger," Jill laughed.

Rebecca giggled in return, "I'll never forget the look on yours, Jules, and Windy's faces!"

Their laughter felt like the perfect way to end a memorable day.

As Rebecca closed her eyes, her thoughts quickly slipped into a dream, although the dream was interrupted when a familiar voice began to speak with her.

"Hello, my darling," the woman's voice greeted.

"Nani," Rebecca greeted. "It has been such an amazing day. Have you been with me today?"

"I was with you through every glorious moment," Nani replied. "I was there when you sang to Jasmine and Violet, when you faced the thieves, and when you met your father. So, it is no surprise that you, such a beautiful, intelligent and gifted young woman, would have two inspiring and loving parents."

"He is the most amazing man I've ever met," Rebecca exclaimed. "I can't believe he's my father. Heck, I still can't believe I even met my father!"

Nani smiled, "I heard you sing two beautiful songs today. I hope you saw how you moved every person who heard you sing. You have magic in your voice, and I do not use the word 'magic' lightly, but I must help you understand that your voice is a magical tool that can positively affect the course of your life. Feel confident in yourself and believe in the power of your voice to make a difference in your life and your world."

"I did see how people reacted to my songs today," Rebecca confided. "In the past, I always thought people were being kind when they complimented me because I never believed I could sing as well as my mother."

"From now on, you are not only the daughter of Mary Anne Clover Fields and Takoda Nemasket," Nani continued, "but also your unique abilities and life experiences. You are the magnificent, one and only Rebecca Harmony Fields. Let nobody tell you otherwise. And most importantly, never tell yourself otherwise."

"Thank you, Nani. You're making a big difference in my confidence." I'm also beginning to connect intuitively with Tempest and Songbird," Rebecca confided, "although I've had very little time alone with them to practice."

"Do not fret, my dear. Tempest, Songbird, and Wisdom

are connected to you beyond the human limitations of time and place." Nani proceeded, "This is my final message to you this night. Not all in the Mystic Land is as it appears. I am not yet certain, but there may be difficult challenges coming. If you should get separated from your animal protectors, remember, you can call them the same way we are speaking now. They have a way to reach you. My time is up. I must go now. Awaken so you remember our conversation, and then you must sleep. Good night, Rebecca," her great grandmother sang Rebecca's name as she faded into the night.

"What kind of difficult challenges, Nani?" Rebecca cried out. "Why would we be separated? I don't understand." Realizing she was alone, Rebecca whispered, "Good night, Nani." She opened her eyes and looked about the room. She could hear Jill's light breathing from where she slept a few feet away. Tempest rested soundlessly by the fireplace as the final glowing embers from the evening log cast red and orange shadows about the darkening room. She thought about her grandmother's messages and then closed her eyes and drifted into a restful sleep.

13 The Storm

Jill and Jules appeared to be asleep when Rebecca awoke. She knew it was morning by the dim rays of daylight filtering through the curtained windows. As she sat up, a piece of parchment paper fell off her blanket to the floor. It read, Come to the Healing Center for breakfast. Use the back door by the garden. We will have food and water for Tempest too. With love, your father. Your father, Rebecca cheerfully thought. I never believed it possible.

Thinking she could quietly make her way to the washroom without waking her friends, Rebecca stood and stretched.

Jill called out, "Good morning, Sleepyhead."

In less than half a minute, the door to the guest bedroom sprung open. "I was beginning to think you two would never wake up," Jules announced with a beaming grin.

Tempest still laid by the extinguished fireplace, paws tucked under her, watching the humans with a sense of amusement.

It did not take long for the teens to clean themselves, clean up after themselves, gather their belongings, and head for the Healing Center. Songbird whistled to Rebecca as they left the cabin, letting her know she was nearby. The sky, barely visible through the thick trees, was overcast with grey. A shimmer of dew covered the ground, and dampness filled the air. Rebecca commented to her friends that it was the first day the sun was not shining since she arrived in the Mystic Land, but she would happily accept grey clouds before the thick, dense fog covering the swamps.

They walked steadily along the tree-covered path to the

opening in the trees by to the magnificent garden. Then, stepping from the shadows into the open space, they walked into a small pack of llamas. The ordinarily calm llamas appeared as startled by the three teens and the cat as the three friends were by the animals. For a few confusing moments, bodies stepped into, over, and through each other, trying to go in opposite directions. Which species gathered their senses first could not be determined, although the pack of llamas was foremost to move away while the humans stood in place, caught their breath, and then broke out in laughter. When Jules pointed out that one of the llamas spit on him, they laughed even harder.

One of the largest llamas let out a bleating sound, comparable to a sheep or goat, then slowly walked back to the bewildered teenagers. It stopped directly in front of Rebecca and began to hum before leaning forward to plant a human-style kiss on Rebecca's cheek.

"Thank you," was all Rebecca could think to say. The llama returned to the pack, and they all meandered away.

Unusual noises emanated through the open air, sounding like loud meowing sounds. Tempest either didn't notice or didn't care, so Rebecca guessed there was nothing to worry about. As the friends continued past rows of tall corn stalks, two peacocks surprisingly flew together into the roadway directly in front of them. One with a massive colorful plumage excitedly greeted the teens with loud screeching noises. The other, slightly smaller peacock with a simpler brown-colored tail turned to face them. Hanging from her beak, she proudly presented a five-foot-long, wiggling green snake on the ground in front of Rebecca. The snake began to slither away when none of the teenagers picked it up. The peacock snatched it up again without letting it go a second time.

"Well, this day is beginning in some unexpected ways," Rebecca commented. She smiled gratefully at the peacocks while she and her friends circled past the big beautiful birds.

Finally turning the corner near the building, Takoda Nemasket excitedly waved his arms as he raced to greet the teenagers. His broad smile beamed from fifty yards away.

"I have never seen him look so happy," Jill whispered to Rebecca. "Likewise, I've never seen Jules looking so happy either. Do you have this effect on all men in your life?" she laughed.

Rather than saying anything in return, Rebecca smiled glowingly at her friend. They giggled and picked up their pace to greet Takoda.

"I see you met a few of our guardian llamas and peacocks," Takoda teased, following their good morning salutations and hugs.

"Guardian llamas and peacocks?" Rebecca inquired.

"At the far end of the garden," Takoda gestured as they walked, "we have a large barn and a barnyard that stretches into the trees. We raise sheep, cows, goats, chickens, ducks, geese, rabbits, mules, and eight horses. In addition, we have eight dogs, sixteen llamas, and a dozen peacocks, which are natural guardians of the other animals and the gardens. That's why the llamas met you when you came out of the woods. And peacocks make more than a dozen different sounds that serve as signals," Takoda informed them. "For instance, today they are making meowing sounds, indicating that it will rain.

"I heard the loud meowing sounds from the woods," Rebecca announced, "but did not know peacocks were making the noise."

"Or that peacock noises had meanings," Jules added.

Did you know that peacocks prey on snakes?" Takoda asked.

"We discovered that in our meeting with your peacocks five minutes ago," Jill laughed. "I think one of the peacocks tried to give a snake to Becca as a gift!"

Takoda laughed. "Come," he said, "We have breakfast waiting for you and a special breakfast for Tempest. And we have people to meet and things to do before you leave this morning." Nearing the back doors to the Healing Center, a young man appeared carrying a tray with three plates covered with various foods and a wide bowl filled with milk. Takoda directed him to set the tray on the ground and announced to Tempest that this breakfast was for her.

The cat curiously sniffed at each plate before selecting one to begin devouring. Rebecca knelt next to Tempest just long enough to tell her that they would return in a short while, then followed Takoda into the building.

"Before taking you to breakfast," Takoda declared, "we have one stop to make." He led them a short distance down a long hallway, passing several rooms before turning left into an open doorway. Racks lined the walls with white staff uniforms. Shelves held piles of folded blankets, sheets, cloth, and materials. In the center of the room, five women sat around a wide table, sewing and making various clothes, curtains, bedcovers, pajamas, and everything imaginable that could be sewn, knitted, or pressed for the Healing Center.

Takoda greeted the women, "Ladies, these are the teenagers I was telling you about. This is my daughter, Rebecca," he proudly announced, "and our twin friends. Jules and Jill, who I am fortunate to have known since the day they were born almost eighteen years ago. Might you have made the pieces I described to you earlier?"

While the teenagers wondered what he was referring to, one of the women reached under a pile of cloth to secretively hand something to Takoda. Then, turning back to the teenagers, he declared, "Jill, these women kindly made a scabbard for you to house your sword." He presented her with a black leather sheath with white stitching. "You can wear it on your belt as the Civil War soldiers wore it or with a strap to carry over your shoulder.

"But the sword belongs to Becca," Jill murmured.

"No," Rebecca said, "that sword was never meant to be mine. That's why I asked you to carry it. While I learned to sing and play sports, you and Jules trained to protect yourselves. So, the sword and the sheath are yours, Jill."

"The women also made a similar but smaller sheath for Windy's long knife," Takoda added. So, Rebecca, would you be so kind as to give it to Windy when you see her?"

"Of course," Rebecca replied. And ladies, we thank you so very much. Your work is beautiful and tremendously appreciated."

"Thank you, Ladies," Takoda concluded as he led Rebecca, Jill, and Jules toward the door. "I must now get these hungry, growing teenagers some breakfast." He led them back to the main lobby. Instead of crossing the open room, they made another turn through a pair of double swinging doors into a large dining area. It reminded Rebecca of her school cafeteria, except this was nicer and made for adults. It held a long buffet-style serving bar covered with fruits, berries, loaves of bread, cooked eggs of varied styles, breakfast sandwiches, oatmeal, pastries, pitchers filled with milk, juices, and teas, and several items that Rebecca did not recognize. People in white clothes and aprons busily helped cook over open fireplaces, served, cleaned, and greeted Takoda and his guests.

During their breakfast, Takoda announced that he would

lead them back to Tempest and introduce them to the two people who would drive the wagon to take them back to the Trader Market.

Jules started to argue that they did not have to drive them that far, but Takoda quickly stopped Jules before he completed his sentence.

"It is already arranged," Takoda explained. "As the peacocks have told you, we have heavy rains coming today. So, we provided a covered wagon for you. Besides, the wagon drivers are dropping off items at the market storage facility for tomorrow's Trader Market. This will assure you will be home before sunset as you promised your mother."

Tempest waited patiently by the back door. The plates and bowl were surprisingly clean. Nobody said anything, but everybody wondered if the cat had eaten all of that food by herself.

Takoda gave them a tour of the enormous barn, introduced each of the dozens of animals by name, and finally brought them to the side of the Healing Center. A pair of extremely large, muscular draft horses were hitched to a long tarp-covered supply wagon, reminding Rebecca of the old covered wagons she had seen in her history books.

"These are our finest Clydesdales," Takoda proudly announced. "They each weigh over sixteen hundred pounds. The larger male is named Strongbow, and the female is Mahogany."

Rebecca immediately went to the front of the wagon to meet the horses. She called them by name and fed them the apples she had brought from the dining room.

Two young adults, a man carrying a large wooden crate and a woman balancing two overflowing baskets, appeared through the side doors of the Healing Center. "These are the last items, Takoda," the man called out, "We are ready to go."

After helping to place the crate and baskets into the wagon, Takoda made introductions. "This hard-working young woman is Luna, and the diligent young man is her younger brother, Leo. They are both students of the healing arts. It is a tradition here that the students work and learn many of the various responsibilities at the center while training as healers. They are both especially gifted at caring for animals. Leo has volunteered his services at every physical task, such as driving this pair of giant workhorses." While introducing Jules and Jill, Takoda proudly told the story of delivering his first twins. Then proudly presented Rebecca as his daughter and Tempest as the cat which is not really a cat. He did not detail further, explaining that he would allow them to tell their stories and get to know each other on their journey that day.

Raindrops were beginning to fall as they said their goodbyes. Rebecca waited to share a few private moments with her father. They both expressed how happy they were to have finally met and to have had the opportunity to get to know each other. They promised to see each other again as soon as possible. Neither wanted to let their hugs end, and they both comfortably expressed, "I love you."

Takoda helped Rebecca climb aboard the back of the covered wagon with Jules, Jill, and Tempest. Then, stoically, he stood outside the doors to the building, watching and waving as the wagon pulled away. He struggled to hide his emotions while his daughter wiped away her tears.

Rebecca quietly considered how the past week had affected her. She completed her junior year in high school, got separated from her brother, lost in the woods, led through a horrible swamp by spirit animals, fought goblins, communicated with the spirit of her great-grandmother, gained the support of a wonderful family, made new friends, discovered her singing voice, and met her loving father. It felt amazing and overwhelming at the same time. A part of her wondered if it was real. Maybe I'm actually in a coma somewhere, she thought, and this is a dream from which I can't wake up!

The wagon pulled to the side of the road where Windy was visiting with her family. Nobody was outside because it was raining, so Jules and Jill left the wagon to find Windy. They had not walked even halfway up the path toward the cluster of Wetu huts when Windy appeared. Carrying a collection of clothes and objects over her shoulders, she waved to her friends before hugging her mother, grandparents, and several other relatives. Then cheerfully raced to catch up with Jules and Jill. After boarding the covered wagon, the friends helped her unload the armful of clothes and belongings and introduced Windy to Luna and Leo.

The resounding excitement of the teenagers reverberated through the wagon. Each had questions to ask and stories to tell. An outsider might have thought these friends had not seen each other in weeks or months rather than hours. Rebecca presented Windy with the sheath for her knife as a gift from her father and told of the kind women who made it. Jill eagerly showed Windy her matching scabbard for her sword while Windy excitedly placed her knife in the new sleeve and placed it on her belt.

As the covered wagon rounded the Community Center and headed south, few in the wagon seemed to notice the increasing patter of rain on the overhead tarp.

Relatively quiet aboard the buckboard seat, Leo remained focused on keeping the horses and the wagon out of holes filling with water. At the same time, Luna responded to friendly questions about her and her brother.

"I'm twenty-three, and Leo is twenty," Luna revealed. "Our father has been best friends with Takoda Nemasket since childhood. As teenagers, they both worked and trained at the Healing Center. While Takoda was interested in helping people, our father wanted to work more with sick and hurt animals. They would often travel together to the Elfin villages to learn about medicines and healing techniques as part of their studies. Our Native American father met our Elfin mother during those visits, and they fell in love. They now run a large animal hospital and boarding ranch, straddling the East River in the Borderland Hills."

"We've been there several times," Jules called out. "Our father says it's the best animal care in the Mystic Lands. I'm surprised we never met."

"It is a big ranch," Luna explained, "and we work all over it. Leo and I grew up working with all animals, but our parents insisted that if we wanted to help with medical care, we must train at the Healing Center for a few years. We've been there for slightly less than one year, but Takoda has been especially thoughtful in mentoring and overseeing our training."

Rebecca was fascinated to learn that they were half-elves but did not feel comfortable asking questions about it. She thought she might sound ignorant to admit she thought elves were only fairy tale stories. So instead, she attempted to observe the features of the brother and sister. Because of the cool rain, they both wore wide brim hats and loose-fitting clothes that covered their bodies. The only visible features were in their faces, which Rebecca thought looked more like they were of Asian descent than anything she imagined resembled an elf. She finally reminded herself that it doesn't matter how people look. I am so fortunate to meet such incredible people, she thought, and that's what's most important.

Leo suddenly pulled back on the reins to slow the horses. Luna called out to the teens, "A man is standing in the middle of the road up ahead."

No sooner were Luna's words spoken when a voice yelled, "You stop right there."

As the wagon drew to a stop, the wet scruffy-looking man wearing an old gray cap reached down to pick up a long, sharply pointed stick. Probably close to ten feet in length, he pointed the spear at Leo as he approached the wagon. Two other men ran out from behind trees on each side of the wagon. They also carried long sticks with sharp points directed at each side of Leo and Luna.

The big man on the left, standing at least six and a half feet tall and likely weighing more than three hundred pounds, held the point of his stick inches from Leo's face. To the right, a small, skinny man muttered to himself as he pressed the sharp end of his stick into Luna's arm.

"Get down off that wagon," the leader called out. "We are confiscating this wagon and anything it carries for the needs and the betterment of our national defense."

The teens in the back of the wagon were beginning to rise, intending to help defend Luna and Leo, but Tempest was quicker. The cat began to grow before she reached the ground. By the time Tempest rounded the back corner of the wagon, she had reached her full size. Within seconds the white tiger met face to face with the big man on the left side of the wagon. One long scratch split the big man's arm from his shoulder to his hand. Another slashed the length of his leg.

His long, pointed stick dropped to the ground before he could use it. He cried out in fear and pain, fell to the ground, and crawled into the bushes.

Tempest bounded past the wounded man to directly confront the talkative leader. Before he realized what was happening, the tiger's gaping maw roared into the scraggly man's frightened face. The big cat's paw pressed on the man's foot, tripping him backward. Tempest pounced. Her four-hundred-pound body slammed onto the man's chest. His bones made a cracking noise as she sat across his legs. The giant cat knitted her long sharp claws into his chest like a kitten preparing a spot to lie down on a warm blanket. When Tempest climbed off the man, all he could do was roll over and drag his ragged body to the side of the road and into the woods.

During those few moments, Jill was the first to hit the ground. She rounded the back right corner of the wagon with her sword drawn. Seeing the tiger at the front of the wagon, the scrawny nervous man who had threatened Luna dropped his spear and turned to run from the scene. But instead, he ran directly into Jill's sword. The sword passed through his right shoulder and came out the backside like a warm knife passing through butter, shocking both the sputtering man and the startled girl. Jill quickly withdrew the sword. The wounded man dropped to the ground, screaming, crying, and wailing like a wounded dog.

Jill yelled, "You've got about three seconds before that tiger gets here. Run," she ordered."

And run he did. He was off the ground and into the trees before anybody could count to three.

The event happened so quickly; Rebecca, Jules, and Windy were still gathering around Jill while Luna and Leo climbed down from the buckboard bench. The brother and sister had observed most of the situation, yet they were still trying to grasp what had happened.

"Did you see that tiger?" Leo questioned.

"Where did that tiger come from? Luna asked quizzically.

"And where did it go?" she implored.

Tempest, now the affectionate little cat, nudged against Rebecca's leg and quietly jumped into the back of the covered wagon. Nobody noticed the nightingale that followed her into the wagon, visited with the cat, and flew back out again.

The group stood in the rain, excitedly describing their experiences. Rebecca explained to Luna and Leo about the protective cat, which was not really a cat. Luna assured everyone that the pointed stick pressed into her arm had not broken the skin. Her experience with the sword still shook Jill, but everybody assured her that she had done no wrong.

While Luna, Leo, and Rebecca calmed the horses, Jules, Jill, and Windy gathered the three long sticks left behind by the thieves, smashed them into pieces, and scattered the splintered segments into the woods. Then the group climbed back aboard the wagon and resumed their journey. It was still barely past noon.

The remainder of the journey became a battle with the weather. Rain splattered noisily on the tarp-covered wagon. Massive puddles and streams formed in the muddied road. Then the winds picked up, delivering sheets of rain in blinding circles. Several times, portions of the tarp began to buckle and lift, causing the friends to make repairs to the damaged framework.

One wheel got stuck in a deep water-filled trench. Jules and Leo found thick fallen branches in the woods along the roadside to pry the wheel from the ditch, while Luna and Jill manned the reins and worked with the horses to pry the wagon loose.

Lightning flashed overhead, and thunder boomed around them as the wagon approached The Trading Post country store. It was a much-needed place to stop. They used the barn behind the store to rest and feed the jittery horses. Leo traded a basket of homemade bread, muffins, fresh vegetables, herbs, seeds, blankets, and towels, in exchange for feed for the horses, the use of the stables, use of tools to make minor repairs to the wagon, hot tea, and a place to rest for an hour. When Leo told The Trading Post owners that the basket of goods came from the Healing Center, they expressed so much gratitude and appreciation for the Healing Center, that it became a challenge to persuade the owners to accept the basket.

Once the lightning and thunder dissipated, everyone boarded the wagon to complete their journey. The rains and wind had lessened but not entirely stopped. Mud-filled puddles and flowing streams covered deep pockets in the washed-out road. Travel was slow, uncertain, and miserably wet.

Jules joined Leo in the driver's seat, allowing Luna to socialize with the girls. She quickly took on a big sister persona to the three teenagers, while Leo and Jules found much in common to bond them as friends. Although the wagon traveled slowly on the hazardous road, the stories and developing friendships helped the time pass swiftly.

Nearing mid-afternoon, they reached the Trader Market. Except for a few groundskeepers, the market was empty of people. Leo drove the wagon to the storage building, where they unloaded their wares. With everybody pitching in, it took only minutes to unload and stack everything into the storage room.

After storing the wares, the friends gathered by the doorway. Rebecca gratefully approached Luna and Leo. "Thank you so much for the ride and everything you've done for us today. I hope we see each other again," she sighed.

"What? Wait. No," Leo stuttered, "We're not leaving you now. We're going to deliver you to Jules and Jill's home."

"Oh, that's awfully kind of you," Jill spoke up, "but that wouldn't be fair for you to drive all that way and then turn around to be back here in the morning."

"Wait a minute," Luna interjected, "let's get this straight. We are not coming back here. Somebody else will be working at the market tomorrow. So, after Luna and I deliver you to your home, we will visit our parents for a few days, then spend a week training at the Elfin Healing Center.

Once Leo and Luna explained their plans, everybody's spirits seemed to rise again, except for Windy. "Since I live only a short distance down the road, I guess this is where I need to say my goodbyes," she said sadly.

"Windy, don't think you're getting away from us that easily," Jules exclaimed. "You're staying with us, at least until the next time we come back to the Trader Market."

"You're family now," Jill grinned, "whether you like it or not."

Windy broke down. "I love it," she cried.

Tears and hugs again broke out among the friends. Tempest watched from inside the opening of the covered wagon. Songbird watched from the branch of a nearby tree. As the friends closed the doors to the storage room and climbed aboard the wagon, only the nightingale and the unusual cat were aware that a more dangerous storm was brewing on the horizon.

14 Alsaahir

Dark black storm clouds moved away, leaving behind a sheet of gray overcast sky. Heavy rains reduced to a steady drizzle. The covered wagon, the Clydesdale horses, and the group of friends were soaked and muddied. They could have had a dozen reasons to complain. But instead, the wagon was abuzz with excitement like a nest of bees.

They decided to travel west through the Trader Market, swing by Windy's apartment so she could drop off some of the clothes and items she brought from her family home, and then head south across the West River to Jules and Jill's home.

While Leo and Jules continued to share the driving, they discovered much in common: hard-working family upbringings, farm responsibilities, protective personalities, and a longing to see more of the world than the Mystic Lands could offer.

The four young women shared stories of their upbringings and their dreams. But, of course, they were most intrigued by the stories Rebecca told. They could hardly imagine such inventions as the automobile, television, telephone, computers, airplanes, and cities with huge skyscrapers. Even clothing fashions and makeup seemed like fantasy stories. And nobody could grasp the concept of money. The idea of trading paper and small coins for land, houses, or anything of value was confusing. The one thing they all agreed on was that they would each like to see Becca's world. Rebecca began realizing how much she had taken for granted.

The wagon rolled along at a slow but steady pace over the wet, muddy path. The billowing winds, torrential rains, flooded trenches, and dangerous obstacles they had grappled with that morning were no longer treacherous in the late afternoon. The rain was reduced to a drizzle, and the wind slowed to a cool breeze, but the ground was still wet and slippery for the horses and wagon.

As they passed along the edge of the Fringes, nearing the final turn toward home, Jules pointed out where they had met Windy and Rebecca, each only a short distance from each other. No sooner had he spoken when two figures dashed across their path and disappeared into the trees less than fifty yards ahead of them.

Leo pulled back on the reins to slow the horses. "Did you see that?" he quietly asked Jules.

"Yeah," Jules responded. "At first, I thought it was two people, but they were not human. I think it might have been a pair of the Sorcerer's mutants. What did you see?"

"I saw the same thing as you," Leo said as he brought the horses to a stop. "They were only silhouettes in the rain at that distance, but both were twisted and deformed."

"Girls," Jules discreetly spoke into the back of the wagon, "we just saw two mutants run across the road ahead of us. Grab whatever you have for weapons. Be prepared if we have any problems."

"I wish we had our crossbow," Jill commented.

"Hello ahead," Leo called out. "Who are you, and what do you want?"

No response came.

"We saw you," Jules yelled in turn. "Come out and show yourselves,"

Still, no response other than the patter of the rain could be heard.

After waiting a few minutes, Leo and Jules decided to

move forward. Cautiously they moved to where they had seen the figures. Still, they neither saw nor heard anything. Finally, after passing beyond the suspicious area of the woods, they picked up the pace as they made the final turn toward the Verne home. The excitement they had been expressing only minutes earlier was now quietly reserved.

"We're only about twenty minutes away," Jill announced. Those twenty minutes felt like an hour, but the wagon finally approached the house.

Suddenly, a small bird landed on the tailgate of the covered wagon, flapping its wings and making a noisy ruckus.

Rebecca immediately recognized the troubled nightingale. "Songbird, what is it?" she called out.

Tempest was on her feet. The hair on her neck and back stood on end.

"Something is wrong," Rebecca announced. "I don't know what it is, but something is wrong."

Leo immediately pulled the wagon into the grass, slightly beyond the view of the house. Jules jumped to the ground, and Tempest had already jumped from the back of the wagon. Both moved swiftly into the trees, moving within view of the house. Rebecca and Jill follow several yards behind, with Leo, Luna, and Windy catching up moments later.

Viewed through the misty rain, the house appeared quiet. The front door stood open, which was not unusual at the Verne home. A dim light shone from within, perhaps from a flicker of the fireplace. Jules started moving forward from within the trees when Leo hastily called him back. He pointed to the far corner between the house and barn, where a one-horse carriage with a black roof and dark green sides hid in the shade. Beside it, a single figure moved in the shadows.

"Do you know who that is?" Leo asked.

Jules and Jill answered simultaneously, "I've never seen that carriage before."

Growing fearful for their parents, Jules impatiently announced, "I'm not waiting any longer." With his knife drawn, he ran toward the front door as fast as possible. Tempest raced ahead of him. By the time they bounded through the open doorway, Tempest had begun transforming into a tiger. Suddenly a dart shot out from within the house, hitting the half-grown tiger in the neck. Tempest dropped to the floor, immediately transforming back into the cat. A large figure struck Jules. His knife flew from his hands as his body landed with a thud next to Tempest.

Rebecca saw Jules and her beloved cat go down from behind the trees. Her heart sank. She cried out and started running. Jill was already several steps ahead of Rebecca with her sword raised. As they entered the house, multiple hands reached out to grab ahold of the two girls. Somebody swiftly took Jill's sword from her hands before she could use it. Rebecca screamed and fought to break free, but the hands holding her were too big and too strong to fight against.

Once their eyes adjusted to the dim light, the girls discovered that at least eight huge figures filled the room. They each stood at least six and a half feet tall, with orange-brown skin that resembled burnt toast. They all had similar-looking faces with large round noses, dark eyes, thick bushy eyebrows, and squared jaws. Some had shaggy, unkempt brown hair; others were bald. Some wore a leather sash across their shoulders and chests, while others were shirtless, revealing massively muscled barrel chests and thick arms. Rebecca struggled to keep from gagging at the odor of the sweaty body that held her.

"Nasty trolls," Jill called out.

One of the trolls had his foot pressed on Jules' back.

"Did you kill my cat?" Rebecca cried out.

A voice answered from the kitchen, "The cat, which we both know is not a cat, has merely been put to sleep. It will awaken in a few hours."

At that time, Leo, Luna, and Windy were forced through the door by several misshapen creatures carrying pointed spears. Rebecca knew these had to be the mutants she had heard described. Each varied from four to five feet in height, with twisted bodies and faces. Some looked as if formed of sticks, others like mud, and others looked like rotted meat. A few had visible eyes and mouths, while the rest seemed to have no noticeable facial features. They all had blackened green mold seeping from their bodies.

To make room for the addition of her friends and the creatures filling the room, the troll holding Rebecca moved closer to the kitchen. There, she was able to see Aaron and Jasmine bound in chairs. Vines wrapped around their chests, and their hands were tied behind their backs while giant trolls stood over them.

A slender man with long well-kept grey hair and beard, wearing a black robe with green trim, stared directly at Rebecca. His deep black eyes looked like the pupils and iris were one solid black color. Rebecca felt uneasy by his intense stare, but she had no choice but to face him from within the troll's muscled arms.

"You must be Rebecca," the mysterious man commented.

"That depends on who's asking," she replied sarcastically. Rebecca already suspected who the stranger was, but she did not like how she and her friends were being treated. She had no clue why he and his collection of trolls and mutants were there, and she felt extremely disturbed to discover that he knew her name.

He laughed mockingly. "Well, you certainly share the contemptuous personality of your grandmother's side of the family,"

Rebecca was growing visibly more irritated. "You and your henchmen are threatening my friends and holding us hostage in their own home. Do you expect us to thank you and greet you with open arms?"

"My sincere apologies, you are right," he granted. "I will release you and all of your friends if every one of you will accept my presence while we engage in conversation. After that, I will send my protectors outside. But heed my warning that any sign of threat or violence will be most regrettable. Do you agree?"

The dark intruder looked at each person individually, waiting for them to say yes or nod in agreement. Then, finally, he instructed his trolls and mutants to release the hostages, including untying Aaron and Jasmine. Once he was sure everybody was calm, he ordered his guards to wait outside.

"Is this more comfortable for you?" he asked directly of Rebecca.

"What did you do to my cat?" Rebecca stubbornly inquired for a second time.

"Your cat, as you call it, was entering the house in the transformative phase of becoming a large white Bengal tiger," he replied. "Its intentions were clearly to attack. One of my trolls used a blowgun to shoot a tranquilizing dart into the neck of the tiger, immediately decreasing its ferocity and size to that of the sleeping feline you can see breathing on the floor. As I previously stated, the cat will awaken in approximately three hours. Now, if I may, I invite you all to find comfortable seating while I introduce myself and my reason for being here in your fine home."

The man spoke respectfully, Rebecca thought, although his contingent of menacing trolls and spear-carrying mutants did not present the most welcoming of introductions.

"My name is Alsaahir," he began. "Some know me as Alsaahir the Sorcerer. I understand that many in this land believe I may be dead. Obviously, I am not. I have been a recluse in my fortress for many years. I grew up in Egypt, where I became a merchant at a very young age. A violent hurricane carried me in a tattered ship to the shores of this land in 1591, almost thirty years before the English settlers known as Pilgrims arrived here. I am now nearing five hundred years of age. I have lived this long through my extensive study of the use of magic. I incorporated that same magic to build the mist around this land to protect it from the violent wars the Colonists perpetrated upon the Native American Indians during the seventeenth and eighteenth centuries. Because some violent people, unfortunately, wandered their way through those mist, I created ways to make it more difficult to pass through, and I built indestructible walled boundaries within the land to separate the warring factions. In the meantime, with the influence of the elves, I added magic to the waters and the soil to help the people produce all they required to survive and thrive here. Still, some attacked and threatened me for their own hateful and selfish reasons. It became necessary for me to create my troll army to protect myself. My home became a fortress, and I became a recluse. Then, almost one hundred years after arriving here, I met and fell in love with a beautiful Native American Indian woman. We married and soon had a daughter. However, my wife became seduced by the magic. In her hunger for power, she neglected her daughter and our marriage. Our daughter quickly grew and had a daughter of her own. I then discovered that my wife had used magic on our unborn child to make her daughter and all of our future granddaughters look exactly like her. Our daughter felt betrayed and became infuriated with her mother's selfish use of magic on her and her off-spring. She took our granddaughter and escaped through the mists. Over the many decades, I have occasionally heard of our descendants appearing in the Mystic Lands. But they disappeared before I had a chance to meet any of them. Until now. You, Rebecca, are my great-granddaughter, many generations removed."

"That does not sound believable," Rebecca protested.

Jasmine spoke up. "It might explain why you look so much like your mother and grandmother at the same ages," she gently reminded Rebecca.

"Rebecca, you look like my daughter did when she was your age," Alsaahir explained, "and she was your age three hundred years ago."

"So, you came here with your gang of trolls and mutants to threaten my friends and their family because you wanted to meet me?" Rebecca angrily asked. "I am not feeling complimented by your gesture. Your goblins attacked me in the mist. When Jasmine, Violet, and my mother came here eighteen years ago, Violet was severely hurt and almost killed by them. And just a few days ago, after my friend Windy delivered a message to you, your mutants attacked her, knocked her unconscious with rocks, and they stole her horse. Now you expect me to be happy to meet you?"

"Again, I sincerely apologize to all of you," the Sorcerer responded. "After too many years of seclusion and mistrusting everyone as being bent on harming me, I have lost my sense of reason. When I was informed you were here, Rebecca, I was so determined to meet one of my descendants that I acted irrationally. With your help, I promise to make amends to you all. Please forgive me."

"How were you informed of Rebecca's being here?" Jasmine asked.

"I believe it might be inappropriate for me to divulge that information," Alsaahir replied.

"Never mind," Jasmine responded, "I have little doubt it was my aggrieved friend, Violet, who betrayed us. What I do not understand is why."

Alsaahir did not agree or deny the mention of Violet's name. Instead, he merely looked dispassionately at Jasmine and then back to Rebecca. "I understand that you are coming from meeting your father," he said. "It would fill an old man's heart if you were to give me the same consideration and come with me to my home so that we too may become better acquainted. Moreover, I believe it would greatly benefit you to learn how your great grandfather lives."

For a moment, Rebecca was speechless. Even with his unusual story and apologies, she felt uncomfortable with this eerie man. She looked around for help from the others, but everybody felt shocked by his unexpected invitation.

It was Aaron who finally broke the silence. "We have plans with Rebecca and her friends for the next few days. Perhaps she could use that time to consider your invitation and visit with you then."

"I fear that if I accept such an arrangement," Alsaahir responded, "I might never see Rebecca again. Please understand that I am an elderly man of great wealth. My life is on borrowed time. I have longed for a relative with whom I might share my earthly resources and assets.

Therefore, I present to you this offer, Rebecca. I will step outside for ten minutes while you speak with your friends. You may come with me at the end of that time, and I promise you a safe return in two days. If you choose not to know me or to discover the opportunities I offer, I will leave, never for us to see each other again."

They all agreed, and Alsaahir left the house. As quiet as they had been while the sorcerer was in the room, they made up for it as soon as he stepped outside. The room erupted in voices speaking over each other.

"Quiet!" Jasmine yelled. "We will quickly go around the room to give each person an opportunity to offer valid opinions. I will start. Becca, I will not tell you what to do, but I will remind you that this is a sorcerer with the powerful magic to create the mists we each came through, the goblins, trolls, mutants, and the indestructible walls that divide us and keeps thousands of people trapped in this land. Also, be aware that even the worst criminals psychologically justify their crimes. That justification is the only way they can live with themselves. And I believe that Alsaahir is doing exactly that."

Aaron added, "There is much that he did not tell or explain in his short story. There is much that you do not know. There are many questions I would prefer he answers before going anywhere with him. It could be an opportunity for you to learn about his magic, but it will be risky. After four hundred years, I doubt Alsaahir will easily lower the mists and free the people. I recommend you stay here and find a way to escape this Mystic Land like your mother did."

"Over the past few days, you have become my sister, Becca," Jill commented. "I will respect whatever you decide, but I prefer you don't go with him. I wish that I could escape this land and go to see the outside world with you."

"I agree with Jill," Windy said. "I've never had a friend like you. And I do not trust the sorcerer. But I respect that you have to choose your own path."

Jules appeared to struggle to speak the words that were on his mind. "Becca, I'm not supposed to say things like this after knowing you for only a few days, but I've imagined my life with you. If anything bad happened to you, I think I would die. I don't care about Alsaahir's opportunities. I don't want you to go."

Leo spoke next. "We only met this morning, Rebecca, so I have no place to offer you advice, but I remind you there are many opportunities in the Mystic Land without accepting the Sorcerer's supposed gifts. I believe that your father can offer many such opportunities for you."

"Like my brother said," Luna added, "we don't know you well enough to tell you what to do, but I will offer one piece of wisdom which has guided me; listen to your gut instincts. If you feel safe taking a chance to learn the truths about the sorcerer, do it. But, if you feel danger in any way, then choose to stay here with your friends."

"My Nani has often advised me to trust my intuition," Rebecca responded. "Although the trolls and mutants scared me, I do not now feel threatened by Alsaahir. I do not believe him to be entirely honest, and I agree with Jasmine that he likely justifies his wrongdoings, but I think he is sincere in wanting to have a relationship with me. I keep asking myself, why else would he have come here to meet me? I believe there is some truth to his seclusion. Based on your stories, nobody has seen him in many years. He probably has regrets about the loss of his family too. I have no interest in his possessions, but I wonder if I might be able to convince him to lower the mists and allow the people in the Mystic Land to return to the world. Maybe I can show him a different perspective. Since he promised to return me here in two days, I feel safe enough to go with him. Thank you all for your counsel. You have become the best of friends and family to me. If I could convince him to lower the mists, it would be the best way for me to show you all that the world has to offer. And Jules, I feel the same way about you. We are only seventeen, so there is no urgency to rush into a relationship, but if we continue to feel this way, I can imagine us together. Are there any other thoughts before we call for Alsaahir?"

Everybody muttered their support for Rebecca but offered no new suggestions.

Rebecca called Alsaahir back into the house. "With your guarantee of my safety and promise that I will be returned here before sunset in two days, I will go with you," she announced. "And I look forward to becoming acquainted with you, Grandfather."

Alsaahir smiled for the first time that anybody in the room had seen. "You have my word for your safety and return in two days," he confirmed.

Rebecca turned to Leo, "My hiking staff and backpack are in the covered wagon. Would you please get them for me? I will leave the staff here but would like to take my backpack with me."

Leo turned to ask Alsaahir if he would be safe to walk past the trolls, but the sorcerer was already at the doorway calling orders to his protectors.

"Bring your covered wagon up here by the house and take care of your horses," Alsaahir offered to Leo. "I assure you the trolls will not be a threat to you, your horses, or your wagon."

"Jill," Rebecca asked, "when Tempest wakes up, would

you please tell her where I've gone, that I will be back in two days, and I prefer she not follow me? She will understand. And would you please feed and take care of her while I'm gone?"

"Of course," Jill answered. "But don't assume I have any control over that cat," she grinned.

"Before you go," Jasmine announced, "I spent most of the day making Becca's homemade granola bars. Would everybody like to try them?"

It had been several hours since the group of friends had eaten. They eagerly attacked the granola bars like starving animals. Even Alsaahir ate one and then returned for a second.

With her backpack over her shoulder, Rebecca hugged everyone goodbye. She took a few extra minutes to express her gratitude to Luna and Leo for all they had done that day, and she promised to see them again.

She stopped in front of Jules, closed her eyes, pulled herself close to him, and kissed him passionately on the lips. After stepping back, she felt shocked at herself for acting so boldly. Then she looked at Jules. He stood there dazed with his eyes closed and his mouth open. Rebecca heard giggles from others in the room, but she resisted the urge to laugh. I suspect that he will eagerly wait for me to return, she thought. If nothing else, I am finally finding that confidence I always wished I had.

Before boarding the carriage, Alsaahir stopped to make an introduction. "This is Pixie, our driver and my most trust-ed assistant," he said. "Pixie, this is my great-granddaughter, Rebecca. She will be visiting us for a few days. Please treat her as our most valued guest."

"Yes, Master," Pixie replied in a soft, almost squeaky voice as she reached out her hand to greet Rebecca. Rebecca was startled to find that Pixie's hand was more like a hairy paw with long pointed fingers than a human hand. She stood no more than three feet tall. She had a snout-like nose and mouth that reminded Rebecca of a type of ferret and large shining eyes with extraordinarily long eyelashes. A small patch of gray hair stood up between round ears that protruded from near the top of her head. She wore a pale green vest, pants that reached just below her knees, and no shoes. Her feet looked much like her marsupial hands. "It is a pleasure to make your acquaintance," Pixie said before climbing onto the driver's seat.

Rebecca's friends stood outside while she boarded the carriage. She sensed their concern but also understood that this was something she must do.

Before joining Rebecca in the carriage, Alsaahir turned to speak to the group of her friends in a voice everyone could hear. "Be forewarned," he called out, "Rebecca is my granddaughter, and I will treat her well, but if any of you try to follow or interfere, I will not hesitate to make you regret that decision. I may be elderly, but there is still nothing in this land that is big enough or strong enough to defeat me." Finally, he turned and climbed aboard the carriage, closing the door behind him.

The rainy grey sky appeared to be clearing. Glimmers of sunlight colored the horizon orange and pink as the one-horse carriage pulled away from the Verne home. The mutants had already disappeared into the surrounding woods. The trolls spread out in a protective circle around the carriage. It reminded Rebecca of a secret service detail around the President of the United States.

Nobody, not the sorcerer nor anybody in his security detail, noticed the nightingale quietly following from a safe distance away.

15 Sorcerer's Fortress

Songbird quietly followed the black and green horse-drawn carriage into the dwindling light of the setting sun. Inside the cab, Rebecca and the sorcerer who claimed to be her four hundred and fifty-year-old great grandfather chattered pleasantly and politely. Although friendly in return, the idle social conversation felt like a knot twisting tighter in Rebecca's chest. She yearned to scream out dozens of point-blank questions of the dubious wizard but resigned herself to observe and learn rather than confront. She might be gaining some confidence, she thought, but she was not comfortable with being confrontational. She remembered her mother and grandmother each repeating the old proverb, "you can catch more flies with honey than with vinegar," every time she had a temper tantrum as a child. She didn't always understand its meaning then, but it felt like wise words at this time.

As darkness settled over the carriage, Rebecca mentioned feeling tired after a long day. Alsaahir waved his hand in front of her face. The next thing she knew, the sorcerer was waking her to tell her they were nearing his home.

Rebecca peeked through the small window. Moonlight glimmered off the rock walls of an enormous castle. She could not distinguish the height or width of the fortress as it disappeared into the night sky. When the horse-drawn carriage clattered across a heavy wooden drawbridge, Rebecca could see the waters in a moat shimmering beneath it. They passed through a tall arched gateway into an expansive courtyard. No light came from the building or its grounds. Only the moon and stars allowed Rebecca to see the shadowed spaces of doorways set within the walls.

Pixie pulled the horse to a stop in front of the largest entryway. It felt to Rebecca as if they had barely stopped moving before Pixie was already opening the door at the Alsaahir's side of the carriage. Rebecca followed Alsaahir out of the carriage and into a darkened doorway. Light filled the entryway with a wave of the Sorcerer's arms, yet Rebecca could not find that light source no matter where she looked. She could only assume that it was the Sorcerer's magic at work.

"Pixie," Alsaahir called out, "I will give Rebecca a brief tour of our home. After taking care of the horse and carriage, please clean yourself, then prepare my daughters' room for Rebecca."

"Your daughters' room?" Pixie exclaimed. "But you've never permitted anyone to stay in…."

"Yes, my daughters' room," Alsaahir raised his voice. "Rebecca is not just anyone. She is my great-granddaughter, and she will be treated as such.

"Yes, Master." Pixie gave a slight bow and moved to do as the sorcerer requested.

Rebecca felt uneasy about the way Alsaahir gave Pixie orders, but again she swallowed her discomfort, deciding this was not the time to confront him. Instead, she calmly reminded herself she was a guest in his home. If she was to influence changes in the older man, she must first observe, learn, and approach him well-informed and prepared. One observation she already recognized is that as his great-grand-daughter, she might be able to influence the man as nobody else could. She just had to hold her tongue for a while and remember to use kindness before confrontation.

Following Alsaahir through the doorway, they entered a dimly lit entry room. It might have been called a foyer or lobby, but Rebecca thought it was too small to call it one of those names. The floor and walls were built entirely with large flat rocks. A few wooden benches lined the walls, and empty tables sat in the corners. No carpeting, pictures, or plants decorated the room. Rebecca felt this was the coldest, most unfriendly room she had ever been in. She was sure this was the guard room a person would walk through to enter a prison.

The sorcerer asked aloud, "Has anything eventful happened that I should be aware of?"

Rebecca jumped when a deep voice answered from a corner to her left, "No, Master, all has been quiet." A slight movement revealed a giant troll standing in the shadows. He stood at least seven feet tall, yet he blended with the rock wall like a chameleon. Only the movement when he spoke and a leather sash across his shoulders and chest revealed his physical presence.

"I thought Trolls could not talk," Rebecca gasped.

Alsaahir chuckled. "Trolls are my soldiers and guardians. They speak only when necessary."

No introductions were made. Rebecca quickly followed Alsaahir across the room and through a set of arched heavy double doors. As they entered the next room, the sorcerer waved his arm. Light emanated from the ceiling and walls. Yet again, Rebecca noticed no lamps, candles, or light source. This room resembled a vast atrium, except there were no windows or skylights. Rebecca quickly noticed the still air smelled musty and old. Alsaahir pointed a finger to the right side of the room. A fire exploded within an immense fireplace. A marble fountain centered the room, although no water flowed from it. Various couches, cushioned chairs, and side tables were positioned around the fountain, with huge vases and urns holding unusual plants and ferns. Wide spiral staircases led to the upper floors on the left and right. An immense bookcase spread across a large section of one wall, although it held mostly objects and few books. All of a sudden, a sense of disgust washed over Rebecca. Severed heads of bears, wolves, bobcats, moose and deer mounted on plaques hung on the walls. Their pained eyes stared down at her. Whole wild animals stuffed and formed into statues stood in the corners. Grotesque black crows, vultures, buzzards, and hawks posed on tables and shelves with absurdly outstretched wings, many with holes or missing patches of feathers, twisted necks, and bulging fearful eyes. Rebecca gasped as the shock of their deaths rushed through her. She looked to the floor to steady herself and hold back the retched nausea from leaving her stomach. Then, spinning away from the menagerie of dead animals, she walked into a four-foot-tall pedestal mounted with the most horrendous-looking bird staring directly into her eyes. It had a snake's green and red face with sharp red eyes, a long scaley neck, broad bat-like wings, a round body and tail spattered with patches of hair that resembled a flying rat more than a bird. Thick, sharp claws gripped the pedestal, except for one talon that pointed straight at her. She screamed before realizing the horrendous bird was not alive.

"One of my favorite pieces," Alsaahir stated calmly, "a rare species from the late Jurassic period of the Mesozoic era, bridging the Pterosaurs with modern-day reptiles and bats."

Rebecca felt relieved to move past the dead animals. Beyond the empty fountain, several arched doorways led in various directions to other rooms, some with closed doors, others open. Alsaahir stopped before an opening on the right.

"This is the formal dining room," he announced. Two overhead chandelier candelabras came alive with light revealing a vast room with red and gold curtains, beautiful oil paintings on the walls, and an extended table longer than Rebecca had ever seen. She quickly counted twenty-four chairs on each side of the table and two oversized chairs at each end. All of the fifty seats had a formal place setting before them. Rebecca wondered how often her great-grand-father might fill this room with guests but did not ask.

As if reading her mind, Alsaahir commented, "It has been well over a hundred years since last filling the room. "Maybe even two hundred years," his voice trailed off with his thoughts.

"Perhaps we could invite my friends for a dinner party," Rebecca cheerfully proclaimed. "It would be a generous first step toward building a new reputation in the land."

Alsaahir smiled but did not respond to Rebecca's comment. The formal dining room lights dimmed as they walked to the next doorway. "This is our private dining room," he continued," where we will have most of our meals."

Light again appeared from the ceiling and walls as they rounded the corner. Although modest compared to the formal dining room, Rebecca still recognized it was larger than Aaron and Jasmine's entire house. A round red mahogany wood table with ten chairs sat in the middle of the room with a long buffet table and china cabinets along two side walls. Instead of the masculine style of the other rooms she had passed through, Rebecca thought the fine antique furniture gave this room an old colonial charm. However, the walls were all built with plain wood panels, and she had seen no windows since entering the castle. They passed through the private dining room and a pair of swinging doors. Rebecca noticed that the mahogany wood doors matched the table, chairs, buffet, and china cabinets.

Rebecca gazed in amazement at the kitchen. It was bigger than her mother's restaurant. Bowls and platters overflowed with fresh fruit and vegetables. Cabinets, counters, and tables held hundreds of cooking utensils, mixing bowls, and pots. Rows of shelves overflowed with bags, boxes, and canisters. The scents of spices and baked goods filled the air. Yet, there were none of the modern appliances, such as refrigerators, freezers, stoves, ovens, grills, or dishwashers, that she used at Clover's Coffee & Tea Café. Instead, it contained an open fireplace, ice boxes, and basins similar to those she had seen at the Healing Center.

"You are welcome to help yourself to anything in the kitchen anytime you want, day or night," Alsaahir invited. "Are you hungry?"

"I might like an apple or pear," Rebecca commented, "but I feel more tired than hungry. I would especially like a bath."

"Take whatever fruit you would like," Alsaahir told her. "Your bedroom has a bathtub with hot water and all the toiletries you might want or need. Pixie should have everything cleaned and ready for you. Come, I will show you the way."

Alsaahir led Rebecca back through the kitchen, private dining room, and the hallway to one of the stairways, where he paused at the base of the steps. "At my age," he snickered, "stairways seem less and less appealing to climb. I did not foresee that as an issue when I created this castle over four hundred years ago." He took a breath and started up the stairs. Rebecca followed a few steps behind. Although he had expressed concern about climbing the stairs at his age, Rebecca thought he bounded them surprisingly energetically.

Reaching the landing, they turned right and followed the hallway to the second door on the left. Alsaahir reached for the doorknob just as the door opened. Pixie dashed out of the room, stopping inches short of running into the tall sorcerer.

"Oh, Master," Pixie exclaimed. "The room is cleaned and ready for the beautiful princess."

"Is there fresh water in the bath, Pixie?" Alsaahir asked in a direct voice.

"Oh yes, Master," she excitedly responded. "I stocked the room with fresh towels and robes and dressed the bed in our finest linens. Is there anything else you or the princess would like, Master?"

Alsaahir turned to Rebecca. "Is there anything else that you might like?" he asked.

"No, you have both been overly hospitable," she replied. "Thank you so much."

"You are released for the night, Pixie," Alsaahir nodded to his petite assistant. "We will see you in the morning."

"Yes, Master. Goodnight, Master. Goodnight, Princess." Pixie bowed and scurried quickly toward the stairway.

Alsaahir took one step into the room, glanced about as if to inspect it, then stood by the door as he gestured Rebecca into it. "I hope you will find the accommodations pleasant," he commented.

"This room looks beautiful," Rebecca replied. "I'm very impressed with your entire home. It's magnificent. And I am grateful for your hospitality, Grandfather."

Alsaahir halted. The endearing term seemed to leave him momentarily speechless. "I will show you more of the castle tomorrow, and we will have much to discuss. Goodnight, Granddaughter," he said as he left the room, closing the door behind him.

Rebecca slowly moved to the bed and took a seat.

For the first time in several days, she felt the peacefulness of being alone. So much had happened in such a short time that it felt overwhelming. She thought about her family back home. Even though she had only been gone for a few days, her life there felt like a lifetime ago. She thought about the people she had met since coming into this Mystic Land, including her father, new friends, and the animals who helped protect and guide her. Dangers she faced in the swamp, goblins, trolls, mutants, and the three thieves who attacked her and her friends raced through her mind.

She raised herself from the bed, momentarily brushing aside the formidable thoughts. Looking about the room, she discovered steam rising from a bath built into the stone floor. It reminded Rebecca of a type of hot tub, except like everything else in this place, this tub displayed no water jets, faucets, plumbing, or any sign of how the water was heated or got into the bathtub.

Pixie had stacked a pile of neatly folded towels on a nearby bench, and white robes hung from hooks on the wall. Rebecca glanced through an open door, revealing a closet almost as big as the bedroom, filled with clothes. Another door led to a bathroom, which included a toilet with no handle, a sink with no faucet, a real glass mirror, and a cabinet with all the necessities a person might need.

Turning to the bath, Rebecca slipped off her clothes and stepped into the soothing warm water. Bowls with soaps and shampoos had been placed next to the tub. After the past few days, Rebecca felt a new appreciation for the luxury of a bath.

After washing, Rebecca relaxed into the warm water, allowing her mind to wander. She thought about meeting her father, the Verne family, Windy, Luna, and Leo, and the possibility of a relationship with Jules. She thought about Tempest, Songbird, and Wisdom. She thought about her brother, Chris, hoping he was okay. For a moment, she wondered if she would ever get back home. Then she remembered that her mother had somehow returned through the mists. Nani had told her that she had the same abilities as her mother to make that return; she just had to discover her strengths and believe in herself. Rebecca knew it would take a while but wanted to return home above all else.

Rebecca finally climbed from the bath, dried herself off, and slipped into a white nightgown that Pixie had left at the foot of the bed. She slid under the bed covers and immediately fell asleep.

"Hello, my darling," Nani's familiar voice greeted.

"Nani," Rebecca responded, "Have you been with me all day today?"

"I have been with you as much of the day as possible," Nani replied. However, there were times when I dared not get too close out of concern of being detected."

"What do you mean, Nani?" Rebecca asked. "Detected by who, or what?"

Nani paused. "Listen closely, Rebecca. These circumstances came faster than I anticipated, but I must speak to you now of the challenges you face. The Sorcerer is your great-grandfather many generations removed and is nearly five hundred years old. Of that, he told you the truth. But many of the things he says are barely half-truths. He will tell you how he supported and protected the thousands of people who spent their entire lives imprisoned in his land. He will justify goblins, trolls, and mutants as protection, yet they threaten those he claims to protect. He will make promises he will not keep and offer opportunities of magic and power that will drain your spirit and drive you to madness. Everything he tells you will sound generous and reasonable, but I implore you to ask one question of everything he says, what does he get out of it? For everything he says and does will primarily benefit only him."

Rebecca shuddered. "Nani, how can I protect myself from a sorcerer with so much power?"

"I'm sorry, my dear. It is not my intention to cause you to fear. I want you to be aware so that he does not mislead you. Do not directly challenge him. To do so will only anger him. Use logic and common sense. Listen to what he says, but withhold any contradictory opinions. Remember that your animal protectors are still nearby. If you need them, you can call them in the same way we are speaking now. They will find a way to reach you. Others will be watching and protecting you too. Trust your intuition to know right from wrong. Also, remember to trust in your song and your connection with the animals. There lies your magic and your power. I must go now, Rebecca. Awaken to remember this message, and then you must sleep." Nani sang as she faded into the night, "Close your eyes, my child, and sleep. Sleep in heavenly peace."

Rebecca forced her eyes to open. She knew that if she passed into a deep sleep, her grandmother's visit would disappear like a lost dream. But her senses warned her that this communication could hold the keys to her future. She had to wake up, even for a minute, if she wanted to remember Nani's messages. She ran the significant points through her mind. Be wary of the Sorcerer's self-serving and half-truths. Do not directly challenge Alsaahir. Use logic and common sense. Trust my instincts. Trust in my voice and my connection with the animals. Others will be watching and protecting me.

Rebecca wondered who the others could be. She then
closed her eyes and fell into the much-needed sleep.

16 Mystic Magic

A knock at the door brought Rebecca out of her sleep. She had no way of knowing if it was day or night in the room with no windows.

"Princess," the voice called through the door.

"Come in, Pixie," Rebecca called back.

The door opened slowly, and Pixie's ferret face peeked in. "Master wants to know if you would like breakfast this morning, Princess?"

"That sounds delightful, Pixie. Please tell Master…, I mean, please tell my grandfather that I will get dressed and come down for breakfast shortly."

"Yes, Princess," Pixie responded as she began to back out through the door.

"Oh, Pixie," Rebecca called out.

Pixie stopped. "Yes, Princess?" she asked.

"How do I turn the lights on in here?"

"Think about the light and wave your arm from left to right, Princess." Pixie waited while Rebecca waved her arm through the air. A dim light began to glow in the room. "Wave your arm again if you want it brighter, or wave it from right to left if you want to dim the light, Princess."

"Thank you, Pixie," Rebecca cheerfully replied. "You are a wonderful help. I think you and I are going to be great friends."

"That would be wonderful, Princess," Pixie timidly responded. Rebecca thought she saw Pixie smile as she closed the door behind her.

She washed and dressed in a loose-fitting shirt and pants she found hanging in the closet. Although the clothes were rather plain in style and color, Rebecca was surprised by how comfortably they fit. She took her personal items from the pant pockets she had been wearing the day before, stuffed them into her new attire, and headed downstairs to meet with her great grandfather. She found Alsaahir sitting alone at the table in the private dining room. He read a book and sipped on a cup of something that Rebecca assumed to be coffee or tea. The table, set for two, held enough platters of food to feed at least a dozen people.

Alsaahir cheerfully greeted Rebecca and invited her to help herself to anything she wanted from the table.

"What do you have planned for us today, Grandfather?" Rebecca asked.

"I would like to show you more of this castle," he answered. "There is so much that you have not yet seen. There are histories and mysteries I would like to explain to you. I believe you will find many of the stories interesting and perhaps even beneficial. Are you interested, Rebecca?"

"It sounds fascinating. I look forward to learning more about you, your magnificent home, and our family history. There is so much I don't know. May I ask a question about the castle?" she inquired between bites.

"Of course, Rebecca," Alsaahir replied. "Do not hesitate to ask about anything. I hope that I may freely ask you about your life as well. Now, what would you like to know?"

"How does everything work here? I mean, lights come on with a wave of your arm, the stone floors feel heated, the water in my bath is hot, you have a kitchen stocked with food and platters of fresh fruit and vegetables on the table, but the only assistant I see is Pixie!"

Alsaahir grinned. He seemed to be stifling a laugh. "It's Magic, my dear. Everything is created with magic. I promise to explain it in greater detail throughout our day."

Following breakfast, Rebecca followed Alsaahir to tour his castle. As they left the dining room, a clinking sound caused Rebecca to look back over her shoulder. Pixie was already cleaning dishes from the table.

As they walked past the dry fountain, Rebecca lowered her head to resist the eyes of the dead animals. Even without looking, she felt nauseous in their presence. Alsaahir said nothing about them, and Rebecca had little interest in asking. For a few moments, Rebecca feared her breakfast would make a regrettable return appearance.

Upon entering the dimly lit entry room, Rebecca immediately looked to see if a troll stood guard. He did. In the dim light, Rebecca was unsure if it was the same troll who was there the night before. He looked the same, but he did not move, and neither the troll nor her grandfather said anything as they passed.

When Alsaahir pushed open the front door, fresh air rushed into the room. Rebecca breathed a sense of relief as she stepped into the daylight. Although the sky was mostly overcast, a few rays of sunlight seeped through scattered spaces between the clouds.

In the daylight, Rebecca could better see her surroundings. Although everything was impressive in size, the details were disturbingly plain. The courtyard grounds contained nothing more than hardened dirt and patches of worn grass. There were no plants, trees, flowers, or bushes in sight. The rock wall surrounding the courtyard stood at least thirty feet in height. Rebecca recognized the silhouettes of trolls standing guard along the top of the wall. Since they primarily stood facing outward, away from the castle, she wondered if they noticed her and Alsaahir in the courtyard. Tall round towers stood above each corner of the wall. Rebecca assumed the doorways at the base of the towers must provide stairways to the upper walkway. An arched gateway stood open at the center of the front wall, but nobody came or went. Overall, Alsaahir's home appeared only as an intimidating fortress to Rebecca. She thought about what it must have been like for Windy and other messengers to have made deliveries here.

Rebecca followed Alsaahir along the front edge of the main building. Neither spoke. He stopped before two tall, heavy wooden double doors and pulled them open. Inside the door sat the carriage that carried them to the castle the night before. The familiar scent reminded Rebecca of the barns at the Verne home and the Healing Center. Beyond the carriage revealed a massive stable with a floor littered with old hay. Rows of open stalls and pens for animals lined each wall, yet only the single horse that pulled their carriage the night before and a few chickens wandered about the room. An empty flatbed supply wagon sat in a corner, and farm tools rested along one wall.

"This stable was once filled with animals, horses, goats, sheep, ducks, and chickens," Alsaahir confessed. "My wife and daughter loved animals, but they became too much of a burden for me to take care of after they left. It was not the animals that were so difficult as managing the staff to take care of the animals. Did you know that humans can sometimes be more difficult than animals?"

Rebecca understood it was more of a comment than a question. "I imagine they can be," she replied. "Grandfather, if you created everything in this castle with magic, why is the up-keep so difficult? Can't you just wave your hand and fix it all?"

Alsaahir paused, quietly contemplating his response. "My dear, magic has given me tremendous power and wondrously long life of almost five hundred years. But like an athlete or a warrior, the ability to create such powerful magic is for the young. So much of what you see in this Mystic Land was created when the energy of youth coursed through my body. Now it is more difficult for me to maintain that magic. But have no doubt, with my magic, there is still nothing in this land that is big enough or strong enough to defeat me. Now come, it is time for me to show you the true reason I brought you here."

They walked past the supply wagon and stopped before a tall wood panel wall. Alsaahir waved his hand, causing the entire wall to slide open. Rebecca could see only a short distance into the dark entryway. Stepping aside as the door began to close behind them, Alsaahir grabbed her arm when she almost fell into a dark stairwell. Again, Alsaahir waved his hand to create a light source, revealing a long hallway ahead and stairs to the right that led below ground.

"I'm sorry," the sorcerer apologized, "I should have warned you about those stairs. They go below the moat to a tunnel leading to the West Woods. It was created as an escape tunnel but now is only used by my wife when she chooses to visit the castle."

"Your wife!" Rebecca exclaimed. "Do you mean the wife who would be my great-grandmother? I thought she had died centuries ago. Is she still alive?"

"Yes, she is your great-grandmother. She is kept alive by the same magic that has allowed me to live all these years. After I discovered that she had used magic on our daughter and granddaughter, we almost destroyed each other. That led to creating a large cabin in the West Woods where she could live separately but still have access to this castle and the life-extending magic."

Rebecca suddenly realized what her grandfather called the

West Woods; Jillian had named the Witch Woods on the map she had drawn. Rebecca slid her hand along the outside of her pants pocket to assure herself that the map was still there. That must mean her great grandmother is the witch, she thought.

"Is there a possibility I might be meeting her while I'm here?" Rebecca asked hesitantly.

"It is possible but doubtful," Alsaahir responded. "She typically appears every three or four weeks. She was here a week ago, before I knew of your presence in the Mystic Land. I believe it best not to let her know that you are here. I fear it could raise too much anger and resentment that once divided us."

Rebecca silently agreed. She thought it might have been best if she had not met her great-grandfather either, but here she is. So, all she can do now is follow, listen, and learn.

No words were spoken while Rebecca followed Alsaahir through the dimly lit hallway. While they walked, Rebecca noticed slits in the left side wall where dim light filtered in. Looking closer, she discovered the spaces looked into the entry room with the troll guard, the massive sitting room, the formal dining room, the private dining room, the kitchen, and a guest bedroom room. To her right was the outer wall of the fortress, which explained why the interior spaces had no windows. She then promptly realized that her upstairs bedroom also had no windows. A sense of disgust washed over her at the possibility that she could have been watched while bathing the night before, but she quickly dismissed it as an unlikely concern.

Alsaahir abruptly stopped and turned to face the wall on his left. He waived one arm, causing a panel to slide open. They entered a large spacious room that appeared to serve as an office. Inside the open doorway sat a large desk with a massive throne-like chair behind it. The desktop held a feathered quill pen with a gold ink well and two large, thick leather-bound books with metal bands and locks wrapped around their binders. Rebecca assumed that the closed double doors on the opposite side of the room must lead into the castle. Long colorful tapestries hung on each side of the doors. Two cushioned chairs and a small table sat against a wall. A pair of glass-door cabinets stood along another wall, with a few books, small boxes, and what appeared to be rolled scrolls in one cabinet and an assortment of unusual bottles, vases, cups, and containers in the other. The most striking piece was a decoratively carved wooden pedestal in the middle of the room, holding a shiny white cloth bag. The bag grabbed Rebecca's attention. Its finely woven silk cloth glittered with tiny gemstones. A similar piece of cloth tied the bag closed at its top. It appeared to contain something oblong or egg-shaped, about the size of a loaf of bread. Most striking was how the bag shimmered with light or energy emanating from within.

Again, Alsaahir waved his arm, and the sliding door closed behind them. He then began the conversation, "I have much to tell you, but I would first like to ask if you have any questions?"

"I have a million questions, Grandfather," Rebecca responded sharply, "but I hope you might begin by revealing everything you've been waiting to tell me. Likely your information will answer many of my questions without my having to ask."

"You are entirely correct, Rebecca," Alsaahir acknowledged. "Let us sit, and I will begin with my history." They seated themselves in the two cushioned chairs with a small table between them.

Alsaahir began, "As a young merchant, I came across two

separate discoveries that gave me incredible magical powers. The first is the pair of locked books lying on that desk," he pointed. "They are journals containing a history of magic covering nearly five thousand years, with writings by more than four hundred owners of those books. Much of the first journal is written in Sanskrit, an ancient Southeast Asian language. Various Eastern languages followed. I am the first to write in Arabic and English. After acquiring those books, it took me many years to learn to read and decipher their teachings. Some I still do not know. Some owners wrote only a few sentences or provided recipes for potions, and others wrote many pages. I suspect that some had the books for a short time, others for many years. Very little was written about the owners' personal lives, only about their discoveries in magic, sorcery, and witchcraft."

Alsaahir paused for a long moment before continuing. He seemed to be considering his words. "The second element is a rock, or perhaps I should refer to it as a large crystal geode, wrapped in the bag on that pedestal in the center of the room."

Alsaahir moved to the edge of the pedestal. While continuing his story, his hands began to unravel the cloth ribbon tying the bag closed. "The power of any magical potion or verse used in its presence is multiplied many times," he exclaimed. "I do not know how it works or where it gets its energy. I do not know if it came from within the earth or from the stars. I only know the force of its power. It is the source of my long life and many of the qualities of life in this Mystic Land. Just opening the bag will change the energy in this room. But be forewarned; without knowledge, there can be unexpected consequences for its use. I tell you this from experience."

As if on cue, the bag fell open. A violent pulse of energy surged into the room. Brilliant light temporarily blinded the stunned girl. Rebecca looked helplessly to her grandfather but saw only a silhouette of the man surrounded by an aura of swirling color. She felt her stomach churn, her head spun, and her legs give way beneath her. The next thing she knew, her grandfather was lifting her from the floor to an empty chair. She glanced toward the pedestal to confirm that the cloth bag was securely closed.

"Grandfather," Rebecca stammered, "are you telling me that the books and the rock in that bag are the sources of all of your magic, the mists, the goblins, trolls, this castle… everything?"

"Yes, Rebecca, but let's be clear, the mists, goblins, and trolls were all created to protect my land and people." Alsaahir rose to a standing position. His entire demeanor changed to one who thought of himself as a dictator or supreme being. His voice raised, "My magic has created perfect soil and clean water for growing the freshest fruits and vegetables. I have eliminated winter snow and summer droughts. When I created the mists, the Colonists and the Indians were at war. My walls separated those who came through the mists, and my people learned to live in peace. My people have flourished here under my magic and my leadership."

Rebecca's mind reeled. She wanted to yell about the inhumanity and injustices she had witnessed in her few days in the Mystic Land. She wanted to scream out about the loss of freedoms and the lives people could have had in the world outside of this forsaken place. Anger washed over her as she thought about the generations of people who spent their lives captured by this delusional man who believed he was protecting them like some deity. And this is her ancestor, she lamented. Yet, she dared not risk angering him. Instead of speaking out, she sat in stunned silence. It felt like minutes had passed before she found the only words she could manage to speak, "Why have you brought me here, Grandfather?"

"As I have said previously," Alsaahir explained, "I have longed to meet my descendants ever since my daughter left with my grandchild many generations ago. I have heard that others, such as your mother and grandmother, had been here, but I only learned of their presence after they had departed. Rebecca, you are the first of my blood relatives I have met in over three hundred years. Secondly, and perhaps more importantly, I wanted to know you. I have already come to believe you to be an extraordinary young woman. Hence, I would like to offer you an opportunity. As my only known ancestor, I would like to bestow everything I have to you, including the rock, my books, and all the power they contain. Of course, there will be much for you to learn. You will become heir to all I own if you serve as my apprentice. The magic, this castle, the entire Mystic Land, and the ability to live for centuries will be yours in only a few years. You will live like a queen. Is that something you would be interested in, Rebecca?"

Her head spun. Although she thought Alsaahir might have ulterior motives in bringing her here, this was not what she expected. "This is a generous offer, Grandfather," Rebecca managed to blurt out. "I feel overwhelmed by the significance of it. May I have a few days to consider such a life-altering decision?"

"Of course, my dear," Alsaahir responded. "However, I must require you to remain here while you decide."

"What? Why?" Rebecca stammered. "You're breaking your promise to return me to my friends by the end of the day tomorrow."

Alsaahir suddenly became visibly angry. "I cannot risk your telling your inferior underling friends about the sources of my magic," he bellowed. "Until I know of your intentions, I must insist that you remain here,"

All at once, Rebecca felt trapped. She immediately realized this pretentious man intended to keep her here as his willing apprentice or unwilling prisoner. It would be best, she decided, if she attempted to calm the Sorcerer's anger. "How about if I sleep on it tonight and tell you of my decision tomorrow?" she asked calmly. "Would that be satisfactory, Grandfather?

Following a few huffs and puffs to display his annoyance, Alsaahir appeared to calm down. "I suppose that is a reasonable amount of time to make such a decision," he exclaimed. "I will give you one day to consider the tremendous opportunity I have offered. In the meantime, please make yourself at home. I will look forward to your response tomorrow. I do hope that you will make the correct decision."

Alsaahir guided Rebecca through the double doors at the front of the room and the hallway that led back to the main room. Rebecca proceeded up the stairway to her bedroom without speaking. Before she had reached the top of the stairs, Alsaahir turned and marched into the kitchen. As the doors swung closed, Rebecca could hear him yelling for Pixie. At that moment, Rebecca felt sorry for the little servant girl.

17 Dire Decisions

Rebecca stayed in her room throughout the afternoon and into the evening. She had no appetite for eating and even less interest in seeing or speaking with the self-serving sorcerer. She knew her answer to his offer to become his apprentice as soon as he proposed it. But she feared angering him with a reply he did not want to hear. Moreover, she feared for her life and the lives of her friends. How did I get myself into this mess? She wondered.

A knock at the door snapped Rebecca to her feet. I'm not ready to be confronted by him, she thought. "What do you want?" she called out.

"I'm sorry to bother you, Princess. I wondered if you might like some dinner?" the meek voice responded.

"Oh, Pixie!" the relieved girl rushed to open the door. No longer naïve to the Sorcerer's potential for deception, Rebecca looked up and down the hallway in both directions before eagerly inviting Pixie into the bedroom.

"Would you like something for dinner, Princess?" Pixie asked.

"I am a little hungry," Rebecca replied. "But I don't want to deal with my grandfather tonight. Could you bring me some fruit and a cheese sandwich, Pixie?"

"Yes, Princess, although you should know that Master is not here."

"Not here! Do you know where he is, Pixie?"

"Not exactly," Pixie answered. "He left in the carriage with some of his Troll guards. He only said that he had some business to take care of. Very unusual of him. Very unusual."

"How long ago did he leave?" Rebecca asked curiously.

"Not long, Princess. Only a few minutes before I came to see you," Pixie smiled shyly.

"Very well, Pixie," Rebecca spoke confidently. "How about if we both go to the kitchen and find something to eat? Given an opportunity to know each other better, I think you and I could become great friends."

As they left the bedroom, Rebecca caught a glimpse of the demure woman wiping her eyes. "Are you okay, Pixie?" she asked.

"Yes, Princess." Pixie sniffled, "Nobody ever said they wanted to be my friend before."

"First, let's not call me Princess anymore. From now on, please call me Rebecca or Becca. That's what my friends call me. Is that okay?"

Pixie smiled sweetly and shook her head to indicate that she agreed.

Rebecca took Pixie's hand. Together they bounced down the stairs and skipped into the kitchen. After realizing she had not eaten since breakfast, Rebecca began eating from a basket filled with apples, oranges, bananas, and tomatoes. Next, she found cheese and bread to make a cheese sandwich, while Pixie brought a whole raw chicken from the icebox. In less than two minutes, the unusual woman devoured the entire chicken, including bones and all. Rebecca felt disturbed by Pixie's dining performance but dared say nothing to disrupt the friendship she was developing with the ferret-faced girl. After finishing the meal, they returned to Rebecca's bedroom.

"Tell me about you, Pixie," Rebecca began the conversation. "How did you become a servant and assistant to Alsaahir?"

"I do not remember much of my life before meeting your grandfather," Pixie confessed. "I was merely a ferret he caught killing a chicken in his barn. He used his magic to turn me into a human. He said he kept my ferret face and hands to remind me where I came from. I have been with him for more than thirty years. He says that I would have lived less than ten years as a ferret and warned that he would turn me back into a ferret if I were ever disloyal to him. I may not have the best life, but it's better than being a dead ferret."

Rebecca took a deep breath and let out a long sigh before continuing. "Well, I think Alsaahir could have given you an even better life if he wanted to. But I am happy that you are here, and I feel very fortunate to know you and call you my friend."

Pixie rose proudly. "I am happy to know you too, Rebecca, and I feel honored to be your friend."

Time passed quickly while the two shared stories of their lives and experiences. Pixie was enthralled by Rebecca's stories about her life outside the Mystic Land. They talked and laughed as if they had known each other for a lifetime.

All of a sudden, the little servant girl abruptly jumped up. Her entire demeanor immediately changed. "The Master is coming; I must go before he gets home." In a flash, Pixie was through the door and down the stairs. Several minutes passed before Rebecca heard even the faint sound of Alsaahir's voice rising from inside the castle. She felt as impressed by Pixie's hearing as Pixie had been by her stories.

After spending a couple of hours with Pixie, Rebecca felt more at ease than she had throughout the afternoon. It dawned on her that if she were to learn her grandfather's magic, she might be able to give a fully human life to Pixie. With those abilities, she could take down the mists, free the people trapped in this sufferable land, and perhaps make a significant difference to thousands of people. But what guarantees did she have that she would ever have that control of the magic? What if the magic corrupted her as it had her grandfather? And Alsaahir could not even be trusted to return her to her friends as he promised. Why did this happen to me? She wondered. I'm only seventeen years old. I want to go home and finish high school. I shouldn't have to be making life-altering decisions like this!

She felt overwhelmed with thoughts, questions, concerns, and decisions. Although Rebecca's mind was racing, her eyes grew weary. She finally dozed off on her bed covers, still wearing the clothes she had been wearing since morning.

"Hello, my darling." Nani's voice spoke from the darkness almost immediately after Rebecca closed her eyes. Her angelic presence appeared like a comforting mother with open arms. Her soothing voice and the glowing light surrounding her provided the vision of an angel.

"Oh, Nani," Rebecca greeted eagerly, "I'm glad you're here. I have so much to discuss with you."

"As efficiently as possible, please tell me what is on your mind, Rebecca."

The words came quickly. "My great-grandfather showed me the sources of his magic. Then asked me to serve as his apprentice for a few years so he could leave everything to me. I don't want to stay here, but I think that if I could learn to use his magic, I might be able to lower the walls of mists and free the people in this land. Unfortunately, I do not trust him, and I'm afraid of what he might do if I refuse his offer. He won't let me leave, and he wants an answer tomorrow. Nani, what do you think I should do?"

Nani paused. "Now that you know more about Alsaahir, I will repeat the message I shared last night. You are correct in your appraisal of his integrity. Many of the things the sorcerer says are barely half-truths. Everything he tells you will sound reasonable at first, but you must listen closely with logic and common sense to recognize the truth or untruth of his words. If you listen wisely, you will discover that most of what he offers is intended to benefit himself. Carefully evaluate everything he says so as not to be misled by him. As for your decision, it is only yours to make. You must follow your path, your intuition, and your heart. Whether your decision follows the path the sorcerer offers or another, do not be prodded into making hasty decisions that you may regret later. You have yet to fully discover the magic of your voice and connection with the animals. There lies your true power. I must go now, Rebecca. Awaken now to remember this discussion, then rest your eyes and sleep. You will know your decision in the morning."

Rebecca quickly opened her eyes. She knew she must remember this conversation. She repeated the messages to herself. Beware of the Sorcerer's half-truths. Use logic and common sense. Trust your intuition. Do not be pressured into making irrational decisions. I still have much to learn about the magic of my voice and my connection with the animals. I have more power than I know. Rebecca thoughtfully reviewed the lessons a few more times, then closed her eyes and fell into a restful sleep.

There was no knock on the door the following morning. Of course, Rebecca could only assume it was morning since there were no windows or a clock to reveal the time. However, she did feel as though she had slept an entire night. Rebecca awoke as she had fallen asleep, on top of the bed covers and still wearing the clothes she had worn the day before.

Her conversation with Nani helped her feel more comfortable and confident about her decisions, although she was in no hurry to meet with her grandfather. Feeling unsure of how the exchange with her grandfather would go, she feared his reaction to anything he might disagree with.

She took her time to take a warm bath, brushed her hair, and browsed through the large closet, picking a nice, simple preach–colored dress for the occasion. Rebecca realized this was the first time she had dressed in anything that could be considered pretty in several days, but it might help if her grandfather saw her in a younger and more feminine light. She wondered how Jules might react to seeing her in a dress. Jules would probably walk into a wall. She giggled to herself at the thought.

Finally, Rebecca took a deep breath, exhaled slowly, stepped out of the comfortable confines of her bedroom, and down the stairs to meet with her grandfather. She found him sitting at the breakfast table in the private dining room, looking as he had the day before. He read the same book and sipped a cup of coffee or tea. The table, set for two, held platters of food. The only noticeable difference today was that Pixie stood patiently next to the door to the kitchen, apparently waiting for an order or signal from Alsaahir.

"Good morning, Grandfather. Good morning, Pixie," Rebecca called out."

"Good morning, Rebecca," Alsaahir responded.

Pixie remained silent. She did not look at Rebecca nor acknowledge her arrival in any way. Quite unusual, Rebecca thought.

"I have some good news for you," Alsaahir cheerfully announced. "Last night, we found the culprits who attacked your friend and stole her horse. Those responsible for the crimes have been punished. I had the horse delivered to the home where we met two days ago with a message of apology. I also clarified to my guards that anyone who comes here, whether to meet with me or deliver a message, is to be treated with the utmost courtesy and respect. Any further reports of disobedience will be severely punished. I promise you they will never commit such misbehaviors again."

Rebecca was stunned by his news. "Thank you, Grandfather! Was Windy excited about having her horse returned? Did you see anybody else while you were there? Is everybody okay?"

"Oh, I did not go to the house personally," Alsaahir admitted. Once we found the horse and the thieves, I returned home. My guards delivered the horse and my message to your friend."

"Well, thank you again, Grandfather. That was quite thoughtful of you. I am sure Windy was most grateful to have her horse returned to her."

"I told you I would take care of that for the girl. I want you to see that I always keep my promises," Alsaahir boasted. "Now, please relax and have your breakfast. Is there anything particular you might like Pixie to prepare for you?"

"No, thank you, Grandfather," Rebecca answered. "There appears to be plenty for me to choose from already on the table."

The two sat quietly while Rebecca ate her breakfast of oatmeal, scrambled eggs, strawberries, toasted bread, and fruit juice. Finally, as she swallowed the last bites of her meal, Rebecca spoke up. "Grandfather, I have made some decisions about your offer and my future. Do you want to discuss it now?"

"Yes, but first, Pixie," he called to the servant girl, "please take Rebecca's dirty dishes to the kitchen for cleaning and stay there until I call you to clean the table."

"Yes, Master," Pixie replied. She picked up the dishes from the table and disappeared into the kitchen as ordered.

"Now, tell me about your decisions," Alsaahir requested.

"Grandfather," Rebecca began, "I feel honored that you already have enough faith in me to offer me the opportunity to learn from you as your apprentice. But I am only seventeen years old, I've not yet finished high school, and I've never even had a boyfriend. I don't yet know what I want to do when I grow up. I may decide that learning about your magic and becoming the leader of this land is a lifetime opportunity. But I am not ready for such responsibility. I want to go home, finish my schooling, and be a normal kid until I grow up enough to make such important life decisions."

Alsaahir was trying to remain calm, but his face turned red as he shifted uncomfortably in his chair. "How long do you expect me to wait for you to make a yes or no decision, Rebecca? I am almost five hundred years old. I may not have so long to live."

"Grandfather, how old were you when you began to travel as a merchant? How old were you when you traveled to America? Please understand that I am too young for this."

The sorcerer became more angered by Rebecca's pointed questions. "For your information, I became a ship's mate at the age of fourteen. By the time I was seventeen, I had become a worthy merchant who had traveled to dozens of countries." Alsaahir's voice grew louder. "I arrived in this country because I was the only survivor when my ship crashed here during a vicious hurricane. I want to know your decision now!" he bellowed.

Rebecca shrunk at his anger. She choked back tears.

"I just want to go home, Grandfather," was all she managed to say.

Alsaahir raised from his chair. "Well, I'm not ready to send you home," he yelled. I am the last and the most powerful of wizards. I can fulfill your greatest dreams or your worst nightmares. You have the opportunity of a lifetime in front of you. It is the opportunity of many lifetimes. And you sit here thinking like a foolish child. Go back to your room until you rethink your decisions or until I decide what to do with you."

For a moment, Rebecca feared that he was going to strike her. He didn't, but she cowered at his forcefulness. She jumped up at his demand and quickly ran from the dining room without looking back. She raced up the stairs and into her room as fast as her legs could take her. She almost slammed the bedroom door but instantly realized that it would do no good to make the sorcerer any angrier. She quietly closed the door and hurried to the bed, where she dropped face-first into the bed covers and began to cry. Dark thoughts filled her mind. He might never let me go. Nobody could rescue me here even if they tried. How did I get myself into this mess? And how am I going to get out of it?

Several hours after running to the room, she changed her clothes and packed her few belongings into her backpack. She thought there was a chance Alsaahir might take her back to her friend's home as he had promised., but as the day wore on, Alsaahir did not call for her.

Rebecca guessed it must be nighttime when a barely noticeable knock came on the bedroom door. She opened the door hesitantly and felt a sense of relief to find Pixie standing there. Pixie held one small finger to her lips as she quietly entered the room. She carried a serving tray with assorted fruits, cheese, bread, and a water pitcher.

"I thought you might be hungry," Pixie spoke quietly after the door had closed.

"Thank you, Pixie. Did Alsaahir send you up here with this food, or is it your idea?

"No, Master did not send me. He has been in an angry temper today, so I dared not bother him."

"Where is he now?" Rebecca inquired.

"He has been in his office for several hours," Pixie answered. "I am not allowed in there, so I do not know what he is doing."

"He had promised to return me to my friends' home today," Rebecca mused, "but it appears that he is not going to do as he said. Do you know if it is day or nighttime, Pixie?"

"Yes, Rebecca, it got dark about an hour ago. I am sorry that he has broken his promise to you." Pixie began to fidget, obviously uncomfortable with the topic and being in Rebecca's room against the Sorcerer's wishes. "I cannot stay here very long, Rebecca. If my master finds me here, I fear he might punish me. But I could not let you be hungry." Pixie removed the food from the tray, tucked the empty tray under her arm, and returned to the door. Before opening it, she turned back again to face Rebecca. "Good night, Princess," she smiled, then left the room, gently closing the door behind her.

Rebecca hungrily consumed the food Pixie had left for her. Unsure when she might eat again, she put an apple in her backpack and drank only half of the water from the pitcher. Feeling uncertain about everything, she decided to sleep in her clothes because she feared being dragged from the room in a nightgown. Climbing under the bed covers, she waved her arm to dim the light in the room as Pixie had taught her. Conflicting thoughts kept her awake for a while before she eventually fell asleep.

Hello, my darling," Nani's soothing voice and angelic
light filled the darkness of Rebecca's dreams.

"Nani, thank you for coming," Rebecca greeted. "I am so
grateful to have you with me."

"How may I help you, Rebecca?"

"I told Grandfather I am not ready to accept his offer to
be his apprentice. He got angry and called me a selfish child.
Then he broke his promise to return me to my friend's home.
He seems to think that if he holds me here, I will change my
mind and decide to stay. But Nani, he scares me. I don't want
to stay here, and I'm afraid he will force me to stay. I don't
know what to do."

Nani paused before she calmly responded. "I see that
you have made a friend in the servant girl. Next time you
are alone together, sing to her. Select a song that is special
and meaningful. Let her know you have chosen this song,
especially for her."

Rebecca felt confused. "What? I don't understand how
that will solve my problem with Alsaahir."

Nani held a finger to her lips. "Shhhh," she whispered.
"I am not certain that it will make a difference, but I feel a
connection between the two of you that I would like to see
nurtured. It never hurts to have a trusted ally on your side.
Furthermore, your friends know you have not returned as
Alsaahir had promised. Like you, they are uncertain about
what they can do. However, your animal friends, Tempest,
Wisdom, and Songbird, are outside this fortress. They are
watching, and they are aware of your circumstances. Those
animals have abilities to help you in ways that humans do not.
Should your circumstances become dire, they will be here for
you. So be patient, my darling. Now, awaken to remember

our meeting, consider a beautiful song for Pixie, then sleep well this night."

"Goodnight, Nani," Rebecca gently called out as her guardian angel faded into the darkness. Rebecca snapped her eyes awake. Sing a song to Pixie? While a thoughtful gesture, Rebecca did not understand how that could solve her problems with her great grandfather. And while there is comfort in knowing her animal guides were outside the fortress, it did not provide a solution to help release her from captivity. Nani's message tonight was more confusing than helpful, Rebecca thought. She briefly considered songs she might sing to Pixie, but no one song immediately stood out to her. I'll think about songs in the morning, she decided, then closed her eyes and fell asleep.

18 Pixie

Morning came too soon for Rebecca. She woke several times during the night, thinking about her plight and how she might get through it. It felt like she had just gone to sleep when a loud pounding came at the door. Becca jumped to her feet at the sound of the abrupt noise. "Who is it?" she called out. Before the violator could respond, she realized what a foolish question it was. Only one person in the castle would beat on the bedroom door so disrespectfully.

Alsaahir shouted through the door, "It's your grandfather. Are you awake?"

"I am now," Rebecca remarked with a twinge of sarcasm. "You may come in."

"I apologize if I woke you," Alsaahir stated as he opened the door. Rebecca no longer felt startled by the man's lack of sincerity. "I have two questions of you," he continued. "First, would you like breakfast this morning?"

"Yes, please," she answered.

"Second, have you had any reconsiderations for my generous offer?"

"I have been thinking of nothing but your offer, Grand-father," she calmly replied. "At this time in my life, I am not ready for that responsibility. And my heart still tells me that I want to go home."

"Very well," Alsaahir spoke decisively, "If you prefer to act like a child, I will treat you accordingly." His anger grew as he spoke. "If you wish to see any of your pitiful dreams come true, you would be wise to reconsider my offer. I will have Pixie bring breakfast to you. I will give you another day in your room to reconsider your decisions," he shouted. Then he stormed through the door, slamming it behind him before she had another chance to respond.

The disappointment was devastating. Tears welled in her eyes. She began to sob; then fell onto the bed. She hid her face in the covers to stifle the sounds of her crying.

Close to an hour passed before a light knock sounded at the door. Unlike Alsaahir's disruptive pounding, Rebecca immediately knew this was Pixie. She wiped the remnants of tears from her face as she anxiously crossed the room. Rebecca flung open the door with a beaming smile, only to see sad tears dripping from Pixie's big eyes. "Please come in," Rebecca invited. She reached to take the breakfast tray from the petite servant girl's hands. "What's wrong, Pixie?"

"Master said he knew I brought food to you last night. He said he saw the dishes in your room," Pixie cried. "Then he told me to bring your breakfast but not come back again today. I'm so sorry, Rebecca."

"It's okay, Pixie. It's not your fault," Rebecca explained. "He's mad at me for not accepting a future as his apprentice. I'm so sorry he's taking it out on you. I wish I could go home, and you could go on with your life, but he's determined to keep me here until I change my mind."

Pixie's eyes widened. "So, you're his prisoner like me?" she asked.

"Well, I can't compare my situation to yours, Pixie, except that we are both kept here by my grandfather. I can tell you that my future has suddenly become more uncertain." Both of the girls were quiet for a moment. Rebecca took a bite of bread and a drink of apple juice from the breakfast tray. Pixie began to say her goodbyes when Rebecca stopped her. "Pixie, before you leave, I have a song I would like to

sing. It's a song that makes me think of you. May I sing it
for you?"

Pixie smiled and shook her head in agreement. "I would
like that, Rebecca."

Rebecca began to sing.

You lift me up
You make me smile
You take my heart away in everything you do
My life would never be the same if I did not know you

Whatever path you choose
You've got a friend in me
You're my best friend
You know that much is true

These words are all I have to give
To show my heart is true
You've made a difference in my life in everything you do
My life would never be the same if I did not have you

I found my greatest friend
The day that I found you
Let's make it last forever
Let's take this road together
Let's make our dreams come true

You're always there
When I need you
You know I'd do the same for you
Let's not end this story now
Let's make our dreams come true

Whatever path you choose
You've got a friend in me
You're my best friend
You know that much is true

I found my greatest friend
The day that I found you

By the time Rebecca finished singing, Pixie was crying. Raindrop tears dripped from her whiskers into puddles on her clothes. "Oh, Rebecca," she sobbed, "nobody has ever been so kind to me. You are the most wonderful person I've ever known."

"Thank you, Pixie," Rebecca countered, "I've never had a friend like you. I believe we will always be special friends for as long as we live. But now, you should return downstairs before the sorcerer comes looking for you."

"Yes, you're right," the little servant girl admitted. "I will return when I can."

Rebecca ushered Pixie toward the door. "Thank you for bringing breakfast to me," she spoke graciously. Rebecca looked into Pixie's big sad eyes as they stood in the doorway. She grinned out of politeness, but inside, she held back tears for her sad friend. Pixie turned and walked toward the stairway. Rebecca started for her bed when she remembered breakfast was waiting for her.

Following breakfast, she took her time washing. A little more than an hour after Pixie left the room, a quiet knock sounded at the door again. Rebecca rushed to open it, surprised to find the little ferret-faced woman staring up at her. Rebecca anxiously welcomed Pixie into the room. "Rebecca," Pixie started, "the sorcerer has gone into his office. He is never there for less than a few hours. Sometimes he spends whole days there. Quickly pack your belongings into your travel bag. I know of a way to get you out of here."

Rebecca was stunned. "Pixie... What?... How?... Isn't this risky for you? she stammered.

"I think I can get you out without my master knowing until tomorrow, and he will not suspect me of helping you. Now hurry. please, Princess."

Fortunately, because Rebecca had packed most of her belongings the day before, she tossed another apple, a single set of eating utensils, a towel, and a pair of socks into her backpack, put on her boots, and was ready to go.

Before they headed out the door, Pixie warned Rebecca, "We will pass Alsaahir's office. Stay very quiet until we are completely clear, okay?"

"Okay, Pixie, I'm ready," Rebecca replied.

They quietly closed the door behind them. Then, gently stepping down the stairs, they tiptoed past the dining rooms to the closed double doors of Alsaahir's office. Directly across the hall from his office, Pixie stepped up to a pair of matching double doors, quietly opened one of them, and stepped inside, gesturing for Rebecca to follow. After closing the door behind them, Pixie waved her arm to signal a dim light into the room.

Rebecca stood in awe at a massive, warehouse-sized storage room. One section to her right was stacked with furniture, desks, chairs, and tables of all sizes and shapes. On her left, rows of shelves held old glass bottles and clay jugs, boxes of all sizes, piles of plates, cups, and cooking ware. The two girls moved through the maze of cabinets, supplies, carpets, tapestries, paintings, old weapons, swords, rifles, knives, saddles, gear for farm animals, and a vast collection of large and small tools for building, gardening, farming, and repair work.

Partway through the room, Rebecca tripped over a rake sticking out into the walkway, screeching as she fell against a pile of rakes and shovels while the tools made a loud clattering noise. Pixie quickly grabbed Rebecca and moved her into a hiding spot behind a pile of tall wooden boxes.

They stayed quiet for several minutes before Pixie finally whispered, "The sorcerer must not have heard the noise since he did not come to inspect it." After a brief pause, Pixie added, "I would have accepted responsibility for the noise if he had come in, but it would have ruined your chance to escape."

"I would have returned to my bedroom before allowing you to be punished for helping me," Rebecca responded.

The pair continued carefully through the menagerie of items filling the warehouse. Finally, they turned right between a row of cabinets and the back wall until they reached a corner where Pixie slid a section of a wood panel wall to the right. It reminded Rebecca of the hidden door at the back of the barn where she had followed Alsaahir into the secret hallway two days before. After closing the door panel behind them, Pixie waved her arm to bring light to a stairway that appeared to drop below ground level. Rebecca counted about fifty steps before entering a long, cold, damp, rock hallway. Another fifty steps through the hall, Rebecca noticed steel doors lining the walls. A sick feeling spread through her as she realized these were prison cells.

She stopped in her tracks. "Where are you taking me, Pixie?" Rebecca held on to the wall in fear. She was preparing to turn and run the other way as fast as possible.

Suddenly realizing the danger Rebecca feared, Pixie

answered, "Oh, no, Rebecca, I would never.... This old dungeon has not been used for many years. We are walking under the moat. We have only a short distance further to get you outside. I promise."

Rebecca took a deep breath and stepped in the direction Pixie led her. As promised, it was only a short distance to a turn in the hall and a stairway leading upward. Rebecca counted another fifty steps until they reached a small landing. Pixie stopped in front of a solid wood door held closed by a heavy steel bar settled into brackets across the front of the door and each wall. Together they lifted the heavy bar free of the brackets. Once the door was pushed open, bright sunlight filled the small landing room. The girls covered their eyes until they adjusted to the glaring sunlight. They had emerged within a small grove of pine trees. Rebecca took a deep breath of the fresh air and lifted her face to the sunlight beaming between the branches of the pines.

"We are facing directly south, Rebecca," Pixie pointed. "If you look back between the trees, you can see the southeast corner of the fortress behind us. That corner will point you in the southeasterly direction you need to go to the Elfin Woods. You will travel for a little more than one mile. Many trees will help keep you hidden, but there are also patches of open land where you should look for troll guards or mutants before you cross through them. If you go too far east, you will come to a wall. Follow that wall to the right. If you travel too far south, you will arrive at the Burg Marsh. Turn left and follow the swamp's edge until you reach the Elfin Woods. The elves will see you coming. After explaining who you are and how you got there, the elves will help you. They are the wisest people in the Mystic Lands."

Rebecca remembered the landmarks Pixie spoke of from the map Jasmine had illustrated for her. The map was in her pocket, but she had studied it enough that she did not feel the need to bring it out.

"Pixie, won't you come with me?" Rebecca implored. "This is your chance to escape too."

"No, Rebecca, I cannot. My master gave me a life. He is old, and he is not well. He will not admit it, but he needs me. I am committed to serving and caring for him as long as he lives. I wish you well and hope we see each other again under better circumstances. I will always remember you and our special friendship. Now go, my Princess."

Rebecca knelt to one knee to give Pixie a long, heartfelt hug. "I will always remember you, my special friend. And our special song will always remind me of you." She quietly sang a few verses as she backed away from the doe-eyed girl.

Whatever path you choose
You've got a friend in me
You're my best friend
You know that much is true

These words are all I have to give
To show my heart is true
You've made a difference in my life in everything you do
My life would never be the same if I did not have you

I found my greatest friend
The day that I found you

Rebecca turned and walked away. At the edge of the pines, she turned back to wave to her friend one more time, but when she looked, Pixie was gone. What an incredible person, she thought; I will always be grateful for Pixie.

19 Elves!

After exiting the pine grove, Rebecca discovered the area to be much as Pixie had described. There were enough trees to provide shade and cover and enough open space between the trees to see where she was going. A look over her shoulder revealed the southeastern corner of the fortress, pointing her toward the Elfin Woods.

It was a warm summer day. The sun appeared slightly more to the west than the east, so Rebecca guessed the time near one or two o'clock. She laughed to herself. Who would have thought I would have to look at the sun's position to guess the time of day?

She glanced upward again as a dark shadow moved across the sky between her and the sun. All of a sudden, she realized it was coming directly at her. It dropped below the treetops, causing Rebecca to fall to the ground as it flew only a few feet above her head. At first sight, she thought it might be an eagle or a hawk attacking her for an afternoon snack. She considered that Alsaahir might have sent a bird of prey to find her. Instead, the large bird landed on a branch only a few feet over her head. At second sight, she realized she knew this bird. Its creamy white feathers, reddish-brown ears and tips of its wings, and large golden-brown eyes stared down at her from behind a band of gray color that wrapped around its head like a bandit's mask.

"Wisdom!" she exclaimed. "Wisdom, is that you?"

Rebecca jumped up excitedly when the owl responded with its melodic "Hoot, Hoot."

"I have so much to tell you since we last saw each other.

But you've probably already heard much of the story. How are you? Have you been on an adventure?"

"Hoot, Hoot," Wisdom replied,

"Nani told me that you, Tempest, and Songbird were outside Alsaahir's castle while I was there. Do you know where they are now?"

"Hoot, Hoot," the owl responded, then spread his wings and flew through the trees in the castle's direction.

Rebecca decided to sit and rest under Wisdom's shade tree. She pulled one of the two apples from her backpack and began to eat. She had barely eaten half of the apple when Wisdom flew back into the clearing, landing on the same branch over Rebecca's head. Less than one minute later, Songbird arrived, landing on the ground only inches from Rebecca.

"Songbird!" she exclaimed. "I've so missed the sound of your beautiful singing." Rebecca used her pocket knife to trim a few apple pieces for the birds, but neither showed much interest. She had just taken a big bite of the apple when a giant white tiger raced into the clearing. Rebecca spit the piece of apple into her hand. She jumped up to hug the massive tiger, but within the few seconds it took them to reach each other, the tiger had transformed into a twenty-pound cat. She grabbed the cat and squeezed her. "Oh, Tempest, I am so happy to see you. When I saw you last, you were unconscious after being shot with a dart. I am so relieved to see you're okay." Rebecca hugged Tempest for several minutes. Surprisingly, the cat did not try to get away. Nor did she seem to mind the chunk of apple stuck to her fur.

Rebecca settled back against the tree with Songbird on one side, Tempest on the other, and Wisdom resting on the branch over her head. Songbird began to whistle a soft melodic tune. Rebecca closed her eyes and drifted into a light sleep.

"Rebecca, can you hear me? Rebecca, it's Nani. Can you hear me?" came the grandmother's voice.

"Yes, Nani, I can hear you," Rebecca replied in her semi-conscious dream state.

"I am happy to see you have escaped from the Sorcerer's fortress. Am I correct that the small servant woman helped you?" Nani asked.

"Yes, Nani. Your suggestion to sing her a song was such a wonderful idea. We truly bonded as a result of it. I believe it was the key to her helping me to escape."

"That is marvelous, my child. Are you okay?"

"Yes, Alsaahir scared me but did not harm me," Rebecca replied.

"Now that you are free of the sorcerer and have reunited with your animal guides, I would like you to open your eyes, look at Songbird while she sings, and listen to my voice."

"Will I be able to hear you after I am awake, Nani?" Rebecca asked.

"That is what I hope for us to learn. Stay calm. Do not lift yourself from your position of comfort. Slowly open your eyes, find Songbird, and listen closely to my voice while she sings."

Rebecca did as Nani asked. She opened her eyes. Songbird stood on her knee directly in front of her, softly whistling her melody.

"Rebecca, can you hear me?" The voice was her great grandmother, but it sounded like it was coming from the nightingale. "Can you hear me, Darling?" the voice repeated. "Yes, Nani, I hear you," the startled girl spoke while staring into Songbird's eyes.

"Wonderful. We are making tremendous progress. This is what I want you to know; I am the spirit within Songbird.

She is the vehicle in which you and I can communicate in your awakened state. In my human life, I was the daughter of Alsaahir and Apani. My mother was a Native American Indian. My birth name was Puyuqumaaraq, which loosely translates as 'Little Bird that looks like smoke.' However, even at a young age, I loved to sing, so my parents gave me the English nickname, 'Songbird.' My mother, Apani, used the magic she learned from Alsaahir on me to make my daughter and all of our firstborn female ancestors look like her. I did not discover that she had used magic on me until after the birth of my daughter. It was then that I fled through the mists. That was many generations ago, yet the magic continues to this day. Side effects of that magic included enchanting singing voices and the ability to communicate with several animals. I once mentioned to you that Tempest and Wisdom are spirit guides. You can communicate with them as you are with me now. Do you have any questions before we continue to the Elfin Woods?"

"Thank you, Nani. Or should I now call you Songbird?"

"I suggest calling me Nani when we communicate in the sleep state, but refer to me as Songbird in the presence of others. Both are respectful names for me. Now, how can we help you, Rebecca?" Nani asked.

"I would like to send a message to our friends at the Verne home to let them know I am safe. Is there a way we can do that? Rebecca asked.

Songbird replied, "Write a note to your friends. I will deliver it, then return to meet you in the Elfin Woods."

Songbird stopped singing, and Rebecca snapped to attention. She found it hard to believe she was conversing with the nightingale. Nevertheless, Rebecca pulled the notepad and a pen from her backpack and began to write a short letter to the Verne family. She wrote that she had safely left the Sorcerer's fortress, Tempest was with her, they were going to the Elfin Woods, and she would see them in a few days. She folded the paper and handed it to Songbird, who quickly flew off to deliver the letter. Shortly after, Rebecca, Wisdom, and Tempest were up and moving through the trees toward the Elfin Woods.

With Wisdom guiding the way, the journey to the Elfin Woods was relatively quick and uneventful. They detoured around one open area, although Rebecca saw no signs of the trolls or mutants. After that, they followed a direct path toward the Elfin Woods. As they grew closer, Rebecca saw that these woods were unlike any she had ever seen. Giant redwoods, like she had only seen in pictures, towered into the sky. She thought redwoods did not grow in New England, but here they were.

A few hundred yards before reaching the forest edge, Wisdom flew ahead. "Wisdom is going ahead to investigate." Rebecca heard the voice but felt unsure where it came from.

"Tempest, did you just speak to me?" she questioned.

"Meow," the cat replied.

Rebecca immediately stopped walking. She closed her eyes, took a deep breath, and asked out loud, "Tempest, if you can understand me, please respond."

In her mind, Rebecca heard a voice say, "You will be safe here." Rebecca opened her eyes.

Tempest stood and began walking toward the trees. Rebecca shrugged and followed a few steps behind. "She may talk, but she still acts like a cat," Rebecca murmured amusingly.

Stepping into the shadows of the tall redwoods made Rebecca feel like she had shrunk in size. She guessed that some of the trees would take five or six people with outstretched arms to reach around them. Treetops extended into the sky like pointed skyscrapers with sprinkles of light reflecting off pine needles and multi-colored leaves. Thick vines wrapped around branches like ropes and ribbons, crisscrossing from tree to tree, binding the forest together like a giant spider web. The path twisted around long waist-high roots securing the massive tree trunks to the ground. Grass covered in purple clover and big colorful flowers spread between the trees. Fresh scents intoxicated and energized Rebecca's senses. Fist-sized bumble bees, extraordinary butterflies, and animated hummingbirds fluttered from flower to flower. The sounds of singing birds and buzzing insects filled the air like a chorus of musical harmonies.

Rebecca excitedly followed Tempest along the forest path. How different is this, she thought, from following the cat through the fog-covered swamp a week before?

A swift movement ahead of them suddenly caught Rebecca's attention. Soaring directly toward them, barely a few feet above the ground, Wisdom drew to an abrupt stop on a nearby tree stump.

"Hoot, Hoot," the owl declared.

Rebecca didn't have time to read the owls' thoughts or guess what he was trying to tell her before a human figure abruptly appeared in the path only a dozen yards ahead of her. "Stop!" a woman's voice called out. It appeared to be a young female, likely close to Rebecca's age, with a beautiful face, shining eyes, and short golden-brown hair. She was relatively petite in height, under five feet tall with a slender build, but with a fit body and forceful body language did not look like a woman to be taken lightly. She wore a dark green vest over a brown shirt with sleeves rolled above her elbows, matching dark green pants tucked into knee-high black boots, a long knife hanging from her belt, a longbow in her hand, and a quiver full of arrows prominently displayed behind her shoulder. "Identify yourself and explain what brings you into this forest," she ordered.

"My name is Rebecca Fields. These are my friends Tempest and Wisdom," Rebecca pointed out as she called their names. I am traveling to my friends' home near the Gypsy Camps," she explained. I hope you might help me get there safely.

"Did you come here through the mists?" the girl asked.

"Oh, no," Rebecca replied, "well, I did about a week ago, but not today. I escaped from the Sorcerer's fortress this morning. I thought this would be the safest route to prevent running into his trolls."

"It sounds like an unusual story, perhaps even a little suspicious," the girl commented, "but it is not my place to make such judgments." She raised a hand to her mouth and made a loud whistling sound. Within seconds, several people dressed exactly alike, even with matching knives, longbows, quivers, and arrows, surrounded Rebecca and her animal friends. "My name is Quinn," the girl introduced herself. "I am the Sergeant of the Guard at the Elfin Woods southern post. These are a few of my fellow guards. We will guide you and your friends to the Elfin Village, where you can tell your story to the Council. They will decide how to help you. Is that satisfactory, Rebecca Fields?"

"Yes, thank you, Quinn," Rebecca graciously replied.

The walk to the Elfin Village took about half an hour. Quinn asked a few questions of Rebecca, but Rebecca's fascination with the Elfin Woods encouraged Quinn to do most of the talking. She explained that most elves built their homes in the trees, yet the average person would never see the homes or the elves there. Once a few treehouses were pointed out, Rebecca began to see them everywhere. Yet, except for the elves accompanying her, she saw no others.

Upon closer observation, Rebecca began to notice more details of the elves. They really did have pointed ears, just as the fairy tales had described. The males and females in the group were all slender, close to the same height, looked as young as teenagers, and could move about extremely fast. When Rebecca asked Quinn how she had become Sergeant of the Guard at such a young age, Quinn asked what age Rebecca thought her to be. She was stunned to learn that Quinn was forty-five years old!

"Elves typically live three-hundred years or more," Quinn explained. "The elves believe in life-long learning. Once we complete our initial schooling, we train in various roles throughout the first half of our lives. If we excel in a role, we may become teachers for a few additional years to develop training and leadership skills. That is how I became a Sergeant of the Guard. Before becoming a Forest Guardian, I had been a gardener, cook, school teacher assistant, worked in construction, and spent two years training to live and move among the trees. Because I've been with the Forest Guard for five years, I expect to be assigned to my next role quite soon."

"Do you know what your next role will be?" Rebecca inquired.

"Not yet," Quinn answered, "but I hope for it to be something that allows me to interact with people outside of the Elfin Woods. I'm embarrassed to admit that you are the first person I've ever met who is not an elf."

"Well, I never would have guessed that," Rebecca commented. "You have been so cordial; I had assumed it was part of your role to greet, communicate, and socialize with travelers and guests."

"Ha," Quinn laughed, "in my five years at the southern border of the Elfin Woods, you are the first person who has entered the forest!"

The group rounded a corner beyond a long row of trees and tall plants, passed under a large overhang of manicured bushes and flowers, and into what Quinn called the "Elfin Village."

Rebecca gasped at the magnificence and beauty of the thriving hamlet. Rows of flowers precisely spaced between apple trees lined a stone walkway that led to the village center. Behind the trees and flowers, gardens overflowing with fruits and vegetables filled yards fronting wood cabin-style homes and treehouses. The scene reminded Rebecca of paintings on holiday greeting cards, except for the missing snow. Massive redwoods towered over the town, hiding it comfortably in their shadows. Elfin people, clad in natural-colored clothes, moved gleefully along the walkway, many carrying bags or baskets of goods, some pushing or pulling carts. Small dogs sometimes paraded next to their owners. Chickens, ducks, geese, peacocks, and assorted birds wandered in and out of the trees, bushes, and flower beds. Rebecca lost sight of Wisdom as he blended with the varied birds and scenery. While Rebecca, Tempest, Quinn, and the guards passed through the village, a passerby would smile, wave, and call out cheerful greetings, but none displayed any particular curiosity toward the group.

Midway through the village, they crossed the road's only intersection. To the left and right, storefronts and shops lined the road as far as Rebecca could see. Crowds of people moved busily in each direction. The crowd thinned after the group proceeded through the junction. They passed a park where couples strolled and children played, then approached what Quinn called the government section of the village. Buildings grew progressively more official in appearance. Most were built with stone rather than wood. Statues and monuments called attention to the history of the Elfin society. The roadway led directly to the front steps of the town's most prominent structure. Although only two stories in height, its width stretched hundreds of yards. A dozen stone columns lined the front of the building. Banners and flags adorned the entryway.

"This is the seat of government," Quinn announced. "The Elfin Council meets here daily. They are officially named the Council of Elders to signify the time and experience of the delegation. Nobody can be selected to the Council before completing all of their roles at one hundred and fifty years of age. After reaching eligibility, a candidate's name can be placed on a ballot for consideration to join the Council of Elders. The people of the village vote every five years. No more than two hundred members sit on the council, and the eldest are selected first to fill the empty seats of those who have died or left the panel. Therefore, many are not chosen for a chair until more than two hundred years old.

"That's fascinating," Rebecca acknowledged. "Is there a President or a King?

"A new Minister of the Council is also elected every five years," Quinn explained. "A Minister cannot be elected more than once, but past Ministers serve as advisors to the new Minister," You will see the Minister and former Ministers seated at the center of the dais at the front of the assembly. We also have honorary members who have received Lifetime

Achievement Awards for extraordinary service to the Elfin community. They've earned titles of Prince or Princess. They too serve as advisors to the council, but they are usually so busy with more important responsibilities, they are rarely seen here unless something significant is being debated."

"So, what should I expect in my appearance before the Council, Quinn?" Rebecca asked.

"You will be asked to tell your story as briefly and clearly as possible in fifteen minutes or less. Tell them what brought you here, what goals you hope to achieve, what challenges you might be facing, and what kind of help you need. You should know that I will be required to present to them my judgment and experiences with you. The council will then ask any questions, discuss your issues, and decide if and how they might help you. The entire process typically lasts no more than thirty or forty minutes. After that, their decision will be final."

As they reached the front doors of the building, Quinn directed her team of Forest Guardians to take two hours to eat, rest, and wait outside when they returned. They scattered quickly, leaving Quinn, Rebecca, and Tempest to enter the Council building. Rebecca did not know where Wisdom might have disappeared but felt it wise not to bring up the subject. They entered a spacious reception area with two wide desks facing the doors and several receptionists coming and going to and from the desks. A few individuals, families, and small groups were seated on benches around the room's edges, apparently waiting for their turn to be summoned into the council chambers.

When Quinn announced to one of the receptionists their names and general reason for requesting the meeting with the council, the entire room quieted.

"We had heard that you might be coming," the receptionist declared, staring directly at Rebecca. "We were not expecting you so soon. The council is anxious to meet you. I will let them know you are here."

Rebecca called out as the receptionist hurried away, "How did they know we were coming?" When she did not respond, Rebecca turned to Quinn. "Did you send someone ahead to tell them we were coming?" she asked.

"No," Quinn replied. "I am as surprised by that comment as you are!"

A few minutes later, the receptionist returned with a tall, muscular, broad-chested elf, bearing swords on his belt at each side of his hips. Before reaching the desk, the man boldly asked, "Are you Rebecca Fields?"

"Yes," Rebecca answered, stepping back somewhat timidly.

"The Council has been hoping that you would come here," he continued, "please follow me."

Quinn had sprung to an upright military position of attention. "Sir, would you also like me and the lady's cat to follow?" she asked.

"Yes, Sergeant," he replied as he turned and bounded back in the direction from where he had come.

Quinn and Rebecca chased after the big man. Tempest followed at a more leisurely, cat-like pace. Upon reaching a pair of tall, ornate doors, the leader opened one door, pointed the pair through, and then waited patiently while the cat casually strolled across the reception area. They had entered a short hall end of the passage.

"My name is Andor," the big man introduced himself, "I am the Captain of the Guard for the Council of the Elders. If you wait here, I will let the Minister and his advisors know you are here. I will return in a few minutes to announce you to the Council." The captain turned and paraded through the doors at the other end of the hallway.

Quinn let out a breath of relief. "Andor is not just the Captain of the Guard for the Council," she murmured, "he recently retired as the captain of the entire Elvin Armed Forces."

Rebecca and Quinn seated themselves on one of the couches. Little was spoken between them while they waited. Tempest sat on the carpet, indifferently licking her front paws as cats will often do.

Fifteen minutes passed before the doors swung open at the end of the hallway. Andor stood at one side, waving Rebecca, Quinn, and Tempest forward. A smaller but similarly dressed elfin man stood by the other door.

"Ladies and Gentlemen of the Council," Andor announced to the assembly, "please welcome our honored guests, Miss Rebecca Harmony Fields, accompanied by her protector and spirit guide, Tempest the Cat, and our Sergeant of the Guard at the Southern Woods, Sergeant Quinn Triewe." The entire assembly stood and clapped while Captain Andor led them to a table and chairs on the right side of the room, facing the council. Tempest jumped onto the table, quickly stretching herself to a laying position while comfortably facing the room. The row of Ministers sat on a raised platform at the front of the room to their right.

The Minister called for the council to be seated and began to speak. "Miss Rebecca Fields, we have heard of your presence in the Mystic Lands. If you are as we have been told, we are most honored to have you here, and we look forward to assisting you in your journey. Please, kindly tell us how you come to appear before the Elvin Council of Elders."

Rebecca nervously stood to speak. "I'm not sure what you heard," she began. "I got lost and came through the mists about a week ago with the help of this fearless cat and a couple of birds. A kind family living near the Gypsy Camps generously helped me until Alsaahir, the sorcerer, claiming I am his distant ancestor, took me to his fortress. This morning I managed to escape. I reached the southern end of the Elfin Woods this afternoon. That's where Sergeant Quinn found me and brought me here. I hope you can help guide me back to my friend's home."

Rebecca had barely finished speaking when the doors sprung open at the back of the assembly.

"Ladies and Gentlemen of the Council," Andor announced, "please stand, as we are honored to welcome Princess Stefani to our council." The entire council stood to applaud while murmurs of startled members grew into an exuberant buzz through the room.

"Quinn leaned into Rebecca to speak excitedly into her ear. "This is an extraordinary occurrence. Princess Stefani is the most highly honored of all of the elves. She is rarely seen outside scientific and spiritual circles and most important events."

A statuesque woman, a vision of eminence, entered the room. Long glittering white hair flowed from under a gold wreath adorned with small white flowers. She wore a simple white dress shimmering with brilliant translucent colors in her light. She moved with elegant grace as if she floated above the ground.

The entire council quieted to near silence as Princess Stefani moved to a standing position directly before the dais.

"My Dear Minister and leaders of the Elfin Council," she began. "I believe I have information of vital importance to you, the Council of Elders, and the future of the Elfin peoples. May I have your permission to address the assembly?"

"Of course, Princess Stefani," the Minister answered positively. The Council of Elders is honored by your presence."

"Thank you, Minister," she responded as she turned to face the audience. "My fellow council members, most respected elders, and friends, I am grateful for your attention. Miss Rebecca Fields, I am honored by your presence in our community and this council."

Rebecca felt stunned that the Princess knew who she was. Considering the murmurs in the room, it was evident that she was not the only person feeling so perplexed by the recognition.

Princess Stefani continued, "I have received information from several highly reputable sources who have led me to believe that Rebecca Harmony Fields is the deity that the elves and the people of the Mystic Lands have foretold would rescue us from our captivity within the mists."

The room erupted in conversation. Rebecca could not believe what she was hearing.

"Please, please allow me to explain," Stefani called out. The council members quieted. "If my information is correct, Rebecca Fields is the maternal great-granddaughter of the sorcerer, Alsaahir, and his wife, Apani. On her father's side, she is the daughter of the Health Center leader, Takoda Nemasket. Takoda's mother is the highly respected Elfin spiritualist, medical, and health expert Haley Janel Nemasket. As a result of her genetic makeup, Rebecca Fields has superior magical powers that even she is yet unaware of. I desire an opportunity to help her discover those powers.

In return, I hope she will help us to free the Elves and people of the Mystic Lands. Next, I would like to introduce you to three of Rebecca's spiritual guides and protectors who will help you to see a small sampling of her powers." Stefani raised her arms outright to the sides of her body. A large white owl with brown tips on its wings and a black band of color wrapped around its head flew into the room and landed on Princess Stefani's right arm near her shoulder. Moments after, a colorful nightingale whistled a song as it circled the room and landed on Stefani's extended left arm.

Stefani called out, "Rebecca, these glorious birds are long-time associates of mine. Might you also be familiar with them, and if so, would you please tell us their names and how you know them?"

"Yes, Princess Stefani," Rebecca timidly answered. "The owl's name is Wisdom, and the nightingale is named Songbird. They have been my guides and guardians since I entered the mists."

"How did you come up with those names, Rebecca?" Stefani asked.

"They told me," Rebecca replied.

Again, conversation broke out among the Council members. Rebecca thought she heard a few snickers, but Princess Stefani abruptly put a quick stop to the rumblings. She whispered to each of the birds. Wisdom lifted from Stefani's arm, flew around the room, and landed on the back of Rebecca's chair. Songbird flew to the desk in front of Rebecca and Quinn, stopping next to Tempest. "Please, Rebecca," Stefani continued, "tell us about the cat by your side."

"Her name is Tempest," Rebecca answered. "She is a cat which is not really a cat. Throughout my journey, she has been a faithful guide, protector, and friend. I would not be alive without her. I owe her my life."

"Rebecca," Stefani inquired, would you please ask Tempest for a brief demonstration of why she is not really a cat and how she has protected you?"

"I will ask," Rebecca commented, "but like most cats, she can be quite stubborn in deciding when to do what she does." Rebecca leaned forward to speak with Tempest. "Okay, Tempest, it is essential for you to show your abilities. Please," she pleaded.

Tempest stood up, yawned, stretched, then jumped to the floor. Within seconds she transformed from a twenty-pound cat into a four-hundred-pound white tiger. As soon as she reached full size, she faced the assembly and growled her loudest and fiercest roar. The entire room shook. The elves sitting closest to the white tiger fell over each other in a futile attempt to flee the ferocious beast. Seconds later, Tempest returned to her twenty-pound cat size. She jumped back onto the table, sat down, and began to lick her front paws as if this was the most natural and unassuming part of her day.

"Thank you, Tempest," Rebecca whispered in the cat's ear.

While the shaken council members cautiously returned to their seats, Princess Stefani continued, "In case it needs explaining, Rebecca has a magical ability to communicate with these animals. She also has a gifted voice which enables her to influence listeners with her songs, including Alsaahir's trolls, mutants, and goblins. However, she has only learned of her magic and ancestral connections since arriving here approximately one week ago. Therefore, with the approval of this Council, I offer a proposal. I will personally take Rebecca under my wing to help her reconnect with her friends. During our journey, I will mentor her to the best of my ability in using her magic."

"Furthermore, I have been informed that her friends may be in danger by Alsaahir and his trolls and mutants. Therefore, I request eight of our best warriors go to Rebecca's friends' home as soon as possible to help protect them. I would also like eight of our best trackers, guides, and guards to serve with us while on our journey.

Finally, I understand that our young Sergeant Quinn Triewe has been an accomplished Forest Guardian for five years and Sergeant of the Guard for more than two years. As it is time for her to transfer to a new role, I would like her to become my guard on this journey, followed by her becoming my Personal Assistant. That is if the position interest you, Sergeant Quinn?"

Quinn appeared stunned. She stuttered, then tried to cover it with a cough before finally uttering, "Yes, Your Highness, I gladly accept that great honor."

Princess Stefani smiled. "You have performed exceptionally in every role you have attempted, Quinn. That is why I have chosen you as one of my closest associates."

Quinn sat with her mouth open. "I did not expect that!" she whispered so quietly that only Rebecca heard the proud Sergeant speak it.

"The significant aspects of my proposal," Stefani concluded, "involve two important considerations. First, I sincerely believe that with proper training and support, this young woman will be capable of defeating the Sorcerer, lifting the mists from our borders, and freeing all of the peoples of the Mystic Lands. For that to happen, the Elves must immediately secure our borders against any incursions by Alsaahir and his army. Second, to be successful in our goals, we must consider and be prepared for the future in a new world. My new companions and I will now leave the council for your discussion and vote. We respectfully await your decisions."

Stefani signaled for Quinn, Rebecca, and her guardian animals to follow her from the room. As soon as the doors closed behind them, the assembly exploded into a deafening cacophony of voices. Calling for order, the distinct voices of the Minister and Captain of the Guard boomed above the crowd.

Rebecca questioned why they would leave in the middle of the meeting. Stefani explained that she had provided all the necessary facts and evidence to the Council. "It is wiser to let the Council members come to the same conclusions among themselves than to confuse the situation with redundant questions and concerns," she reasoned.

While the Council of Elders debated their fate, Princess Stefani led the group to a dining room in the government building. The sight of Princess Stefani with a forest guard, a non-elf girl, a cat, an owl, and a nightingale, received several awkward glances and staring eyes, but they dined uninterrupted. The dining room had food for every taste, including meals for the three animals. The conversation was upbeat. Princess Stefani felt confident that everything she had proposed to the council would be accepted. Rebecca wished she could feel as confident in Stefani's appraisal of her inherited magical abilities.

While eating, Stefani handed Rebecca a note that Songbird had brought from Jasmine. It read, "Dear Rebecca, we are happy to hear that you escaped Alsaahir's fortress. We are all fine here. Tempest left the morning after you departed with Alsaahir. A horse was delivered here two mornings ago with a letter from Alsaahir stating that he was returning Windy's horse. Windy says it is not the same horse, but she is grateful. We all miss you and hope to see you soon. You should be safe with the Elves. Love, Jasmine."

Before returning to the Council for their decision, Stefani joined Quinn to meet with her team of Forest Guardians outside of the front doors. The Guardians were excited to meet Princess Stefani, thrilled to be told they could stay in the village overnight, and curious when Quinn advised them to return in the morning for further information.

Andor, the Captain of the Guard, paced impatiently outside the double doors when the group arrived back at the Council assembly. "Decisions have been made. They await your return," the captain said as he opened the doors and led them through the hallway. He paused at the second set of doors while waiting for them to gather together. Finally, he sprung open the doors and announced, "Ladies and Gentlemen of the Council, please welcome back our most honored guests, Princess Stefani, Miss Rebecca Fields, Sergeant Quinn Triewe, Tempest the cat, Songbird the nightingale, and Wisdom, the owl. The entire assembly rose from their seats to give them a standing ovation while Captain Andor led them to the front of the room.

As the room quieted, the Minister raised his voice to speak, "It has been an unusually long day for this Council of Elders. Therefore, I will make this announcement brief. Princess Stefani, while we are not entirely convinced that Rebecca Fields has the powers to defeat the sorcerer and eliminate the mists, your presentation has convinced the Council to take a chance for our future and our freedom. Therefore, we have voted to provide you with all the resources you require to accomplish the daunting tasks you endeavor to achieve. At sunrise tomorrow morning, six of our bravest guards will travel to the home of Miss Rebecca's friends for their protection. We would like for you to brief them before they depart. Throughout the day, the Council of Elders and the Captains of the Elfin Forces will be at your disposal to organize plans, assemble forces, select your guardian team, acquire weapons and supplies, and prepare for your journey. Sergeant Quinn Triewe, effective immediately, you no longer carry the title of Sergeant of the Guard at the Southern Woods. You are now the personal guard and assistant to Princess Stefani for a minimum of three years. Send a message to your company captain suggesting names of notable guardians for promotion to your position as Sergeant of the Guard at the Southern Woods. We will all meet here tomorrow at sunrise. This meeting is now adjourned."

20 Stratagem

Although adjourned, the assembly was still abuzz. Rebecca suspected it had been generations since anything this compelling had come before the Council of Elders. Every member had questions, concerns, considerations, congratulations, and opinions to offer to Stefani, Rebecca, and Quinn. However, nobody spoke to Wisdom or Songbird or dared to go near Tempest. Finally, Princess Stefani gathered her small company together and led them from the Council chambers more than an hour after the meeting had concluded.

Once outside, Stefani invited Rebecca, Quinn, and the animals to spend the night at her cottage. It was a short ride by horse and carriage to her home at the edge of the nearby woods. Wisdom and Songbird flew rather than ride in the carriage, and both chose to spend the night in the trees outside the cabin. Stefani used the large cottage less as a home and more as a place of business and study. She quickly moved pages of notes, books, maps, and various tools and equipment to make room for her guests, lit a small fire in the fireplace, and heated a pot of water for tea. After finally sitting down, Stefani asked what questions Rebecca and Quinn might have of her.

"How did you know so much information about me?" Rebecca was curious to know.

"Two days ago," Stefani began, "Songbird delivered an urgent letter to me from friends of yours and students of mine, a brother and sister named Leo and Luna. The letter detailed the circumstances and events of the previous few days. It expressed the concern for the safety of your friends and you in the custody of Alsaahir the Sorcerer. Much like you, Rebecca, I can communicate with spirit animals. You were born with innate abilities through the inheritance of magic to connect with animals. Unfortunately, you have been unaware of your abilities and have not developed them, while I had to study, practice, and learn over many years to develop communication skills with animals. While you appear to connect with all animals, my abilities are limited to spirit animals who carry the spirits of past human lives, such as Songbird, Wisdom, and Tempest. Through the contact with Songbird, I learned more about you and your connections to the sorcerer and my respected friend and associate, Takoda Nemasket. Over the next several days, I hope for us to explore and improve our skills in communicating with the animals."

"Well, how did you know about me?" Quinn asked. "I only met Rebecca today. I have no spiritual connections to the animals. And I've been living in the southern woods for almost five years."

Stefani laughed. "You may be surprised to know that it was Wisdom, the owl who came to me while you escorted Rebecca to the Council of Elders. He spoke highly of your careful consideration for her. As a result, I briefly researched your history before racing to the assembly. I learned that you were ready for a new assignment, and after watching you in the Council chambers, I felt assured that you would be a perfect addition to our party as my guardian and assistant. You are a much more gifted young woman than you yet know, Quinn! If you strive to learn all that I want to teach you, the day may come when you will be known as Princess Quinn, the Greatest of the Elves."

Quinn felt speechless. The recognition and support

Princess Stefani offered felt more than she could imagine.
She barely managed to speak the words, "Thank you, Princess
Stefani."

Stefani raised one hand. "First rule, Quinn," she stated,
"while it is respectful for you to call me Princess Stefani in
public forums, such as the Council of Elders, in private or
outside the Elfin community, please just call me Stefani."

Quinn nodded her head in a gesture of understanding
and agreement.

"We have a sunrise meeting and hectic days ahead,"
Stefani continued. "I would like the two of you and Tempest
to stay close to me. There will be times that I require your
views. And times when you need to watch, listen, and learn.
Also, if you see anyone or anything that appears suspicious
or out of place, let me know. We will have opportunities to
speak following our meetings and again at the end of each
day. If there are no urgent questions, I suggest we attempt to
get a good night's sleep."

Stefani showed them to their rooms. Tempest followed
along and immediately lay on the floor next to Rebecca's
bed. Quinn was given a large room with a big bed. When
Stefani informed her that would be her home for the next few
years, Quinn remarked that she was afraid to fall asleep. After
spending most of the past five years sleeping in the woods, she
feared she would awaken to discover this was only a dream!

It didn't take long for the house to go quiet and everybody
to fall asleep. As Rebecca's eyes closed, a familiar voice
spoke her name.

Hello, Becca," Nani greeted. Her essence filled the
darkness with light.

"Nani! I'm so happy to see you," Rebecca greeted.

"Rebecca," Nani began, "you now know I am the spirit within Songbird. With Stefani's help, you will be developing your ability to connect with me at ease. Therefore, this will be the final time I will come to you uninvited as you fall asleep. I remind you that I am only a thought away. If you need me, just close your eyes and call my name. As the nightingale, I can see you and hear your words. As you develop your abilities, you will be able to hear me as easily as you hear me now. Likewise, you will have the same connection with Tempest and Wisdom. You have also made valuable connections throughout the Mystic Land with people who will be coming together on your behalf. Stefani will be your teacher. Others will serve as your guardians, supporters, mentors, assistants, and loyal friends. They will risk their lives to stand by your side. Stand confidently by their sides in return. Awaken now to remember this message, then sleep well, my child. I will see you in the morning.

"Goodnight, Nani," Rebecca called out as her guardian angel faded into the darkness. Her eyes opened. She thought about the people she had met since coming into the Mystic Land. She felt concerned for Pixie's safety. Learning that Luna and Leo had sent the urgent message to Stefani was a surprise. How impressed she is with her father. She considered her fortunate in meeting the Verne family, her shared attraction with Jules, her bond with Jill, and the message Jasmine sent with Songbird. Rebecca grinned at the image of Windy getting a horse that was not the horse taken from her. It struck her that she was feeling more robust bonds with a dozen new friends here in barely one week than she felt about friends she had known her entire life. In her concern for her mother, stepfather, and brother, she wished there was a way to tell them she was okay. As Rebecca closed her eyes, she whispered to her mother, "I am safe in the Mystic Land."

As she drifted into the space between thoughts and dreams, her mother spoke to her, "Thank you for reaching out to me, Becca. Wisdom came to me a few days ago to tell me that you had safely passed through the mists. We miss you, love you, and await your safe return home."

Again, Rebecca's eyes snapped open. Was that real or just a dream? Now she knew where Wisdom had gone those few days ago. Wisdom was not helping someone else; he was still helping her. It suddenly dawned on her that her mother must have inherited the same magical powers that she is only now discovering. Why didn't her mother tell her about this? she wondered. Rebecca knew she would not get the answer to that question tonight. She had to let it go for now. Finally, she closed her eyes and drifted into a deep, restful sleep.

"Time to wake up, Rebecca," Stefani called to her. Once again, the morning seemed to come too quickly.

By the time Rebecca got dressed and made it to the kitchen, Stefani and Quinn were already seated at the table. Tempest was eating from a large bowl on the floor. Fruits, vegetables, loaves of bread, tea, and juices covered the table. Rebecca was immediately attracted to the scent of hot cinnamon-covered apples. "Yum, it's like apple pie for breakfast," she exclaimed.

While they ate, Stefani recounted their plans and responsibilities for the day. After breakfast, they cleaned the table and dishes, refreshed themselves, gathered their belongings, and left for the Council building. To signal their presence, Wisdom hooted, and Songbird whistled as they flew nearby.

Daylight appeared at the edges of the horizon as they arrived. A group of eight elves with horses greeted them by the door. Each elf, dressed in the green and brown guardian attire, carried a bow and quiver filled with arrows, a sword, and knives hung from their belts. They introduced themselves as the team who would be protecting Rebecca's friends at the Verne home. Stefani quickly invited them into the lobby area to inform them about the threat posed by the sorcerer and his trolls. Rebecca described each of her friends and showed the map that Jasmine had illustrated to help provide directions to their home. Once all of the instructions were clear, they swiftly departed, promising that they would arrive at the Verne home by mid-morning,

Quinn and Stefani then met with Quinn's team of Forest Guardians, who were excited to learn of Quinn's new assignment. They were sent back to their post at the southern woods with a letter to the captain of the guard explaining their circumstances and a list of suggestions for possible promotions to Quinn's position as Sergeant.

Members of the Council, administrators, and workers began appearing in the lobby. Some passed through to jobs and assignments, others grouped for meetings. Messengers had been dispatched to captains at posts throughout the Elfin lands the night before, warning them to be alert for any incursions by the Sorcerer's trolls and mutants. Some of those messengers were now returning with information for the council.

Few citizens had heard of the events from yesterday's meeting, but the presence of Princess Stefani and other dignitaries appearing at the government center sent murmurs of interest through the crowd that began gathering at the building. Stefani and her entourage quickly decided to move into the council chambers for further meetings. Rebecca was surprised to find Songbird and Wisdom already at the table where they had been seated the night before. Of course, Tempest stayed by Rebecca's side everywhere she went.

Multiple plans were made throughout the day. First, Rebecca provided details of the layout of the Sorcerer's fortress. She described the courtyard, entryway, placement of the rooms, stables, the hidden walkway around the interior of the building, dungeons, the secret doorway where she escaped, and placement of the troll guards. Next, she told of Alsaahir's office, his books of magic, powerful magic stone, and their locations.

A decision was made to depart the following morning, accompanied by a group of scouts, guards, warriors, and messengers. They determined there was too much risk in returning Rebecca to the Verne home. Instead, an assembly area would be formed where the East River meets the Borderland Hills in preparation for an attack against Alsaahir's fortress and army. They now had a plan for the people of the Mystic land to gain their freedom.

The Council sent messengers to leaders in the Native Village, Colonists Village, and the Gypsy Camps with information and updates. With the Colonists' Governor and his wife in mind, the Council issued warnings to prevent information leaks. In addition, messages were sent to the Verne's, Luna and Leo, and Takoda Nemasket to update them on Rebecca's circumstances.

Meetings that did not require the Princess's attendance allowed Stefani, Quinn, Rebecca, and their animal protectors to break for meals and personal discussions. Rebecca became fascinated by how Stefani included Songbird, Wisdom, and Tempest in the group conversations. Rebecca thought she understood a few responses from the animals, but Stefani translated the most necessary information for her and Quinn.

Returning to the assembly following a late dinner, Rebecca witnessed Stefani and Songbird staring into each other's eyes in what appeared to be a deep-thought conversation. Moments later, Stefani stood to call for the attention of the assembly.

"Ladies and gentlemen, dignitaries, Minister, and respected members of the Elfin Council of Elders," Stefani called out, "we have a request that our guest of honor, Rebecca Fields, sing us a song. Many of you have heard that Miss Fields has magic in her voice. It is suggested that we are provided a demonstration of her remarkable gift."

A voice called out from the middle of the room, "If it's anything like the magic of that cat, we can do without a demonstration."

Some in the room laughed. Others nodded their heads in agreement.

Stefani smiled broadly, "Rebecca's singing voice is embedded with fairy magic as we have only heard of in tales of our distant ancestors. So, Minister, would you permit us a few moments to enjoy the gift of our talented guest?"

The Minister nodded his head in agreement. "Miss Fields," he announced, "please come forward and honor us with the gift of your song."

This surprising request stunned Rebecca. Stefani had not indicated that she would invite her to sing. It suddenly occurred to her that Songbird presented this idea to Stefani in their mindful conversation. While she walked toward the front of the room, Rebecca turned and stuck out her tongue at Songbird. She thought she glimpsed the bird grinning back at her. Her grandmother's voice entered her mind, "Bring these Elves to tears," Nani encouraged. Make this one of the most moving and inspiring songs you've ever sung."

Rebecca paused before stepping to the front of the room. After considering for a moment, she began to sing,

I will climb every mountain to reach for that star
I will cross every ocean no matter how far
This is the quest I fight for you
To make the impossible possible
The dream we wish to come true
Through the light of day and the dark of night
I will fight for what's right
This I must bravely do
To make the impossible possible
The dream we wish to come true

For the freedom to dream
I am willing to fight
For the glorious cause
To stand up for what's right

And the world will know that I gave my all
To fight for our lives, our freedom, our rights
Through the light of day and the dark of night
I climbed that mountain to reach for that star
I crossed every ocean, no matter how far

To fight for what's right
It is what I must do
To make the impossible possible
The dream we wish to come true

Rebecca opened her eyes. Every person in the assembly sat in stunned silence. Some openly cried. After what felt like an eternity to Rebecca, Stefani stood and began to clap her hands. The Minister, Quinn, and others quickly followed. In seconds, the entire room of more than two hundred elves was out of their chairs. Rebecca received a standing ovation unlike any she could ever have imagined. She stood proudly, accepting the applause for several minutes. Inside, she wanted to place her face in her hands and cry tears of joy. Even while slowly walking back to her seat, the assembly applauded.

She heard Nani's voice tell her, "That was perfect, Rebecca."

Stefani reached out with open arms to hug Rebecca. Then, with a gentle kiss on her cheek, Stefani whispered, "My child, you are a precious gift."

As she rounded the table to stand by her chair, Rebecca saw Quinn's face covered in tears. "That was spectacular, Rebecca," Quinn managed to say. "I've never heard anything so moving in my life."

Finally, the room quieted. Members of the council began to settle into their seats.

The Minister rose to speak, "Thank you, Miss Rebecca Harmony Fields, for a magnificent performance which could never be described with mere words. He then announced that he would adjourn this day's meetings if there were no further necessities to discuss. Nobody spoke, so he requested that everyone gather again one hour after sunrise the following morning. He banged his gavel and called out, "Meeting adjourned."

Several elders approached Rebecca to express their appreciation for her musical talent and her moving song, but Stefani only allowed about fifteen minutes to pass before leading her group toward the doors. Once clear of the assembly, Stefani reminded them that they had another early morning ahead. They still needed to pack and prepare for traveling the next day, and she wanted them all to get a good night's sleep.

Rebecca laid in bed that night thinking about the meetings and events of the day. She thought about the days ahead. And especially the applause that still echoed in her ears. Perhaps, she thought, all the people who had ever told her she had a magnificent singing voice were telling her the truth.

Rebecca closed her eyes. For the first time since leaving home, Nani did not speak with her as she fell asleep. Nevertheless, the night did not pass without a dire warning.

21 The Quest

"Wake up, Rebecca."

"It can't be morning already," Rebecca muttered to whoever was within the sound of her voice. She forced her eyes open, then quickly sat up in bed when she realized Princess Stefani and Quinn were both looking at her. Even Tempest was staring at her from the foot of the bed. "What? What's wrong?" she asked.

"You're right; it is still more than an hour before sunrise," Stefani confirmed. "I received a message from Songbird. A company of the Sorcerer's trolls has been spotted along the edge of the Elfin Woods. We believe that they are searching for you. Our guardians have been ordered not to confront them unless they enter the woods. The Minister, his advisors, and the Captains of the Elfin Guard were notified. They are meeting in the Council building at daylight. We should be there too. Wisdom has left to observe the trolls, while Songbird maintains watch outside for us. Wake yourself up and get your pack ready to leave. I will prepare a light breakfast."

There was little conversation while they ate and packed their bags. It was still dark when Stefani, Quinn, Rebecca, and Tempest left Stefani's cottage. Songbird whistled a few musical notes from the low branch of a nearby tree to let them know she was there. Moments later, Wisdom flew into the yard directly in front of them. Stefani and the owl appeared to hold a silent discussion for the next few minutes. Afterward, Wisdom flew ahead into the trees.

"As reported, the trolls are patrolling along the outer edges of the Elfin Woods," Stefani whispered. "No trolls have been seen here or in the Elfin Woods, but to be safe, let's remain quiet until we get inside the government center."

As they neared the Council of Elders, Rebecca was surprised to see a company of uniformed elves with saddled horses milling about outside the front doors. Stefani, Quinn, Rebecca, and Tempest moved swiftly to the assembly room, where approximately twenty dignitaries and government officials engaged in vibrant discussions. As soon as the four entered the room, the chatter quieted.

Andor, the Captain of the Guard, immediately announced, "Ladies and Gentlemen, our honored guests have arrived."

"Let us begin," proclaimed the Minister. "During the night, at least one company of the Sorcerer's trolls was discovered patrolling along the southern edges of the Elvin Woods. They are still south of the Glades, and none have entered our forest. Therefore, we decided not to confront them unless they encroached on our territory. Nevertheless, our guardians are watching them closely. As a result, we will hasten our guests' departure and increase the size of the team escorting them to fourteen. While Princess Stefani is in charge of this operation, Captain Nisse will oversee the Elfin Guard and be responsible for all communications and messengers.

"For safety's sake, the team will travel inside the Elfin Woods to the northern point of exit, then skirt the edge of the mist and through the Borderland Hills to the assembly area at the northern point of the East River. Over the next few days, Elfin forces will man staging points along the East River, within the Elfin Hills, and along the edges of the Elfin Woods. A force from the Native Villages will soon be joining our warriors at the assembly area. In addition, Colonists and Gypsy volunteer forces will gather in the wooded areas along the West River, north of Mystic Lake. If weather and operations proceed as planned, we will move to attack the Troll Camps and The Sorcerer's Fortress at dusk, five days from today. Further details will come. Although our activities will raise interests within the Elfin community, this plan must remain secretive for security purposes until we of the Council permit it to be shared. Are there any questions?"

A few questions and concerns were raised and quickly answered. Next, Captain Nisse introduced himself to Rebecca and Quinn. Stefani and the Captain already had familiarity with each other. Then they moved outdoors for introductions to members of the Guard escorting them on this trek. Finally, Captain Nisse gave instructions to his company. The scouts and trackers immediately mounted their horses and headed down the main road through the village. The remainder of the company began gathering and walking their horses.

Captain Nisse informed Stefani, Rebecca, and Quinn that horses were also provided for them. And although the soldiers will walk their horses through the village, the women could choose to ride if they preferred. All three women firmly responded that they would walk as far and as long as the rest of the company walked.

Tempest kept close to Rebecca, purposefully staying away from the horses' hooves. Since Captain Nisse said nothing about the cat, Rebecca assumed he had been warned about her protective abilities.

Daylight barely began to appear in the sky behind them. Most buildings were still dark, and the company passed only a few people on the road leading through the Elfin Village. Except for the sound of the horses, the company remained quiet. In this morning silence, Rebecca contemplated everything that was happening. Although perceived as a central figure in an attack against her great-grandfather, she had no clue what was expected of her. She had no military experience, and her magic could not compare to that of Alsaahir. The sorcerer appeared unbeatable with his magic books, the mysterious, powerful rock, an army of trolls and mutants, and his massive fortress. She remembered Alsaahir's warning, "Nobody in this land is big enough or strong enough to overpower me." Just thinking about challenging him made her feel uneasy.

Princess Stefani suddenly appeared at Rebecca's side in what felt like a sense of clairvoyance.

"Have no fear, Rebecca," Stefani spoke in a calm, assuring manner. Your presence has awakened the elves to the possibility of freedom from the Mystic Land. However, nothing is expected of you that is beyond your abilities. As the leader of this expedition, I promise to stay by your side, to help guide and protect you. Over the next five days, we will have significant time to discover some of your unique skills.

They reached the gate at the edge of the village. Everybody mounted horses, except for Tempest, who clearly preferred to remain on her own four feet. The company headed north along a twisting path among the massive trees. Rebecca and Stefani continued their conversation where the trail was wide enough for two horses to ride side by side.

"Stefani," Rebecca inquired, "tell me about the elves. Outside of the Mystic Land, elves are considered characters in stories and fables. So how are you here?"

Stefani smiled. "Elves have been on the Earth for hundreds of thousands of years. But, while many human races battled for supremacy, the elves withdrew into hiding and self-reliance in the deep forests. We found like-mindedness with the natives throughout the North and South American continents before the Europeans arrived. Despite our warnings, the natives decided to share the land with the Europeans. However, out of selfishness and greed, it did not take long for the Europeans to wage war against the natives. Many elves argue that we should have fought as allies with the natives to defend their lands. But most elves recognize that the Europeans would have destroyed us with the natives. Our arrows and swords could not compete with their guns, rifles, and cannons. As it was, the elves were driven from many of our forests when the Europeans developed their cities and towns."

"I understand that your great-grandfather was one of the first to come here," Stefani continued. "However, he impressed the natives with his magic, and they happily gave him this spacious land. When the Colonists arrived and began to wage war against the natives. Alsaahir closed off his property with his magic. He did not know then that a colony of elves lived in the nearby woods. We became trapped within his mists, much as the ancestors of those you have come to know."

"I was told there is no way to forge steel or metals in the Mystic Land. So how do the elves have so many swords?" Rebecca asked.

"Elves have had swords for nearly five thousand years," Stefani explained. "While we have always strived to live in peace, we also knew that we must be able to defend ourselves. As children, we grow up learning to use swords and shoot arrows with bows. Our swords were here before the Mystic Land was closed to the rest of the world. The greatest conflict for the elves in this battle is whether we are being an aggressor or a defender. With your arrival, we decided now is the opportune time to earn our freedom."

"But I'm just a seventeen-year-old girl," Rebecca began to protest. "How am I supposed to make a difference in a battle against a powerful sorcerer?"

"That is what we will discover during the next few days, Rebecca," Stefani assured her. "That is why I am here. But, for now, let's enjoy the ride through the Elfin Woods. If you look closely, you will see sights I doubt you will ever see anywhere else."

Stefani was right about that! Rebecca saw beautifully designed cottages nestled high in the redwoods. Whole gardens tucked into the crevices at the base of the trees. Giant colorful mushrooms grew among the pine needles and brilliant flowers spread into the branches. Stunning butterflies, some nearly as big as her, fluttered among flowers. Fireflies sparkled in the shadows with flickers of light. They passed a rainbow-covered waterfall, which fed into a flowing stream that wove through the woods. The beauty and fresh scents of nature filled Becca's senses. She knew that she would never forget these stunning woods.

By mid-morning, the company reached the northern edge of the Elfin Woods. Still hidden within the shadows of the trees, they dismounted from their horses for a rest. Several scouts and messengers reported to Captain Nisse. The captain told Princess Stefani that no trolls had been spotted this far north. Wisdom appeared to confirm that the Trolls were still along the southern area of the Elfin Woods bordering the Elfland Hills. Songbird returned from scouting the trail into the Borderland Hills with similar assurances that their path ahead was clear. Less than an hour later, the company remounted their horses.

Breaking from the cover of the forest into the glaring sunlight, Rebecca was astonished to discover they were barely a hundred yards from the edges of the mists. She had not seen the wall of thick fog since the day she had arrived in the Mystic Land. She found herself uncomfortably watching for goblins to appear. Fortunately, they did not.

The company traveled for less than thirty minutes before turning west into a valley bordered by low hills covered with tall grass, colorful flowers, and a scattering of trees. They came upon an extremely surprised Elfin couple who said they were returning from the Trader Market. The couple excitedly exclaimed that meeting Princess Stefani and an Elfin military escort is not something that happens every day! They encountered no other travelers; and passed no homes until they reached a spacious ranch with four huge barns, fenced corrals with horses, cows, goats, sheep, pigs, chickens, and various animals. The main ranch house was as big as any of the four barns. In addition, several small cabins were visible around the grounds. At least two dozen workers moved about the property, feeding and tending to the animals, building and repairing structures, and moving supplies. A few people looked up from their work, but nobody appeared surprised to see the approaching company.

As Rebecca and her companions drew close to the ranch, a young man and woman appeared from the main building, waving and running toward them. It took a few moments for Rebecca to realize it was her friends, Luna and Leo. She eagerly dismounted from her horse to greet the brother and sister. The three friends excitedly talked over each other for a few minutes while they hugged and sang their greetings. Rebecca started to make introductions, although it turned out that the siblings already had familiarity with Stefani, Captain Nisse, and almost everybody except Quinn and a few of the younger elfin guards. Ranch workers and elfin guards led the horses to a stable for feeding and cleaning, while Luna and Leo led the rest of the company to the ranch house to meet their parents. Over refreshments, they began to discuss their plans and arrangements.

Unbeknownst to Rebecca until now, this ranch was the planned staging area for the forces to gather.

Several hundred volunteers were expected to arrive over the next five days. Details first needed to be arranged for food, sleeping, washing, outhouses, animals, and medical care. Throughout the afternoon, rules, regulations, leadership, organization, responsibilities, cautions, and concerns were all subjects of discussion and planning. The team decided to delay military planning for one day until leaders from the other villages arrived.

By early evening, scouts delivered reports and messages from leaders of the Gypsy, Elfin, Colonists, and Native Villages. Wagons with food, tools, building materials, supplies, and people began to appear. Captain Nisse had created planning maps of the area and set up a chain of command to provide directions and maintain order. Tents went up in specified sections of the surrounding fields.

Rebecca felt astonished by the organization and attention to detail, but concern for the dangers they faced and the speed at which everything was happening left her uneasy. She was the primary reason a war was brewing against her great-grandfather, yet she had no control over that decision. It felt like a tornado was spinning around her, and she had nothing to grab ahold of. She glanced at Tempest, who sat nearby licking her front paws. Well, I have a cat to hold on to, Rebecca thought, and she did not appear very concerned.

Rebecca closed her eyes and concentrated her thoughts on the cat, "Thank you for being here by my side, Tempest. You are my rock in this craziness."

"There is no place I would rather be," the voice spoke to

Rebecca. She opened her eyes to discover that Tempest was sitting directly in front of her. The cat stared into her eyes. "We are in this together," she heard Tempest speak.

Rebecca looked around the room. Nobody else appeared to be looking in her direction. Although Princess Stefani was in a discussion over maps on the table, she briefly glanced at Rebecca with a knowing smile. For that moment, the teenager's uneasiness fell away. She reached out to pet the cat. "I'm not alone," she thought.

Rebecca, Stefani, and Quinn were each provided individual bedrooms in the ranch house. Captain Nisse was invited to sleep inside, although he chose to stay with his troops. Guards were posted around the outside of the home and the outer perimeter of the property.

Voices and activities could be heard throughout the night. Still, Rebecca felt awed in the morning to see a few hundred people on the property who had not been there the previous evening. Men with horse-drawn wagons, carriages, and carts were delivering supplies. Tents and outbuildings of all shapes and sizes were being built. The scents of campfires and foods wafted through the air.

Despite the enormity of it all, Captain Nisse appeared to be at the center of everything, directing his lieutenants with a clear vision of his objectives. The lieutenants, in turn, led the activities. The implementation of their plans was impressive.

Luna, Leo, and their father held the enormous responsibility of caring for the horses and assorted animals that came and went at the ranch. Their mother took care of the ranch house, including cooking, cleaning, and overseeing the hospitality for their guests. The large home became more like an inn for the leaders and dignitaries arriving at the ranch. Of course, the family had workers and volunteers assisting them in those responsibilities, but it was still a whirlwind of activity for everybody involved.

Stefani directed Rebecca and Quinn to stay close to her, although they were often given tasks that separated them from the Princess. Quinn and a few Elfin guards trained Rebecca with bow and arrows, swords, knives, self-defense, and fighting fundamentals. It didn't take long for her muscles to ache, but she enjoyed the physical and mental aspects of the training. Luna and Leo gave her horse riding lessons. Stefani spent a couple of hours each day working with Rebecca and her animal guides to improve their communications. Stefani stressed that Rebecca strengthened her natural magical abilities, as they could provide valuable tools to defend against the Sorcerer's magic.

By the end of their second day at the ranch, Rebecca enjoyed entire conversations with Tempest, Songbird, and Wisdom. She also noticed a greater connection with other animals as well, especially the horses. Between lessons, Rebecca practiced her singing. Animals watched her intently. Birds seemed to flock to her. Ducks, geese, chickens, and small animals followed her. She began to feel like a Pied Piper! Most importantly, her self-confidence multiplied.

Rebecca's third day at the ranch began much like the first two days with meetings, lessons, training, and practice, but surprises were coming her way this day. She was helping Luna and Leo wash and feed the horses following riding lessons when a familiar voice spoke her name. She turned to find her father, Takoda Nemasket, standing only a few yards behind her. With nary a thought, she rushed to hug him, forgetting she was soaked in sweat, dirt, water, and the scent of the horses. But, of course, he never complained. Their embrace was all that mattered at that moment. Luna and Leo also fondly greeted their highly-admired mentor. They led him to the ranch house for greetings, meetings, and lunch. Takoda was assigned to head a medical group comprised of medical and surgical professionals from the Native and Elfin villages. And he was invited to sleep in the ranch house to ensure that he and Rebecca would have opportunities to spend time together over the coming days.

That evening, Rebecca, Luna, Leo, Quinn, and Tempest sat under a large willow tree at the top of a hill overlooking the ranch. They watched the collection of people move about the property below while lanterns and campfires sparked to life in the evening's first shadows. When the silhouette of a gypsy wagon entered the long roadway to the ranch, Rebecca didn't have to squint her eyes very hard to recognize Aaron sitting on the driver's seat behind his two workhorses. Without a word to her companions, she excitedly jumped up and ran down the hill to greet the big, warm-hearted man. With Tempest keeping pace at her side, she reached the wagon as it came to a stop by one of the large barns.

"Aaron, Aaron," Rebecca called out. She thought she would surprise him with her presence at the ranch, but the surprise was on her. The back door to the wagon sprung open. Jasmine stepped to the ground, followed by Jill, Windy, and Jules. The emotion so overwhelmed Rebecca that she dropped to her knees with her hands held over her eyes while crying tears of joy.

Luna, Leo, and Quinn quickly joined Rebecca and the group of friends. Quinn was the only person needing introductions. Once Rebecca told the story of meeting Quinn, it did not take long for the friends to cheerfully welcome Quinn into the fellowship.

While Leo and Jules took care of the horses and wagon, the friends moved to the ranch house to meet and greet Stefani, Takoda, Captain Nisse, Luna and Leo's parents, and several other guests whom Rebecca barely knew. The house was getting crowded, although nobody complained. Three and four people slept in each room. Even though the reason for the gathering was to battle the sorcerer and his army, a spirit of excitement filled the air. Everybody wondered what it would be like to be free of the Mystic Land, and Rebecca was the key to answering that question.

Aaron reported that the Elfin guards had arrived at their home a few days before. Since the horse was delivered to Windy, no trolls or mutants had been seen. But, in case they were being watched by the Sorcerer's scouts, the family traveled their usual route to the trader market that morning. Then, instead of returning home that afternoon, they traveled southeast into the borderland hills to arrive at the ranch before nightfall. No trolls or mutants were observed along the route.

Aaron also confirmed that a company of Elfin warriors is working with the Colonists and Gypsy volunteers in preparing for the attack on the western side of Mystic Lake. So far, everything appeared to be progressing as planned.

That evening, under a moonlit sky with shining stars peeking out from behind scattered clouds, Jules and Rebecca finally snuck away for some alone time. He told her how much he had worried for her safety. She told him how much she had missed him. Then, hand in hand, they strolled to the same tree on the hill where Rebecca had earlier sat with her friends. For the first time, they expressed affection for each other without interruption or doubts about the other's sincerity. In this most unusual time and place, Rebecca discovered that magic did not have to involve mists or monsters, wizards with mystical books, or powerful rocks. This is the magical moment she would most dearly hold in her memories no matter what the future brought. The only disappointment was that the evening had to end much too quickly.

The fourth day brought overcast skies, drizzle, and scattered showers, but the spirit at the ranch remained high. Rebecca and her friends enthusiastically took to their training, tasks, and preparations. Much of the day passed in a blur for Rebecca, whose thoughts continually strayed to her previous evening with Jules. She wondered if her glow was noticeable, although nobody mentioned it. But, of course, there were more critical responsibilities for everybody to focus on than Rebecca's glowing love interest!

More people, horses, and supplies continued to arrive at the ranch throughout the day. Windy was incredibly excited and proud to see several family members arrive. They brought Windy's horse with them, which she could hardly wait to show Rebecca.

That evening, Princess Stefani and Captain Nisse led a full briefing that included more than one hundred leaders, planners, and dignitaries. Rebecca felt astounded when details of the Sorcerer's fortress, which she had provided several days before at the Elfin Council, became a significant part of the attack plans. Questions asked were thoroughly discussed and answered. By the end of the briefing, everybody knew their responsibilities. Captain Nisse sent messengers to the western camp with detailed plans. The following day would involve movements and preparations for an attack that would begin at dusk.

22 Sorcerer's War

Rebecca didn't sleep much that night. She wondered if anybody did. Going into a battle was not something she could ever have imagined doing. Never mind that she would serve as a leader in a war against her five-hundred-year-old great grandfather, a sorcerer with unimaginable magical powers. How did I get myself into this crazy mess? The only rational consolation is that she would be helping to free the people from their entrapment in the Mystic Land. Still, she feared how many could die for the others to be free. It was a burden she was unsure that she could bear.

She shared her room this night with Jill, Windy, Luna, and of course, Tempest. Although daylight was beginning to seep through the window curtains, nobody had yet stirred. Perhaps, Rebecca thought, they too are all laying there in thought while waiting for someone else to make the first move. Sure enough, everybody jumped at once when a knock came on the bedroom door.

Princess Stefani entered the room with Quinn following closely behind. In her direct and reassuring manner, she calmly asked if anyone had any questions before she spoke. Everyone just shook their head, no. She again explained the sequence of events about to unfold that day. "Most of the camp will move into the Elfland Hills during the day. Many people and supplies have already moved overnight. The first wave of fighters will cross over the eastern and western walls at dusk to attack the Troll Camps. A second, larger wave on horseback will attack the Sorcerer's Fortress. Finally, the third force, including Rebecca, Tempest, their friends, and a company of Elfin warriors, will be led by Stefani to the fortress to retrieve the Sorcerer's rock and books of magic. With luck, those sources of magic will be the key to dropping the mists and freeing the people of the Mystic Land. Any of this fellowship of friends are welcome to join us." Stefani emphasized, "We do not know what hazards or traps we might encounter. It could be perilous. So, let's agree now, anyone who chooses not to join us in battle will never be criticized for your decision."

.

None of the young women in the room flinched in their promises to stand together in this endeavor. Again, Stefani asked if there were any questions. Again, nobody asked questions. "Let's get on with our day then," Stefani called out encouragingly. She turned and left the room with Quinn following close behind.

The room was quiet for a few moments before Rebecca spoke up. "No matter what happens tonight, I am eternally grateful for your friendship and the support of each of you. I could never imagine such...."

"Oh, don't get mushy on us," Jill interrupted. "We might change our minds, so we don't have to listen to your blubbering!"

Everybody in the room broke out laughing. It was precisely the mood change they needed. Laughter and conversation swirled as the girls began preparing for their day.

They met with Jules, Leo, Jasmine, Aaron, and Takoda in the dining room for breakfast a short while later. The entire group of friends, including Stefani and Quinn, were to travel together with an Elfin company of guards to the meetup point in the Elfin Hills. Only Leo and Luna's parents stayed behind with their ranch hands and some medical personnel to tend to the ranch.

Takoda, Aaron, Jasmine, and Jill rode with Rebecca and Tempest in Leo and Luna's covered supply wagon. Others rode individual horses. Wisdom and Songbird flew nearby. They crossed the East River at the northern bridge, just south of the Borderland Hills, then skirted the river for a short distance before turning south through the center of the Elfin Glades. The glades consisted of farms and grassy meadows separated by thick canopies of trees. Takoda explained that many foods are grown in the Elfin Glades. The path through the Glades twisted and turned between patches of trees, which made a perfect cover for the movements of the immense force of people, horses, and wagons.

By late afternoon the forces were settling into the valleys within the Elfland Hills. Because the plan was for a surprise attack, everybody remained quiet. There was no cooking and no campfires. They kept horses further back to help keep sounds to a minimum. Everybody held a watchful eye toward the sun as it slowly inched to the horizon.

Finally, as the last specs of sunlight faded into night, the first row of warriors and volunteers quietly moved over the lower hills to line up at the wall. Under a nearly full moon and clear night sky, hand signals were given for the men to move forward. From Rebecca's position behind the row of hills, she expected to hear yells of men charging into battle, yet the warriors remained eerily quiet.

The cavalry quickly brought their horses forward as soon as the first line of men moved over the wall to attack the troll camps. Within minutes, more than two hundred horses and riders charged through the opening in the wall, each focused on attacking the Sorcerer's Fortress. Still, only the sounds of the horses' hooves could be heard racing into the distance.

Finally, Stefani and her company of forty Elfin warriors with Rebecca and her friends mounted their horses. Their assignment was not to charge into battle but to quickly and cautiously make their way to the fortress. Still, armed with swords, knives, bows, and quivers filled with arrows, they were prepared for any encounters.

Under the moonlight, they steadily moved over the low hill toward the opening in the wall. The silence felt unnerving. A movement overhead caught Rebecca's attention. A large owl flew past their company into the night. She could always depend on Wisdom, she thought. Looking about, she discovered Songbird circling above. A massive white tiger suddenly appeared beside Rebecca and her horse. Rebecca glanced at the faces of her friends. Most of those faces displayed intensity and focus, but none showed any sense of fear.

One face looked back at her. Jules smiled and silently mouthed the words, "I love you."

Rebecca grinned and mouthed "I love you" in return. A renewed sense of strength and purpose washed over the young woman. I am surrounded by people and animals who care about me, she thought. They were all there to protect her in a quest to free them from generations of captivity. With these fearless friends by her side, she knew she should be the least afraid.

Princess Stefani signaled the company to move forward. Several warriors led the way through the opening in the wall. Rebecca's friends followed the leaders, each paired with an Elfin warrior. Rebecca followed Stefani and Quinn with a warrior on her left and her white tiger on her right. Aaron and an Elfin warrior followed immediately behind them. Another company of Elfin guards followed at the end of the procession.

As soon as they passed through the open gateway, the moonlight suddenly disappeared into darkness. Barely fifty yards later, a heavy cloud of fog enveloped them. The company slowed in an attempt to stay together. However, the deeper they proceeded into the mist, the thicker it became. The riders struggled to see other riders directly ahead of them. To their sides, fighters who had led the first lines of battle laid upon the trampled ground, many with their horses lying beside them. The company zigged and zagged to keep from crushing the fallen warriors.

Suddenly, glowing red, green, and blue mists rose from the ground in swirling motions. A few of the horses stopped abruptly; others stumbled into each other. Rebecca saw a few people fall, although she could not distinguish who was in the confusing mess. A feeling of dizziness washed over her. Desperately fighting to stay atop her mount, she grasped her horse's mane with one hand and the reins with the other. She saw Windy laid across the back of her horse, desperately wrapping her arms around its neck while the animal bucked and spun in circles. Stefani's horse stumbled and fell; the princess rolled to the ground beside it. Bodies of people and horses littered the field. In the darkness and swirling mist, all sense of direction seemed lost.

A deafening roar and a row of fire unexpectedly flashed up directly in front of them. The sudden bright light felt blinding. Then, behind the flames appeared an immense, angry, snake-like green and red face with blood-red eyes, followed by a long thick, scaly neck. Broad bat-like wings spread across the entire width of the field, lifting a massive blackened body covered with patches of burnt hair, pieces of feathers, and deep dark scars. Short arms and thick legs carrying enormous heavy claws with long pointed talons swatted at the flames as the fierce animal passed over the wall of fire. Its long rat-like tail passed through the fire without a grimace.

Screams echoed across the field. Rebecca gasped. She recognized this terrifying rat-bat creature from Alsaahir's atrium in his fortress, magically brought to life and transformed into this monstrous dragon.

In a flash, the immense dragon vaulted over the burning fires and plunged itself upon them. Flames tore from the dragon's jaws. It knocked riders from their mounts. Horses toppled to the ground. Rebecca valiantly held her sword above her head as the ferocious predator passed overhead. She could feel the surge of wind and the pressure through her entire body as the beast's claws grazed the tip of her sword. The mist swirled more violently. Her dizziness increased. The yells of warriors clouded her hearing.

Her horse stopped moving forward. Rebecca could feel it stumbling. She turned to see the dragon circling back. This time, she knew it was coming for her. What to do? Indecisiveness raced through her dizzying mind. Should she stay atop her steed or dismount to face the attacker? As the powerful enraged beast drew closer, its hot, flaming breath, razor-sharp fangs, and claws with long sharp talons filled her vision. Again, Rebecca bravely raised her sword, but to no avail. The blade twisted from her grip as hardened claws wrapped around her body. The beast effortlessly lifted her from her stallion while knocking the horse helplessly to the ground. Her last thought was, "This is how I'm going to die."

23 Dark World

Rebecca's eyes opened. Or did they? Is it pitch black, she wondered, or am I blind? Her head and body ached, and her mouth was dry as dust. She must be alive. If she is alive, where is she?

In a face-down position, she began to move her hands and arms. First, she made sure her body had no critical injuries. She could feel bruises from the dragon's claws but no severe wounds. Then felt the ground around her. I'm on a hard rock floor, she thought. Cautiously, she reached out one hand, touching a wall only a few inches beyond her head. Slowly she lifted her head and upper body from the floor. Then moved to sit her body against the rock wall. There she sat, trying to gain some semblance of order, recognition, and understanding in the blackness.

Long minutes passed before Rebecca began to remember details of the battle, watching several friends fall to the ground within the thick rolling fog. The dragon, monster, creature, or whatever came for her. She remembered. So how did she end up in this black room, she wondered. Where is the monster now? Could it be watching her? And why is she alive? Could the beast be saving her for a meal? Her thoughts froze her from moving.

After at least an hour of sitting in the blackness and not hearing a sound, Rebecca realized she needed to move. She crawled onto her knees and followed the wall to her right only a few feet before reaching a corner. Crawling along that wall for about ten feet, she came to a second corner. That wall she followed for only three feet before touching a metal wall or perhaps a door. Yes, a steel door. She could feel a space of about two inches beneath the door, although no light came from whatever was on its opposite side.

Fearing what might be waiting for her to awaken, she did not dare call out. Instead, she felt along the bottom edge of the door until her hand bumped into a pie-shaped dish. Her fingers brushed something wet in the pan. Guessing a pan with water might have been slid under the door, she touched her fingers to her lips. Yes, water. Rebecca cautiously sipped a small amount, then continued to follow the wall another few feet until she came to the fourth wall.

It was now apparent that she was in a small room that measured approximately ten square feet. She crawled along the fourth wall until her hand dropped into a hole in the floor, probably no larger than eight inches in diameter. It took only a moment to realize this hole was her toilet, and she was in a prison cell.

Rebecca moved back to her previous spot along the back wall, facing the steel door she now knew was there but could not see. She remembered the prison cells in the corridor below Alsaahir's fortress. She now assumed that's where she was. If so, how did she get there? Alsaahir is not strong enough to carry her. And how long was she unconscious? Hours? Days?

Several long hours passed before a dim light appeared under the door. The sound of footsteps approached. A key fumbled in the lock, and the heavy metal door slowly creaked open. Although the light was not bright, Rebecca had to cover her eyes until they could adjust. The thought crossed her mind that at least she now knows she's not blind.

Alsaahir stood in the doorway. An extremely large troll stood a few steps behind him. Rebecca now knew where she was and who had most likely carried her to this prison cell.

She did not have to be told.

"You disappoint me, Granddaughter," Alsaahir began. "I give you the comforts of my home, and you can't express a word of gratitude. I offer you my kingdom, and you create a rebellion against me."

"Are my friends all dead?" Rebecca blurted out.

"Every one of your friends is alive," Alsaahir responded sarcastically. "Some may have injuries from their falls from horses, but I assure you, my defensive actions killed none. I spared their lives just as I am doing with you. My mists merely put them to sleep. Like you, they are waking up today with body aches, headaches, and a sense of confusion. The only difference is that my precious bird brought you here while they stagger off their battlefield, unaware that you are not among them."

Rebecca dared not raise her voice against the angry sorcerer. Calmly she asked, "What do you want of me, Grandfather?"

Alsaahir quickly responded, "I want to give you one more opportunity to consider my offer. Will you willingly accept the opportunity to be my apprentice? Or will you choose to spend the rest of your life in this wretched dungeon?"

"I want to go home, Grandfather," Rebecca cried. "Why won't you let me go home?"

"You started a war against me!" Alsaahir raised his voice in anger. "How can I trust you? I warned you several times that nothing in this land is big enough or powerful enough to defeat me. Now you have forced me to prove it to you."

"I did not start the rebellion, Grandfather. The people here want their freedom. They want to live full lives and see the rest of the world. They are trapped here only because they were born here. They thought I might be able to help them because of my relationship with you." Rebecca paused before continuing, "Now I see how I got caught up in it. We approached the situation the wrong way. We should have come to you to discuss their problems."

"Their problems?" Alsaahir yelled. "Their problem is that they do not appreciate all I have done for them. They know nothing of the outside world. I protect them from the chaos and the dangers of the outside world. Governments send their people to die in wars, pollution poisons foods, air, and waters, there are diseases with no cures, billions suffer the selfishness and greed of a wealthy few, millions live in poverty, and the ignorant spread of hate simply because some people have different colored skin or their God has a different name than the God they idolize. It's a tragedy. My people are not prepared to survive in that world. They would not have a chance out there."

Rebecca sat quietly. Perhaps Alsaahir was right; they are not prepared for the outside world. But whose fault is that? She wanted to argue for human rights and freedom of choice. But an argument with the sorcerer would not help her escape this prison cell. "You have brought up valid points, Grandfather," she acknowledged. Although there is much good in the world too."

After a moment of silence, Alsaahir calmly continued. "Rebecca, I admit that my knowledge of the world outside the mists comes only from people who come here through the mists, such as yourself and your mother's friend, Violet. Perhaps you are the person who can teach them how to survive out there. I'm giving you one more chance to reconsider my offer. The best thing you could do is to learn about my magic and help to prepare my people for the outside world. I'll give you a day or two to decide. I have a plate of food and fresh water for you." He turned to the giant troll, who handed him a covered plate and a pitcher. Alsaahir placed the dish on the floor and poured water into the pan by the door.

Alsaahir started to turn away before stopping and turning back. "By the way," he said, "don't expect your friend, Pixie, to rescue you. She betrayed me. She's now a ferret living in the stables." He backed out of the door, slammed it shut, and locked it behind him.

Rebecca sat in stunned silence. Tears welled in her eyes, but she refused to cry. Although it was a small consolation, the light in the hallway stayed lit. At least dim light filtering under the doorway was better than absolute darkness. She crawled to the dishes of food and water. Not knowing how long it might be before she might see food again, she ate sparingly. She then sat back against the wall and closed her eyes.

"Rebecca. Rebecca, can you hear me?"

"Nani!" Rebecca anxiously replied. "Yes, I hear you. Are you okay? Is everybody okay?"

"I am fine, My Child. We are all okay," Nani spoke in a calming voice. "Everyone on the battlefield was put to sleep by the Sorcerer's mists, including the animals. Everybody woke up with foggy minds, scrapes, and bruises, but nobody was seriously injured. I am sorry that Wisdom and I did not see it soon enough to warn you. It took us a while to discover that you were not on the field with us. Where are you, Rebecca?" Are you okay? Have you been harmed?"

"I seem to be unharmed, Nani. But I'm being held captive in a dungeon under Alsaahir's fortress. He says he's giving me one more chance to choose to become his apprentice, but I fear that it might be a long time before he lets me out of here."

"Can you give me any more information about your location?" Nani asked.

"I think it's under the southeastern corner of his fortress," Rebecca answered. "When I escaped from the fortress last week, I passed a row of prison cells in a hallway. So, I'm probably in that same place. There is a solid wooden door hidden in a pine grove on the south side of the moat. It leads down into the dungeon, but the door is bolted on the inside by a heavy steel bar."

"Stay calm, Rebecca. We are coming," Nani assured her. "I think that is enough information for us to find you."

"Thank you, Nani." Rebecca fell into a restless sleep. She would awaken, then fall asleep again. There was no way of measuring the passage of time. She did not know if it was day or night or if she had been there for hours or days. She occasionally ate bites of food and drank sips of water until the plates emptied. Time passed, and Alsaahir did not return to fill them.

The only comfort Rebecca could find was in her dreams. Her waking time felt never-ending. During one of those waking times, a small white mouse crawled through the space under the door.

"Hello, little mouse," Rebecca greeted. "Thank you for visiting with me. I've not had many visitors here. I would love to invite you for dinner, but I'm sorry to tell you that my cupboard is bare. You are welcome to any crumbs or sips of water you might find."

All of a sudden, the mouse began to transform. Rebecca gasped to see Tempest, the cat standing before her.

"Tempest! Oh, Tempest, I'm so happy to see you," she exclaimed. Rebecca reached out her arms in a gesture to embrace the cat. Incredibly, Tempest came to her, nuzzled against her, and began to purr. Rebecca thought it was the most affection Tempest had ever displayed. But, of course, it may have come when Tempest sensed that Rebecca most needed the companionship.

For the first time since awakening in the dungeon, Rebecca felt a sense of relief. Rebecca closed her eyes. The image of an Elfin woman with shoulder-length white hair and bright turquoise eyes stood before her.

"Do you recognize me?" the woman asked.

"Of course, Tempest," Rebecca answered. "I'm delighted to see you again in your human form. How are you?"

"I am sorry that I did not foresee the Sorcerer's mist on the field or find a way to warn you," Tempest replied. "By the time the dragon appeared, I was incapable of moving. Fortunately, nobody was fatally hurt. I am here to help you escape, although it seems that we must wait until Alsaahir returns to the cell. I suggest we not speak aloud so as not to give him any warnings."

"Thank you for coming to my rescue again, Tempest," Rebecca responded. "I owe you my life several times over."

Rebecca opened her eyes. While she and the cat sat quietly, Rebecca imagined how shocked Alsaahir would be to find a massive tiger in this prison cell. Then she realized that the sorcerer would probably sense the tiger's presence before opening the door. She remembered his warning, "Nothing in this land is big enough or powerful enough to defeat me." Alsaahir's Trolls had tranquilized Tempest once before. He might harm Tempest with his magic before the door is even opened.

The sound of footsteps echoing in the hallway jolted her upright. Tempest immediately became a mouse and scurried to a corner behind the door. Rebecca stopped watching the little mouse as the footsteps drew closer. A shadow appeared through the opening under the door. The footsteps stopped, and the sound of a key opening the lock vibrated through the small room. Rebecca squinted at the light and covered her eyes with her hands as the door creaked open. When she could open her eyes again, Alsaahir stood in the open doorway. A pitcher and a food dish sat on the floor by the far wall. This time no troll was with him.

"Have you had enough time to consider my offer?" Alsaahir bluntly asked.

"It seems I have little choice but to accept your offer, Grandfather," Rebecca responded sarcastically.

Alsaahir raised his voice. "That is not the attitude I want to hear from you. If you want to help the people in this land, I am the only person with the knowledge to guide you. If you want to live a long life, I am the only person with the power to teach you. Look at me," he yelled, "I can teach you how to be more powerful than anybody in this land. Don't you want that power, Rebecca?"

At that moment, a small white scorpion dropped from above the doorway onto Alsaahir's shoulder. In a flash, it bounced to the Sorcerer's collar and embedded its tail into his neck. The scorpion venom infused with Tempest's powerful magic entered the carotid artery in Alsaahir's neck, surging immediately to the Sorcerer's heart. He had no time to react. His body stiffened, then trembled. His eyes bulged as his legs gave way beneath him. Finally, he groaned, and a strange gurgling sound left his throat as his body dropped into a heap in the middle of the doorway.

Not until his body stopped seizing did the scorpion remove its stinger from Alsaahir's neck. Then it jumped to the floor, quickly returning to the form of the white cat.

Rebecca sat in shock. "Is he dead?" she managed to ask.

Tempest looked into Rebecca's eyes but did not respond with a sound or a gesture. Still, Rebecca knew the answer was obvious. After a moment, the cat turned and jumped over the still body into the hallway, then turned and looked back at Rebecca. Although still shaken, Rebecca stood up for the first time since she had awakened in the prison cell. Cautiously she stepped over the body of her great grandfather. The two started down the hallway toward the steps and the doorway leading out of the fortress. Before climbing the steps, Rebecca stopped and returned. She picked up the water pitcher from the floor, took a long drink, then hurriedly grabbed the food dish and began to eat while she ran to catch up with the waiting cat.

The heavy metal crossbar was still across the closed door. Putting the half-eaten food dish on the floor, Rebecca slid the heavy bar through the brackets and pushed the door open. Much like the last time she had opened that door with Pixie, she had to cover her eyes while they adjusted to the bright sunlight. Rebecca took a deep breath of the fresh air and followed Tempest into the daylight. Her eyes were still adjusting to the light when she glimpsed the shadows of silhouetted figures surrounding her. Trolls, she gasped and quickly stepped behind Tempest. Once again, she depended on her protector to defend her.

24 Necromancy

After several days in the dark fortress dungeon, the glaring sunlight was blinding. With her hands covering her eyes, Rebecca could only see the long shadows of bodies surrounding her and the cat standing on the ground in front of her. Her only hope was for Tempest to transform into the four-hundred-pound tiger. But Tempest did not change. Instead, the cat sat!

Rebecca felt dismayed. For a brief moment, she considered dashing back into the fortress. But, on second thought, she doubted that she could be quick enough to shut the heavy door behind her before the troll guards caught her.

Several voices began speaking simultaneously. Rebecca's sense of resignation turned to a sigh of relief when she realized the shadows were not of trolls but her friends. Princess Stefani was the first to reach her, followed by Quinn, Aaron, and Jill. Jules watched and waited patiently by a nearby tree before he finally took his turn to greet Rebecca. He lifted her from the ground in a passionate embrace with a kiss that left no doubts about how he felt. Several of the Elfin guards keeping watch cheered Rebecca from the edges of the pine grove. Everybody excitedly talked at the same time. It was a joyful moment of celebration.

Stefani informed Rebecca that nobody in their attack force had made it to the Sorcerer's fortress. The swirling mists put every human and animal to sleep. No trolls or mutants were encountered on the battlefield that night or the following day. There were no fatalities, although several people had lesser injuries by falls from horses, being trampled by horses, horses falling on them, or other accidental injuries. Within Rebecca's group of friends, Windy suffered a sprained arm, and Leo had a bruise on his head, but neither injury was severe.

Leo and Luna returned to their extensive duties assisting their father and his animal care team at the ranch. Likewise, Takoda and his team were quite busy helping the injured people. Jasmine is helping Leo and Luna's mother with cleaning, cooking, and hospitality at the ranch house.

Rebecca quickly related her story of being locked in the dungeon, Tempest's rescue, and the death of Alsaahir. The group expressed gratitude toward Tempest, but the modest cat turned and walked to the side of a tall tree, preferring to sit and lick her paws. Rebecca laughed. "Tempest has never been one to bask in glory or attention," she acknowledged.

Seconds later, Songbird and Wisdom flew into the clearing, joining Tempest at the tree. Stefani and Quinn immediately left the group to join the animals. After a few minutes, Stefani interrupted the celebration to inform the group that she and Rebecca must re-enter the fortress to collect the Sorcerer's books of magic and the mystical rock. She decided that Quinn, Tempest, and four Elfin guards would join them. Aaron, Jill, Jules, Wisdom, Songbird, and the other members of the Elfin guard were to remain behind until they returned. Stefanie warned that Wisdom and Songbird had seen a company of Trolls in the courtyard and atop the walls guarding the fortress. She requested they remain vigilant while making plans for a return to the ranch, reminding them that they could encounter any possible dangers on that journey.

The group of eight who would enter the fortress discussed their plans. Rebecca described the dark stairway they would take under the moat, the hallway through the dungeon, the location of Alsaahir's body, stairs, doors, and the massive warehouse-sized storage room they would pass through before reaching the living area. Finally, she recounted the building's interior, troll guard positions, and office location where the Sorcerer's magical rock and magic books were kept. She warned of the hidden hallway between the walls that led from the office to the stables and the unknown possibility that trolls, mutants, or other characters could be present within the fortress. They refreshed themselves with food and water, gathered their belongings, and shared supportive well-wishes with the friends who would remain behind. Stefani insisted that if they were not back by sunset, the friends and the Elfin guards would return to the ranch to inform Captain Nisse. She reminded them that Wisdom and Songbird could quickly deliver messages requesting help if danger arose.

The small company passed through the shadowed doorway, down the stairs, and into the dank hall leading past the rows of prison cells. Two Elfin guards, Jory and Leif, led the small procession, followed closely by Tempest Rebecca, Stefani, and Quinn. The two largest guards, Espen and Nielsen, were tasked with watching their backs and carrying Alsaahir's body into the fortress. They found him lying in the same position where he had fallen. Stefani pressed her hand into his neck, checking for a pulse, before confirming that the sorcerer was indeed dead. She also searched his wardrobe for pockets and anything hidden within his clothing. She found nothing. Espen and Nielsen lifted the body, placing Alsaahir's arms over their broad shoulders while closing the cell door behind them.

They continued following the hallway until they reached the steps leading upward. Rebecca whispered at the top of the stairs that the wall before them would slide to the left.

Before the door was even half opened, Tempest quickly jumped ahead. She listened cautiously for any sounds, although everything remained eerily quiet. They followed the prudent cat through a dark corridor stretching between a long row of tall cabinets and the back wall. At the end of the row, they turned left into the warehouse. Rebecca mentioned that she knew how to light the room, but Stefani did not want to risk alerting anyone to their presence. Without light, it was not easy to see any distance ahead. Although Rebecca had described its size, nobody in the group was prepared for the enormous collections of weapons, tools, furniture, housewares, tapestries, paintings, and supplies stored here. She heard several gasps as they passed rows, stacks, and piles of items, many of which these Elves had never seen anything like in their lives.

Colorful glassware glinted on rows of shelves, even in the dark room. Rebecca recognized some of the green and yellow decorative depression-era dishes, white milk glass vases, ruby red drinking glasses, and old blue bottles found in antique stores and flea markets back home. But people in the Mystic Land had never seen such unusual glass. Quinn briefly stopped to admire an old blue medicine bottle. While holding it up to better see through the glass, Stefani pulled at Quinn's arm to keep her attention on their task. The bottle dropped, smashing on the rock floor. The sound echoed through the entire warehouse. The group froze. Stefani directed them to hide between a row of cabinets while they waited to see if anyone came to investigate the noise.

Rebecca could hear her heartbeat in the silence that followed. Several minutes passed, but nobody came. Eventually, Stefani signaled for them to continue. Quinn whispered an apology, but Stefani put her finger to her lips in a signal to remain quiet.

Leif suddenly jumped back and drew his sword. A suit of armor with a raised sword in its steel hand stood over them. It took a few moments to realize there was no life in the empty shell. Still, the tension grew as the group moved forward.

Finally, they reached the double doors that led to the living quarters. Espen and Nielsen placed Alsaahir's body to one side. With his sword in one hand, Jory slowly opened one door a few inches. Light immediately seeped into the storage room. He peeked into the lit hallway but neither saw nor heard anything. Slowly opening the door, Jory paused before sticking his head into the light. Everybody stood to either side of the doors, weapons in hands, waiting for an explosion of trolls to come barreling in on them. Fortunately, it did not happen. The quiet was deafening. Tempest squeezed past Jory and through the open door. One by one, each of the members cautiously followed.

Rebecca pointed at the closed door to Alsaahir's office, but they did not enter. Led by the Elfin guards, they continued down the hall, stopping at each door to listen for sounds of life in any open rooms. They stopped at the stairway to the upper floor, but everything sounded quiet, so they did not go up the stairs. Instead, they passed through the sitting room and stopped in the atrium with the bodies and heads of dead animals. Rebecca quickly looked for the tall pedestal mounted with the dragon-like rat-bird. Although the pedestal stood in the same place with the evil-looking vulture perched upon it, the creature was now in a different pose and position. Its green and red snake face and burning red eyes stared directly at her. She shuddered at realizing that the horrendous beast had been brought to life by her great grandfather strictly to apprehend her. She breathed a sigh of relief to see that the animal was again lifelessly mounted on the pedestal.

The Elfin guards chose not to check the entryway, deciding it best not to draw attention if any trolls were present. The group was not there to create a battle; they were there to collect the magic rock and books. Now assured that nobody else was in the living quarters, Espen and Neilsen returned to pick up Alsaahir's body from the warehouse. They brought him to the sitting area, where they laid him on a long couch to appear to be sleeping.

While the others turned to walk away, Rebecca whispered, "Rest in peace, Grandfather."

The group took only a few steps into the hallway when the sound of a door opening and closing behind them caused them to stop abruptly. A troll guard sauntered through the front door; his attention focused on a large envelope he received for Alsaahir. The troll looked up from the package in his hands to see the Sorcerer sleeping on the couch. By the time he noticed the movement in the hallway, it was too late. Jory shot an arrow into the middle of the troll's heart. In the same instant, Leif fired an arrow through the center of the troll's throat. The guard's only sound was a thudding noise as his body hit the floor.

The small company moved quickly toward the office, except for Rebecca. She ran to the fallen troll and took the blood-splattered envelope from the grip of his hands. Addressed to Alsaahir the Sorcerer, the sender was listed as First Lady Violet Pendergast. Rebecca almost tripped over Tempest standing at her feet when she stood up. Always close by. Always protecting, she thought. Rebecca quickly folded the envelope and tucked it into her pants pocket, then dashed to join the others who waited patiently near the closed double doors that led to Alsaahir's office.

Rebecca had previously described the room's layout, the secret door behind the big desk, and the magic books and rock locations. For security reasons, the four guards insisted on entering the office first. Unlike the slow, cautious way they had entered the hallway from the warehouse, this time, they quickly opened both doors and rushed in with swords drawn. In front of Rebecca, Stefani, and Quinn, Tempest stood prepared to transform and defend them in any way necessary. Fortunately, it was not required. Nobody occupied the room. More importantly, there was no sign of the books of magic or the magic rock. The pedestal was still in the middle of the room, but the cloth bag with the rock was gone. The large desk was in the same spot near the back wall, but the books were not on it. The group searched through drawers, shelves, and cabinets to no avail.

Stefani decided to search the Sorcerer's bedroom. While many personal artifacts were found, the books and magic rock were not. They located secret hiding places, sliding wall panels, and hidden doors behind curtains, cabinets, and paintings, but none revealed the magical items they sought.

Time passed quickly. They knew they had to return to their friends who waited outside, but Rebecca had one more place she needed to go before they left the fortress. They returned to the office and slid the hidden wall panel aside. Then cautiously followed the dimly lit hallway where light filtered through the peephole slits in the walls. The hallway ended at a sharp, almost pitch-black corner. Rebecca signaled to each member to be cautious of the stairway that dropped off to one side, then motioned for Espen and Neilsen to quietly and carefully slide the wooden door aside. As soon as they were able, they glanced into the stables to ensure no dangers awaited them, then further opened the door and walked through. While the guards watched for trolls, mutants, or other creatures, Rebecca looked for a ferret.

Assured that no dangers were within the sound of her voice, Rebecca quietly called out, "Pixie! Pixie, are you here?" After neither seeing movements nor hearing a response, she moved close to the empty horse stalls to try again. "Pixie, can you hear me? It's Rebecca." Finally, she began to sing a heartfelt song.

Whatever path you choose
You've got a friend in me
You're my best friend
You know that much is true

These words are all I have to give
To show my heart is true
You've made a difference in my life in everything you do
My life would never be the same if I did not have you

I found my greatest friend
The day that I found you

A clump of hay began to move in the corner of a horse stall. A small patch of fuzzy gray hair popped through the hay, followed by a furry head with large shining eyes and a little round black nose. A sense of recognition washed over the little ferret. She dashed from the pile of hay into Rebecca's waiting arms, excitedly laughing and making ferret dooking noises.

"Oh, Pixie, I so wish I could understand what you're saying," Rebecca said aloud.

Seconds later, Stefani touched Rebecca on the shoulder.

"Pixie is trying to communicate with you. Sit here in the hay, relax, close your eyes for one minute, and focus on the sounds she is making. Then, when you open your eyes, you will understand."

Rebecca did as Stefani had suggested. Still holding Pixie in her arms, she settled into a comfortable position along a side wall, with her legs crossed in a lotus position. With Stefani seated next to her, Rebecca closed her eyes, took a few relaxing breaths, and focused her thoughts on the ferret. "I've missed you, Pixie," she spoke aloud.

At first, Rebecca only heard chirping, clucking, and chittering noises sounding much like laughter. Then, as she focused on the sounds, she heard words intermingled within the noises. "Worried... Safe... You... Becca... Song..." Soon the terms blended into sentences, "The happiest I've ever felt..., Your kindness made it all worth...."

Rebecca opened her eyes to look into the face of her friend. "I am so sorry, Pixie. I didn't expect Alsaahir to know you helped me. And I never thought he would hurt you."

"He was angry," Pixie responded, "but there is no pain in being turned into a ferret.

"Alsaahir is dead now, Pixie," Rebecca compassionately informed her friend. "He was stung by a scorpion. We've been searching for his books and the sources of his magic. If we could find them, we might be able to turn you into a full human. Do you have any idea where he might have hidden them?"

"No, Rebecca, I think he kept his magic potions in his office, but he never allowed me to go in there."

Rebecca sat quietly for a moment before asking, "Pixie, would you like to leave here with me? I don't know exactly where I'm going, but I would love to have you go with me."

"Oh, Becca," Pixie smiled, "you are the kindest and most wonderful person I have ever known. I've been fortunate to experience many years as a human and especially to meet you. Now I get to be with my grandchildren in the grasses, the woods, and tunnels in and out of these stables. Thank you for your generous offer, but this is my home and my family. So, I choose to stay here."

Rebecca felt tears leaking from her eyes. "I will always remember you, Pixie."

"I will always remember you too, Rebecca." The little ferret reached up and gave the girl a ferret kiss on her cheek, then jumped from her arms and hopped the few steps to the hole in the hay. She disappeared down the hole without looking back.

"Goodbye, Pixie," Rebecca whispered.

Stefani helped Rebecca to her feet, then signaled for the rest of the company to gather for their return through the fortress. They left the stables, closing the sliding door behind them. Making their way back to the office, they quickly inspected the room to ensure everything was as they found it. Then, they crossed the hallway into the warehouse and found their way through the maze of shelves and supplies to the dungeons. Up the stairs and through the doorway leading to the outdoors, they joined their friends as the sun was nearing the orange-colored horizon.

25 Reflections

After closing and hiding the back door into the fortress, Stefani decided to eat and rest until dark. Rather than risk encountering trolls or mutants on a direct path to the ranch, they would travel southeast to the Elfin Woods, follow the wooded trail north to the Borderland Hills, and west to the ranch. Stefani determined they could be there by sunrise if they traveled through the night. With that path through the Elfin Woods, they could also pass messages to the Elfin Council about their journey and plans to meet up with Captain Nisse at the ranch.

While eating dinner, Rebecca opened the blood-splattered envelope that had arrived at the fortress for Alsaahir. She informed everyone that the letter had come from Violet Pendergast, the wife of the Governor of the Colonists' Villages, then she began to read it aloud.

My Dear Alsaahir,

I congratulate and commend you on handling the treasonous rebellion perpetrated by our citizens. Your ability to defuse the attack without a single fatality is beyond reproach. You have proven that nobody is big, strong, or intelligent enough to defeat you. In my opinion, you should be recognized and honored as the most brilliant military mind in the history of the world.

Kindly remember it was I who warned you of their treacherous plans. I could never stand the thought of living in this Mystic Land without the values of your thoughtful and generous leadership.

Sincerely,
Your Loyal Servant,
First Lady, Violet Pendergast

A conversation erupted among the friends about how Violet should be punished. Some thought she and the Governor should be publicly reprimanded and removed from their positions. Aaron reminded them there was no proof that the Governor was involved, only Violet. One of the guards suggested imprisonment. Another proposed that Violet should be sent into the mists. That idea was immediately rejected as an unjust punishment, condemning her to death. Rebecca reminded them that Violet was correct in her view that Alsaahir had defused the attack without a single fatality. Jill commented that perhaps Violet's betrayal no longer mattered since Alsaahir was now dead. Then Jules reminded her that the betrayal occurred before the sorcerer died, and they were lucky that none of their friends were fatally harmed.

Aaron chuckled, "Do you realize the irony of Violet's statement that nobody is big enough, strong enough, or intelligent enough to defeat the Sorcerer? It was a little scorpion that defeated him!"

Finally, Stefani commented that the subject of punishments would be brought up with the leaders of the Mystic Land colonies, and it is they who would decide the fates of Violet Pendergast and the Governor. "Meanwhile," she reminded them, "we need an hour of quiet rest before we travel."

Two guards stood watch while everybody else found a place to rest. Of course, Songbird and Wisdom also watched from overhead. Jules joined Rebecca on a soft patch of pine needles. Tempest rested near her feet. Rebecca felt exhausted. She knew one hour of sleep was greatly needed before an all-night hike.

"The trolls are coming! Wake up, Rebecca. Wake up," a male voice called to her. She opened her eyes to discover Wisdom flying only an arm's length over her head. She looked around the pine grove. Stefani was also jumping up.

"They found Alsaahir and the dead troll guard," Stefani called out. "Patrols are coming around both sides of the fortress. We have only a few minutes to get out of here." Everybody raced to grab their weapons and belongings. "This way," Stefani called out as she followed Wisdom and Songbird to the southeastern corner of the clearing. It took less than a minute for everyone to join them.

The company ran for about ten minutes, crossing at least half a mile through the maze of trees before slowing to a quick, steady walk. The bright moon in the clear sky allowed the company to see their path and each other easily. Unfortunately, however, it could let the trolls see them too. They heard no sounds behind them, but the trolls were known as silent trackers who could quietly surround and attack their unknowing prey. Rebecca caught a few glimpses of Wisdom circling overhead, although no warnings sounded from the protective owl. Tempest stayed by her side. She did not see Songbird but did not doubt that the nightingale was watching closely for any dangers. Rebecca felt comfortably safe as long as her protectors were nearby.

It did not seem to take long before they entered the southern point of the Elfin Woods. A few of their Elfin guards raced ahead of the group. Within minutes they returned with an entire company of Elfin warriors to escort them through the woods. They all knew Quinn, and everyone was impressed and honored by the presence of Princess Stefani.

Stefani informed the Sergeant of the Guard that the company needed to be through the Elfin Woods and arrive at a ranch in the Borderland Hills by sunrise. She requested four of the best messengers to write her verbal messages while they walked. The sergeant called out orders. Horses were considered, but the guard did not have enough horses for the entire group. The Sergeant explained that most of their horses were with the Elvin forces at the ranch. So Stefani requested that they maintain their steady pace on foot.

Stefani provided information to the four messengers in pairs. Warning them to stay watchful and prepared, the first two messengers immediately mounted horses for delivery to Captain Nisse in the Borderland Hills. The second two were to deliver their messages to the leaders at the Council of Elders at sunrise.

When the company reached the gates to the Elfin Village, a company of Elfin guards waited with fresh horses. Stefani stopped there to inform the guards traveling with them that they were released to their homes. That included the four guards Rebecca had come to know in their return through the fortress, Jory, Leif, Espen, and Nielsen, and the four who stood guard outside the Sorcerer's fortress with their friends. The Princess requested that the guards deliver their reports to their company commanders and the Elfin Council in the morning. The friends thanked, praised, and hugged the guards while saying their goodbyes.

At Stefani's request, the new company of guards would escort the group of friends to the ranch. She stressed that speed and caution were both of vital importance. She expressed to everyone that she feared retaliation by the trolls for the deaths of Alsaahir and the troll guard. The arrows that killed the troll guard would be easily identified as Elfin. Therefore, Stefani thought it essential they must get to the ranch as quickly as possible.

Rebecca felt so impressed by Stefani's organization of thoughts and actions. She possessed abundant knowledge, experience, logic, and reason yet consistently strived to listen and learn. Always supportive and encouraging to others, Stefani saw the best in everyone while utilizing those skills to help them grow and improve as individuals and within a team. Rebecca wondered if she could ever truly emulate the Princess. The one thing Rebecca did know, Stefani would always inspire her example of an extraordinary leader.

While maintaining a quicker pace on horseback than on foot, they still had to be cautious of tree roots, rocks, and uneven ground in the Elfin woods. Moreover, the moonlight that appeared so bright earlier now only peeked between branches of the tall trees. As a result, the beautiful cottages, flowers, and animals Rebecca had admired on this path a few weeks before were seldom visible tonight. The fireflies still sparkled in the dark, and the fresh scents still tingled her senses, but the one-time visions within these woods were missing. Even Tempest only appeared like a flash of movement when she passed through an occasional spot of moonlight. Wisdom and Songbird were unseen, although Rebecca thought she heard Wisdom's hoot a few times, likely to remind her they were still nearby.

When the company reached the northern edge of the Elfin Woods, still within the cover of the trees, they dismounted from their horses for ten minutes to stretch and grab a quick bite of food and water supplied by the guards. Scouts reported to Princess Stefani and the Sergeant of the Guard that no trolls or mutants had been spotted in the area. Wisdom and Songbird appeared with similar assurances that their path ahead was clear.

Breaking from the cover of the forest into the bright moonlight felt like a mixture of relief and concern. It was a relief to see more clearly, yet concerning that they could be seen more clearly. After less than thirty minutes in the open, the company turned west into the valley between the low Borderland Hills. No people were encountered until they neared the ranch, where several sets of guards maintained watch. The sun had not yet risen when they finally came within sight of the huge barns, fenced corrals, cabins, tents, and the big ranch house. Even at this early morning time, several workers moved about the property. Some looked up from their work, but nobody appeared surprised to see the approaching company.

Stefani ordered Rebecca, Aaron, Jules, Jill, and Tempest to go directly to the ranch house for much-needed sleep. Meanwhile, she, Quinn, and the Elfin guards reported to Captain Nisse at the commander's tent before taking their opportunity to rest.

Rebecca finally laid her body down on the soft bed, immediately falling into a deep sleep. Disturbing nightmares of the monstrous rat-dragon, imprisonment in the dungeon, her grandfather's death, and the dead troll guard mingled with pleasant dreams of Pixie, Jules, and celebrations with her friends. Yet, she slept so soundly that all those dreams and nightmares were merely faded memories once she awoke.

Rolling onto her side on the comfortable bed, Rebecca slowly opened her eyes. Tempest sat on a small carpet, staring back at her while licking her paws. Rebecca grinned at the cat and decided it was time to get up. The first thing she wanted was a washroom to clean herself. After several days without a bath, Rebecca began to smell herself, which was not a pleasing odor. Genuinely surprised to find her backpack sitting by the door, Rebecca grabbed her toothbrush, hairbrush, and change of clothes before jaunting to the washroom. A collection of voices rose from downstairs. Not disruptive, but in a tone of excitement and celebration. She recognized most of the voices as those of her friends.

She took her time washing. It felt like weeks of dirt and grime had become layered upon her skin. With no such thing as shampoo here, Rebecca did her best to wash her hair, brushed, and wrapped a long rawhide string around her head in a headband style. Rebecca thought the look proudly displayed her native heritage. She returned to her bedroom, tossed the dirty clothes into a small pile on the floor next to her backpack, straightened the bedcovers, called for Tempest to join her, and headed downstairs.

The ranch house was abuzz from the kitchen to the dining room, the sitting room, and the front porch. It felt like everybody in the Mystic Land was there, and they were all talking at once! Rebecca was greeted first by Jasmine, then Windy, who was so excited to see her and show off the sling on her sprained arm. Luna and her mother quickly offered food and drink. Rebecca graciously declined the hospitality, saying she would find her way to the kitchen or dining room in a while. She found her father in a deep discussion with Stefani. Jules and Leo were laughing out loud over shared jokes. Aaron was hitting it off with Captain Nisse, while Luna and Leo's father shared stories with Windy's parents. Rebecca briefly joined Quinn and Jill, who talked about the embarrassing clothes they had each been forced to wear as teenagers.

People moved around, and conversations changed, but the atmosphere was energizing. Finally, Rebecca made it to the dining room, where she found assorted sandwiches, vegetables, fruits, cakes, pies, juice, milk, and water to drink. When Tempest appeared at her feet, Rebecca poured some milk, water, and assorted foods onto bowls for her. The cat did not appear to be too selective, as she went after everything with total abandon. Rebecca put more food and drink into the bowls, and Tempest ate that too!

Rebecca was surprised to learn that the sun had set almost two hours earlier, which meant she had slept more than fourteen hours. Of course, it also meant she would likely be awake through the entire night, but that's okay, she thought, as it appeared that everybody else would be awake too.

An hour into the celebration, Captain Nisse began calling, "Attention! May we have your attention, please." Once everybody quit speaking, he announced, "Ladies and gentlemen, let's all step out to the porch where our friends and neighbors can join us." Once outside, he called loudly for anyone within hearing range to gather around. After a few moments, he continued, "The past few weeks have been an extraordinary, eventful, memorable, and historical period in the Mystic Land. We have all played important roles in the battle for our freedom. We experienced extreme challenges, successes, disappointments, and difficult lessons learned in that process. It is my honor to introduce a person who, without her leadership, this quest could have become a disaster. Please help me thank Princess Stefani."

Everybody clapped and cheered as Stefani stood for the acknowledgment. She raised her hand in a modest gesture to quiet the crowd. Then she began to speak, "My friends, as Captain Nisse said, we all deserve recognition for our efforts. In the end, we had successes, and we had some losses. Fortunately, on a positive note, we had no serious fatalities. And, the sorcerer was defeated, not by an army bigger and stronger than he, but by smaller and more determined individuals." Again, the crowd clapped and cheered. Sadly, we did not find or acquire the magic that keeps us trapped within the mists. But we will never give up our efforts to gain our freedom. Whether it is our generation or the generation of our children's children, we will find a way." Everybody clapped and cheered.

After the cheering receded, Stefani continued. "Finally, we all came together from each village in a united effort to fight for what is right. We made new friendships and created strong bonds that should last throughout our lives. One person here is most responsible for bringing us together. She has been in the Mystic Land for less than two months, yet she has inspired and transformed all of us in that short time. She risked her life over and over. She fought by our sides, and she made a difference in the lives of every person and animal she came in contact with. I am honored to introduce Rebecca Harmony Fields."

Rebecca felt stunned by Stefani's proclamation. She stepped next to Stefani but did not know what to say except, "Thank you!" Rebecca started to walk away, but Stefani would not allow her to withdraw that easily. Instead, she pulled Rebecca close, wrapped an arm around her shoulders, and began to ask some simple questions.

"Rebecca, is it true that you came through the mists about six or seven weeks ago?

"Yes," Rebecca replied.

"Would you mind telling us about your experience in the mists?"

Rather than look at the faces in the crowd, Rebecca stared into the trees. She was comforted to see Songbird and Wisdom watching her from a low branch. Their presence gave her a sudden surge of confidence.

"I am seventeen years old," Rebecca began. "While picking berries with my younger brother, we became separated. I got lost in the woods and wandered into the mists. Within that mist was a cold, ugly swamp, through which I was guided and protected by an owl named Wisdom, a nightingale named Songbird, and a cat which is not really a cat, named Tempest. Together, they fought off goblins who attacked me and guided me to safety here in the Mystic Land. Without them, I would not have survived. Since I met them, they have been my friends and protectors."

The crowd gasped, then clapped, although Rebecca could sense some doubts about her story.

Stefani spoke up, "Her story is true. In fact, the animals she speaks of are with us now." She pointed, "Wisdom the owl and Songbird the nightingale are sitting on the branch of that tree."

Both birds flapped their wings, rose above the branch they had been resting on, then settled back onto it as if bowing to the audience.

Again, the crowd gasped and applauded. People began chattering, but Stefani quickly quieted them.

"Ladies and gentlemen, the cat, which is not a cat, is also here with us." She pointed to the porch floor where Tempest sat next to Rebecca, licking her paws.

The crowd began to laugh. A few non-believers yelled sarcastic remarks.

Stefani leaned into Rebecca's ear. "Do you think Tempest could be persuaded to transform into a tiger for this crowd?

"I can only ask," Rebecca answered. "What she chooses to do or not do is entirely up to her." Rebecca knelt next to the cat. "Tempest, would you be willing to transform into a tiger for me again? I understand if you don't....

Tempest stood and moved a few steps in front of Rebecca. Within seconds she transformed from a twenty-pound cat into a four-hundred-pound white tiger. As soon as she reached full size, she faced the crowd and roared. Her friends on the porch who had already experienced Tempest transformations remained calm. The group in front of them fell backward, some tripping and falling over each other. Nobody was laughing now. Seconds later, Tempest returned to her standard cat size. She moved back to Rebecca, sat down, and began licking her front paws as if this was the most routine part of her day.

"Thank you, Tempest," Rebecca whispered to her faithful friend.

"Thank you, Tempest," Stefani said loud enough for the entire crowd to hear. Then, again she waited for the group to quiet. "My point in calling you all here," Stefani continued, "is to give respect where respect is deserved. Rebecca was the central figure in the attack against the Sorcerer four nights ago. She just spent three days in the Sorcerer's dungeon. She is a hero."

The crowd cheered and loudly applauded.

Stefani continued. "Her friends, these animals, and the people you see on this porch went to her rescue. They risked their lives. They are heroes.

And all of you who participated in our battle against the sorcerer in our quest for freedom, whether as part of the force or the support, are heroes. Thank you all. Tonight, we celebrate!"

The crowd cheered, clapped, and celebrated for the rest of the night.

The next day people began dismantling tents and out-buildings and returning to their homes. Aware of the threat still posed by the trolls and mutants, the leaders decided to quietly keep the Elfin forces on guard but not incite fear in the community. The people of the Mystic Land had united in a fight for their freedom. It was best to maintain that camaraderie for as long as possible.

Rebecca and her friends stayed for two more days helping Leo and Luna's family clean up and return the ranch to normalcy. Finally, it came time to say goodbye. Stefani, Quinn, Captain Nisse, and most of the Elfin forces returned to the Elfin Woods. Only a company of guards and messengers stayed behind. When Takoda Nemasket and his assistants returned to the Healing Center, Windy's family traveled with them. Windy chose to return home with her family, at least for now. Luna and Leo planned to stay with their parents for two more weeks before going to the Elfin Healing Center for training.

When asked about her plans, Rebecca told everyone she was staying with the Verne family, although she knew she would soon have to move forward with her life in one way or another.

Tempest stayed with Rebecca, although Songbird and Wisdom were seen much less, which concerned Rebecca that the birds might not be available if she made the journey back through the mists. So, a week after returning to the Verne home, Rebecca decided to discuss her plans with the family. She wanted to make the journey back to her own home. But, of course, that meant going back through the mists.

Jules was especially shocked by Rebecca's decision. He offered every reason for Rebecca to stay. Then he offered to go with her. Jill also wanted to go, but for different reasons.

"Jules," Rebecca responded, "I know you love me and want to protect me. I have fallen in love with you too. But we are too young to make a lifelong commitment. I have learned that my voice has the magic to help me make it through the mists. With Tempest by my side, I will be safe. Jill, I know you want to see the world outside the Mystic Land, but you and your family need each other. I will return to my home with proof of this place and the people trapped inside the mists. Somehow, I will find a way to help free you."

Jasmine suggested, "the shortest distance and safest passage through the mists is at the northern edge of the Wampanoag Woods. More people have arrived there than at any other spot, including myself, Violet, and your mother. That is also where your mother left to return home."

The Verne family decided to travel the next day to take Rebecca to the Native Villages. Rebecca would have an evening to visit with her father before leaving the following morning. Then they could all be there to see her off. They packed food, clothing, and a long knife in her backpack and gave her a bow and quiver filled with arrows for added protection. Finally, Jill reminded Rebecca that her walking staff was left in the gypsy wagon when she had left with Alsaahir. She proudly presented Rebecca with her walking staff, now finely carved with their names and art reflecting Rebecca's time in the Mystic Land.

"It's beautiful," Rebecca acknowledged, "I will cherish it forever."

That night, while she lay in bed, Rebecca silently called out to her great-grandmother to inform her of her plans. Nani agreed with Jasmine's perception that they could get through the northern section of the mists between sunrise and sunset if weather and conditions were agreeable. However, there are no guarantees about how agreeable those conditions might be.

"In fact," Nani warned, "it is wise to be prepared for difficulties, dangers, and delays." She reminded Rebecca of the magic in her voice. And she promised that she and Wisdom would be there with Tempest to help guide and protect her on this journey.

26 Savage Swamp

They awoke at the usual early-morning time to feed and care for the animals, prepare the horses for the trip, and have a light breakfast. Two hours after sunrise, Rebecca, Tempest, and the Verne family left for the Native Villages in their Gypsy wagon. Rather than take their usual route across the West River to the Trader Market, they passed through the Gypsy Camps and followed the road north. Aaron stopped briefly to give a message to one of his friends in the camp. Otherwise, the trip passed with no delays and no problems. The sky was clear. The summer weather felt warm and comfortable. The people they passed on the road were cheerful and friendly. Aaron drove the wagon through most of the three-hour trip. Jasmine took turns riding in the driver's seat with her husband and in the back with the teens. Jules relieved Aaron of the driving duties for a short while, but everybody knew Jules wanted to spend as much time as possible with Rebecca.

It was close to noon when they passed through the center of the Native Village and stopped for a surprise visit with Windy and her family. The mood was festive in celebrating the gathering until learning of Rebecca's decision to leave. Underlying those sentiments was a deep concern for her safety in passing through the mists. Everybody in the Mystic Land knew the stories of the creatures and the dangers in the swamps, although nobody wanted to express those fears to Rebecca. Windy fought back the tears. She truly felt that she was losing her best friend.

By midafternoon Rebecca and the Verne family said their

goodbyes to Windy and her family. With Tempest in the lead, they reboarded the wagon for the short ride to the Healing Center, where they knew Takoda would likely be hard at work. As expected, the receptionists, who remembered Rebecca, Jules, and Jill from their previous visit, informed them that Takoda was in surgery but should be available in about an hour.

Just as predicted, one hour after their arrival, the tall, handsome man with the beaming smile entered the room. His arms raised in a welcoming gesture of friendship; he almost ran to greet them. It reminded Rebecca of watching him cross the room that first day she met him. However, there was no hesitancy this time as she raced to embrace her father. The Verne's gathered around to share the greetings, smiles, and hugs.

Finally, the time came to tell Takoda what brought them to the Healing Center. Takoda clearly felt disappointment and concern in learning that Rebecca had decided to leave. But he smiled and held her hand, then invited them to come to his home for the night. He led them to the Healing Center dining room for their dinner while he dealt with work-related responsibilities. They agreed to meet on the road behind the Healing Center in one hour. By the time Rebecca and the Verne's had eaten, fed Tempest, and drove their wagon to the back of the building, Takoda Nemasket stood waiting for them with a llama, two peacocks, and several farm animals all gathered around him.

The conversation was festive into the evening at Takoda's home, even though they knew they had to rise early to be at the edge of the mists before sunrise. Aaron and Jasmine slept in the guest room, Jill, Rebecca, and Tempest shared a pile of blankets on the floor in the sitting room, and Jules made his bed in the wagon.

Rebecca awoke several times during the night. She began to doubt her decision. Memories of the attack by the goblins in the swamp came back to haunt her. She awoke from a nightmare that she would spend the rest of her life with worse physical and emotional scars than Violet had endured. But then, whenever she considered staying in the Mystic Land, she felt Tempest by her side. That cat which is not really a cat, a nightingale with the spirit of her great grandmother, and a wise old owl would be there to guide and protect her. That knowledge was comforting enough to let her fall back asleep.

"Wake up, Rebecca," she heard the assuring woman's voice. She opened her eyes. The room was still dark. When she turned her head, Tempest stood inches away, staring fixedly into her eyes.

Rebecca could only smile at the face of the vigilant cat. "Thank you, Tempest," Rebecca whispered, "I can always count on you." Rebecca reached across the pile of blankets to shake Jill awake. "Hey, Sleepyhead, it's time to wake up," she laughed.

Jill groaned and tossed the blankets at Rebecca. "You have a way of ruining the nicest dreams," she joked.

"Good morning," Jill shouted to awaken her parents and Takoda, while Rebecca skipped out to awaken Jules. She thought this would be a perfect opportunity to surprise Jules with a wake-up kiss. Instead, she was surprised to find him reading an old book under candlelight, but that didn't stop her from having a private moment with the handsome young man.

While they held each other close, Rebecca spoke what she felt must be said. "I have never loved anyone as I love you. I cannot promise that I will ever be able to come back here. I can only promise that I will try. Outside of the mists, nobody is aware that this place exists. And since the mists only randomly appear, I might never get another chance. So please do not wait for me. Go on with your life. Dance with those girls in the Gypsy Camps who so adore you. Maybe fate will bring us back together one day, but until then, become the best man you can be."

"You are returning through the mists because you dream of a better life," Jules replied. "I promise to strive to be the man you deserve if you promise to become the woman you dream of being." No other words were spoken. Instead, the two hugged and kissed, then left the wagon to join the others in Takoda's home.

Together, they prepared some breakfast. Jasmine gave Rebecca a letter addressed to Clover and a couple of illustrations of the family members she had drawn. She tucked the pages into her notebook inside of her backpack. Takoda quickly wrote a short note, also to be given to Rebecca's mother. Then he gave her more fruit and a flask with juice for her journey. Rebecca jokingly commented that her pack was getting quite full for a one-day hike, but she was grateful for the thoughtfulness everybody generously offered. Finally, they gathered their belongings and headed out the door.

It was barely a half-hour ride to the northern-most spot where the Wampanoag Woods met the mists. A surprise awaited Rebecca on their arrival. As she exited the Gypsy wagon, a cheer went up. A crowd of nearly fifty people waited to say their goodbyes. Unbeknownst to Rebecca, Aaron's friend in the Gypsy Camps delivered Aaron's message to several of Rebecca's friends. Luna, Leo, and their parents, Princess Stefani, Quinn, Jory, Leif, Espen,

Nielsen, and Captain Nisse, were all there to express their goodbyes. Windy was there with her entire family of nearly twenty family members. Others Becca had barely come to know all turned out for the young woman.

As the light glistened on the eastern edges of the sky, Rebecca knew it was time to give her final farewells. Windy approached Rebecca with a cloth backpack in one hand, a sword, and her oak-handled knife in its leather sheath in the other hand.

"I cannot carry another backpack, Windy," Rebecca responded as kindly as possible, "and I already have a long knife, a bow with arrows, and my walking staff. So perhaps it would be best if you kept those items."

Windy grinned. "I'm not giving you these items," she spoke confidently, "I'm going with you."

"What? No. Windy, you can't...." Rebecca stuttered as she tried to grasp Windy's statement.

Windy had her mind made up. "Becca, I love my family, but I have been searching blindly for my path for three years. Meeting you changed my life. I do not know what waits for me on the other side of that mist, but I know it is where my future lies. So, Rebecca, I am going with you, either by your side or following behind you. You are not leaving without me."

Rebecca hugged her friend. "Well, Windy, this could be the greatest decision or the biggest mistake of your life, but you are certainly in for a life-changing adventure. And I am honored to stand side by side with you no matter what the future holds."

At that moment, a nightingale landed on a nearby branch. It whistled a few notes to let Rebecca know she was there. Less than a minute later, an owl gave a loud "hoot" as it landed on the branch next to the nightingale.

Rebecca turned to her crowd of friends. "Our guides and protectors are here. Thank you all for coming to say your goodbyes to us. If it is at all possible, I will return to help you all gain your freedom. No matter what the future brings, know that I love you, and I am forever changed by your friendships."

Windy and Rebecca waved and called out their goodbyes as they walked the remaining yards into the wall of mist. Tempest marched beside them. Wisdom flew past to disappear first into the thick fog. Songbird circled overhead, pausing to enter the darkness simultaneously with the girls. The crowd of friends watched as the girls quickly faded like ghosts in the haze.

Rebecca was the first to speak once they passed into the fog, "Windy, if we are going to survive, it is vitally important for me to tell you a few important details. First, you know about my connection with Tempest the cat, Wisdom the owl, and Songbird the nightingale. I can communicate with these animals because of the magic inherited through my ancestry with Alsaahir, the sorcerer. Today, they will be our guides, guardians, and protectors from the goblins and any other creatures that may live in the swamp. Wisdom best knows the path; he will scout ahead. Songbird will watch from directly overhead, and Tempest will always be in front of us or beside us. At times the trail will be thin, the swamp will be deep, and the mist will be so thick we will have to hold on to each other because we will not be able to see. Furthermore, I have a magical gift of song that will keep the goblins from attacking us. Our animal guides will tell me when to sing. If I start singing, it is for our protection. Just hang on to my belt or clothing with one hand, your knife or sword with the other, and do not let go of me. Do you understand?"

"Yes," Windy timidly replied. Rebecca thought it was the most apprehensive she had ever seen Windy. For a while, no other words were spoken.

Before long, the hilly ground began to level. The trees became darker and more numerous. The fog became thicker, and the sky disappeared into the darkness. Except for the occasional sound of frogs or bugs, the woods were quiet. Rebecca would hear Wisdom hoot every few minutes to tell the girls they were traveling in the right direction. Songbird often circled closely overhead to show the girls her presence. Tempest strolled casually no more than two steps ahead of them. The cat appeared to show no concerns in this early part of their journey.

When Tempest suddenly made a quick jump to the right, Rebecca missed it and stepped into her first muddy puddle of swamp water. Fortunately, the water was not deep enough to enter her boots. She was immediately reminded of how wet and miserable she felt on her first journey through the swamp. She warned Windy, "Stay out of the swamp water for as long as possible."

That first puddle was just a hint of what was to come. Soon, every step felt as if it was in wet mud. The girls squeezed between wet black moss-covered leafless trees, stepped over and around old, dead, broken logs jutting out of the muck, and ducked beneath dead branches that hung from trees like skeleton arms with long pointed fingers. The air was hot. It felt as if the heat was rising from the wet swamp. The smell was worse than Rebecca remembered it on her previous path through the mists. She realized that the summer heat had likely made the swamp more pungent than when she passed through in May. Windy pulled Rebecca to a stop once to throw up. Afterward, Rebecca doubted anything was left in Windy's stomach to throw up a second time.

The fog began to thicken and swirl around them. There was no path, only spaces to step between clumps of dead trees, sticky mud, and black oily water. Movements skittered in and out of the mist. Glowing eyes watched as they passed. Strange noises sounding like screams of an animal in distress, a sudden splash in the water, and other indistinct sounds fought for their attention. Rebecca grabbed Windy's hand and placed it on her belt while she focused on Tempest, instinctively knowing that one look away could be a dire mistake in this noxious maze. The cat seemed unnerved by the sounds, visions, or anything around them. She never altered her pace or her shape. When movements or noises distracted Rebecca, she focused on the cat's footsteps. Songbird's whistle or a hoot from Wisdom reminded her that they were going in the right direction.

In a rare moment of losing sight of Tempest in the fog, a long thick snake dropped from the branches of a tree directly onto Rebecca's shoulders. In seconds it coiled around her body, pinning her arms to her side. She started to scream out, but a part of the thick, greasy snake had covered her mouth while choking the air from her lungs. Its large head sprung up in front of her. Fierce red eyes stared victoriously into Rebecca's frightened face. Its open mouth, with long yellowed fangs and slithering tongue, hissed its warning as it prepared to attack the helpless girl.

In a split second, it sprung. In the next instant, the face disappeared before Rebecca's eyes. Windy's knife slashed through the snake's neck, severing its head from its body. Green slime and dark red blood splattered across Rebecca's face. Rebecca choked for air, her eyes blinded and arms pinned to her sides. The seconds felt like long minutes while Windy desperately ripped the snake off her friend. As soon as the snake's body had fallen to the ground, Windy sliced a piece of cloth from her shirt to wipe the blood and slime from Rebecca's face.

The ground was so wet, and the dead tree stumps so covered in sludge that there was no suitable place to sit without soaking the muck into their clothes. The girls stood facing each other while Windy wiped away the remaining pieces of blood and green slime.

"You saved my life, Windy," Rebecca managed to speak. There was nothing that I, Tempest, Songbird, or Wisdom, could have done that would have saved me from that snake. Without you here, I would surely be dead."

Windy paused for a moment before responding. "Thank you for letting me come with you, Becca. I'm glad I could make a difference for you." Windy picked up the body of the snake. "This thing looks like it's about twelve feet long," she gasped in astonishment as she tossed it into a nearby pond of bubbling black water.

Suddenly, the swamp seemed to come alive. Skittering noises, guttural sounds, and growls grew in the surrounding fog.

A giant white tiger miraculously appeared between the young women and the bubbling water. Tempest was there to protect them, but the noises came from every direction.

A flash of movement raced past them. Rebecca immediately recognized it as a goblin. About two feet in height, bald head, glowing red eyes, long pointed nose, and a wide mouth displaying visibly sharp teeth behind a wicked smile. Twisted arms with overly large hands stuck out from under pieces of moss and tree bark in place of clothing. The creature stabbed a long sharp stick into the dead snake. Then, lifting it triumphantly over its head, the Goblin screeched as though it had achieved a great reward.

The next second, a hideous form of tattered wolf jumped out of the mists to attack the helpless goblin. The beasts' sharp claws, wolf fangs, and wild boar tusks ripped into the goblin, tearing it into small pieces. The wolf watched the tiger and the girls carefully while chewing on the bloody, mutilated slabs of goblin and snake.

All of a sudden, the seething black water abruptly exploded around the startled wolf. The animal struggled to escape before a massive mouth of turbid slime wrapped itself around the frightened animal, pulling it under the erupting water. In seconds, gurgling bubbles were all that was left on the swirling surface. Then, the sounds in the mist went silent.

Songbird flew to the branch above the girls' heads where the snake had been only minutes before. Wisdom appeared only seconds after the nightingale. Tempest, still in the form of the white tiger, turned and looked at the girls.

"I think we need to get moving," Windy urgently requested.

Wisdom lifted from the branch, circled for a moment, then, choosing the necessary direction, he disappeared into the thick fog. Tempest looked about; remaining in the form of a tiger, he slowly followed Wisdom's path choice. Neither Rebecca nor Windy hesitated to follow the massive white tiger into the mists. Songbird waited and watched from the branch before following overhead.

"Sing, Rebecca," she heard Nani's voice call out to her.

Rebecca reached back to make sure Windy's hand was on her belt. While they walked, Rebecca sang.

You can set my world on fire
I will fill my life with rain
You can threaten me with danger
But I will not feel your pain

We reserve the right to live in peace
I choose not to feel your hate
My wings are strong. I will fly
My world, I will create

Your war will end
I will live my life with love
While you struggle with your burdens
I will fly like the freedom dove

One song led to another. Rebecca sang for more than an hour. When she stopped singing, Songbird whistled as she flew in circles over their heads. Rebecca listened for a message from the nightingale, but none came. The swamp was silent. Windy still held on to Rebecca's belt. Tempest had reverted to her traditional cat form, although Rebecca could not remember how long ago the transformation had occurred.

Eventually, the ground began a gradual rise out of the swamp. Rather than continuous blackened sludge, damp brown leaves appeared in patches on the ground. Trees with dark brown bark and green moss slowly replaced dead trees and oily slime. Tiny fragments of light occasionally filtered through the mists, allowing them to see more than a few yards ahead.

In a daze, the girls walked for at least another half hour, one step following the next, still entranced as they followed closely behind Tempest. Finally, Wisdom called out loudly from overhead. Rebecca looked up. It startled her to see the owl and the nightingale sitting side by side on the low branch of a pine tree. She reached back to take Windy's hand from her belt.

Holding Windy's hand in hers, Rebecca lifted their arms toward the birds. "Windy, we're almost there," Rebecca announced. "Our guides are telling us to rest, eat and drink. We should be out of the woods soon."

They stood in a small grove of pines. Brown pine needles and pinecones covered the ground. There was still mist in the air, but the sunlight could sift through the fog-covered treetops. The fresh scents of the pines replaced the stench of the dead swamp.

Rebecca, Windy, and Tempest seated themselves under the same tree where the birds were perched. They each withdrew food and drink from their backpacks. Neither of the girls had eaten since early that morning. And Windy had lost her breakfast early in the day. Several hours had passed, but it was only now that they thought about food. The girls carried enough food to feed all five travelers at least three full meals. The birds joined them on the ground, where they all ate vigorously.

Through the mist and the tall trees, they could not tell where the sun was located in the sky, only that it was still daytime. However, they still hoped to get through the woods before nightfall. So as soon as they finished eating, they packed up their belongings and continued their march. Rebecca and Windy felt a surge of energy and excitement as it became easier to see and move, knowing the trek was nearing its conclusion.

27 Outside World

A half-hour after eating, they came to an old stone wall with twisted vines and trees with knotted roots growing out of the rocks. The wall stood close to four feet high and stretched from left to right through the forest as far as they could see. Although Rebecca knew this was in a different location, she immediately recognized it as the same wall she had crossed when she became lost in the woods two months earlier.

Windy was the first to speak. "Except for the trees and roots growing out of it, this wall reminds me of the walls separating the villages in the Mystic Land."

Rebecca was intrigued by Windy's revelation. Could Alsaahir have created this wall to mark the outer boundary of his property? If so, this wall represents the Sorcerer's doorway in and out of the mists. Rebecca felt a cold shiver roll up and down her spine. "Windy," she said, "I think we will have officially departed the Mystic Land when we cross over this wall."

Rebecca and Windy anxiously climbed over the wall as quickly as they could. Stepping their feet on the ground felt exhilarating. Of course, Wisdom and Songbird flew over the wall. Tempest followed a little slower, as cats tend to do. Almost immediately, the mist was gone. Sunlight shined upon them.

The birds led the way through the woods for another fifteen minutes. As they walked, they quickly grew closer to the rumbling sounds of motorized engines. Rebecca knew they were nearing a road and the sounds of passing cars. It was a sound that was unfamiliar to Windy. Rebecca excitedly hastened her pace while Windy curiously followed. When they arrived at the side of a road, Rebecca knew precisely where she was, on Route 44 in Rehoboth, approximately one mile west of Anawan Rock.

Windy stood back in shock. "What are those?" she asked, pointing at the cars and trucks speeding past.

"Those are cars, Windy," Rebecca explained. "Approximately one hundred years ago, cars replaced horses and wagons. Be prepared; there will be many things here that will be new to you. It will be like stepping more than a hundred years into the future. But don't worry, Windy, I will be with you and help teach you. It will be fun and exciting, and I look forward to sharing every moment with you."

"Thank you, Becca," Windy grinned a beaming smile. "I hope I will always be your friend."

"Windy, we went through something today that will bond us forever," Rebecca responded. "You saved my life today! Without you, I would not even be here. No matter what happens in the rest of our lives, I will always be grateful for you. I promise I will always be your friend. If you ever need anything, all you have to do is call me."

"Call you?" Windy inquired.

"That's another invention you will learn about soon," Rebecca grinned. "Come on; we have a couple of miles to get to my home. So, let's get walking."

Wisdom and Songbird already knew where Rebecca lived. They had a long history with her mother and grandmother. Tempest knew the women but had never been to their homes. So, while Rebecca, Windy, and Tempest walked, Wisdom and Songbird flew overhead. Rebecca explained to Windy that their sword, bow and arrows, and long knives had to stay hidden from people and passing cars.

While they walked, Rebecca explained several phenomena that Windy found unfamiliar, such as telephones, electric lights, stop lights, glass windows, grocery stores, plastic bottles, and kids playing a game called baseball. Rebecca knew many everyday items would astound Windy as fascinating and glorious inventions. However, she looked forward to explaining every modern invention as Windy discovered them.

They walked past Clover's Coffee & Tea Café. Rebecca thought about stopping to see if her mother might be there but quickly decided that neither she nor her traveling companions were appropriately dressed, even for a hippie-style atmosphere. Becca tried explaining to Windy how she had grown up in her mother's restaurant, but Windy had difficulty grasping the concept of a restaurant.

I can't wait until the first time Windy experiences a grocery store, a department store, or a shopping mall, Rebecca thought. But first, Windy will have to learn about money. In fact, there will be a lot for Windy to learn, but I look forward to teaching her. Rebecca wondered what it would take to prepare Windy for school or a job, but she was not yet ready to discuss such concepts.

Rebecca remembered Alsaahir's argument that his people in the Mystic Land were not prepared to survive in the outside world. "They would not have a chance out there," he had said. In a sense, he was right. If the few thousand people in the Mystic Land were suddenly released into the outside world, they would have many difficulties and challenges to overcome. But nothing could justify keeping generations of innocent people imprisoned under a mistaken belief that he was protecting them. They deserved their freedom, and she would do all she could to see they got it. People in this world take so much for granted, she thought. Then it occurred to her that she did not realize how well she had it until she lost it.

The summer sun was nearing the horizon when the friends approached the street to Rebecca's home. To Windy, every house they passed was bigger, more colorful, and grander than anything she had ever seen or imagined. Rebecca could hardly wait for Windy to find out she would live in one of these houses. If only people could see through Windy's eyes how well they have it. What a different world this would be.

As soon as she reached her home, Rebecca led her friends across the nicely mowed front lawn to the front porch of the two-story ranch-style house. Wisdom and Songbird immediately settled on the wooden railing at the front of the porch while Rebecca, Windy, and Tempest climbed the few steps to the door. She almost knocked but quickly decided to turn the door handle first. It opened, so she walked in with Windy and Tempest close behind.

Her brother, Chris, sat on the couch. Although the television was on, he didn't look like he was watching it. Instead, he stared blankly at the floor. He looked sad, as if depressed, Rebecca thought.

Rebecca spoke calmly, "Hi, Chris."

He looked up for a moment, then looked back at the floor. It took a few seconds to register that Rebecca really was there. His head jerked up. He jumped from the couch. Before reaching her, tears already poured from his eyes. He was crying so hard he could not speak. He grabbed his sister around the waist and hugged her so hard it took her breath away. She told him how much she missed him, but it did not feel as emotional as his joy at having her home.

After a few minutes, she finally asked if their mom and dad were there. He pointed toward the kitchen but seemed in no hurry to let go of her. Gently peeling Chris's arms from her waist, she took him by the hand.

She turned to wave for Windy to follow but found her friend staring at the television with her mouth opened. "Windy," Rebecca called as she tapped her on the arm, "I'll explain that to you later. But, first, come meet my parents."

They turned the corner to find her mother, stepfather, and grandparents sitting at the dining room table. They seemed to be holding a serious conversation, but the conversation stopped the second Rebecca, Chris, Windy, and Tempest appeared in the doorway. For a moment, the room was shockingly quiet, followed by an eruption in celebration. Cheers, hugs, kisses, introductions to Windy and Tempest, and an overwhelming number of questions ensued.

No longer the doubtful teenager who left two months earlier, a confident young woman now stood before them. Rebecca raised her hand to gather everybody's attention. "I cannot answer all of your questions at once," she exclaimed. "I expect we will have plenty of time to tell our stories. But, for now, I will say this, Mother and Grandmother, we have a lot to talk about."

At the time of the publication of this book in 2022,
Scott Howard is writing a sequel to
Into the Mystic:Sorcerer's Magic
with a goal for publication in 2024.

A prequel, the story of Alsaahir the Sorcerer,
is planned to follow, hopefully in 2026.

I like to believe,
with a little luck and the grace of God...

"You can be and do
anything you put your mind to."
- Scott Howard

About the Author

In the Creative World, Scott Howard is a well-recognized graphic designer and illustrator, a children's book author and illustrator, a dynamic public speaker, and now a fantasy-fiction novelist.

Scott grew up in Rehoboth, Massachusetts, the setting for *Into the Mystic*. Following high school, he served three years as an illustrator and graphic artist in the U.S. Army. He then earned his Associate in Arts degree at Monterey Peninsula College, California, and a Bachelor of Arts at California State University, Fullerton.

Throughout his career, Scott worked as a graphic designer and art director at advertising agencies, businesses, corporations, and as a self-employed freelance artist. In 2008, he sought new creative ideas, resulting in his first children's book, *Artsy Ant Alphabet Art Adventures*, and joined Toastmasters in 2009 to develop competency as a public speaker.

Since then, Scott has been in demand as an entertaining and inspiring speaker in venues from schools and children's charities to workshops, seminars, and corporate events. In addition, he has continued to illustrate children's books, such as *Hooray for Breezy*, by Wendy A. Williams, and multiple graphics projects, including logos, book covers, and package design.

Scott lives in Tampa Bay, on Florida's gulf coast.

His primary website is www.MyScottArt.com

Made in United States
North Haven, CT
30 November 2023

44761028R00182